FRANCISCO NIEVA
AND
POSTMODERNIST THEATRE

KOMLA AGGOR

UNIVERSITY OF WALES PRESS
CARDIFF
2006

© Komla Aggor, 2006

British Library Cataloguing-in-Publication Data
A catalogue record for this book is available from the British Library.

ISBN 0-7083-1961-0

All rights reserved. No part of this book may be reproduced, stored in a retrieval system, or transmitted, in any form or by any means, electronic, mechanical, photocopying, recording or otherwise, without clearance from the University of Wales Press, 10 Columbus Walk, Brigantine Place, Cardiff, CF10 4UP.
www.wales.ac.uk/press

The right of Komla Aggor to be identified as the author of this work has been asserted by him in accordance with the Copyright, Designs and Patents Act 1988.

Printed in Wales by Dinefwr Press, Llandybïe

To my father and
in memory of my mother

The ability to temporize tradition is the attribute of great writers.

Francisco Nieva

CONTENTS

ILLUSTRATIONS

ACKNOWLEDGEMENTS

I owe many thanks to several persons and institutions that contributed in special ways toward the making of this book. A George E. Grauel Faculty Fellowship and a Summer Research Fellowship granted by John Carroll University afforded me time to define this project in its early stages and to complete it. I am grateful to Don Francisco Nieva for his remarkable kindness and friendship – for all the research data he made available and the interviews he accorded me. Phyllis Zatlin made it easy for me to know this great man. Juanjo Granda, José Pedreira and Julia Trujillo shared with me their experiences on Nieva's performance projects. Juan Francisco Peña, Graciela Lacueva and Keith Nagy helped in important ways to advance this project. I am especially indebted to Yaw Agawu-Kakraba for his perceptive comments and the dedication with which he reviewed the manuscript. To my dearest trio, Dale–Aseye–Eli, I say a big Thank You for your steady support throughout this long process.

Excerpts from this book appeared previously in *Revista Hispánica Moderna* (1998), *Estreno* (1999), *Hispanófila* (1999) and *Hispanic Review* (2000). I thank the editors for permission to reproduce portions of these articles. My thanks also go to Madrid's Centro de Documentación Teatral for making available photographs of Francisco Nieva's stage productions. Don Francisco granted me permission to make citations from his *Teatro Completo* (1991). The Circulation Desk staff and the interlibrary loan department of John Carroll's Grasselli Library facilitated my research a great deal by promptly making available the numerous books I needed to consult. Finally, thanks are due to Sarah Lewis and all the staff at the University of Wales Press for the efficiency with which they always responded to my requests.

INTRODUCTION
IS POSTMODERNIST THEATRE POSSIBLE?

This book is about postmodernist theatre, specifically about the role that Francisco Morales Nieva (b. 1924) has played in its development. Because of the controversy that exists over the theorization of this theatre category, this study hopes to establish the validity of such a concept by presenting Nieva's work as a legitimate representation of what could be termed postmodernist theatre. In order to carry out this objective, the study grounds itself in the theoretical parameters of *Postismo*, a 1940s Spanish neo-avant-garde movement of which Nieva has been a prominent advocate.[1]

A member of the Spanish Royal Academy and the first playwright ever to be awarded the Príncipe de Asturias de las Letras Prize (considered to be the Hispanic Nobel Prize), Francisco Nieva is one of Spain's most innovative living playwrights. A designer, painter, director (of opera, ballet and drama), pianist, academic, essayist, translator, actor, dancer and a playwright, Nieva is commended by the distinguished critic Carlos Bousoño as one of few examples of the 'universal' artist in the twentieth century (see Bravo 1986, 57). Luis María Ansón, his Academy colleague, calls him the highest representative of Spanish culture in contemporary Spain (2002, 3), and Francisco Umbral dubs him the Castilian Marquis de Sade who in half a century stands as the only genuine Spanish writer to pay a legitimate tribute to the surrealists (1989, 4). Still, Nieva has not garnered the attention he merits internationally from theatre artists and critics, a neglect to which Rosett C. Lamont refers as a scandal (1995, 40). To date, Juan Francisco Peña's *El teatro de Francisco Nieva* (2001) remains the only broad-based book on the playwright, and no such work exists in English. With respect to *postismo*, the major studies – Jaume Pont's *El postismo* (1987) and María Isabel Navas Ocaña's 2000 book of the same title – present useful documents on the history of the movement but do not make any links with postmodernism.[2]

Contextualizing Nieva as a postmodernist has relevant intellectual and historical implications not only for Spanish theatre but also for dramatic theory and practice in general. Since the post-modern literary debate was engaged in Spain toward the late 1980s, the tendency has been to overlook or underrate local connections to the postmodern phenomenon. Examples of such studies are Antonio J. Huerga Murcia and José Tono Martínez's *La polémica de la posmodernidad* (1986), Francisco Umbral's *Guía de la Posmodernidad: crónicas, personajes e itinerarios madrileños* (1987), Josep Picó's *Modernidad y postmodernidad* (1988) and Jesús Ballesteros's *Postmodernidad: decadencia o resistencia* (1989). Even José Luis Pinillos's *El corazón del laberinto: crónica del fin de una época* (1998), arguably the most comprehensive study on the topic to date, does not affirm clearly Spain's vital role in the evolution of this cultural trend. Eric Bou and Andrés Soria Olmedo attribute the slow pace of academic interest in postmodernism to a certain suspicion on the part of Spaniards about the concept of postmodernity in general. In their view, this is because the process of modernity itself came under extremely problematic circum-stances complicated by the transition from the Franco dictatorship to democracy (1997, 399). Notwithstanding this lukewarm critical response, mention must be made of a few North American critics whose work demonstrates that Spain has not been oblivious to the postmodern tendency: Gonzalo Navajas (1987), Andrew P. Debicki (1988), Jonathan Mayhew (1994), Mario J. Valdés (1994) and Vance R. Holloway (1999).[3]

Of the literary genres, Spanish theatre has suffered the most glaring isolation from the discussion on postmodernism. Alfonso de Toro is the one critic who perhaps paved the way for a critical dialogue by proposing in 1990 a semiotic model for the study of Latin American and Spanish postmodernist drama. In his illus-trations, however, Toro devotes his attention mostly to Latin American drama and not to Spanish plays. It was not until 1996 that Ignacio Amestoy Egiguren explored the connection between Spanish theatre and postmodernism. In that essay, Amestoy paints what I believe to be an incomplete picture regarding the chronology of what could be termed postmodernist theatre in Spain. This playwright and critic inserts what he calls the Generation of 1982 within the literary culture of postmodernism and characterizes this group of writers as belonging to a new realism closer to 'reality's effect' than to reality itself (1996, 91).[4] In his bid to distinguish the 1982 Generation from the 1970s experimental playwrights of neo-avant-garde orientation (some-times referred to as the New Wave, Underground playwrights, or the Symbolist Generation), Amestoy provides a list of the writers who compose this latter group and affirms: 'They were those who brought the Spanish avant-garde to our (real or imaginary) stage. After them came the post-avant-gardists, the postmodernists' (91). Amestoy's classifications are problematic because they suggest that postmodernist Spanish theatre begins with the 1970s. That is, if one should go by his assertions, one would have to exclude Nieva, whose theatre chronologically precedes that of the 1970s Generation. And, of course, the Symbolist Generation is neither associated directly with the 1920s avant-garde movement nor with what Antonio Sánchez calls 'the contemporary avant-garde'.[5] Even so, the contours pegged by Amestoy at the early 1980s – a period dominated by a theatre defined by social realism – has also become the vital point of departure for Wilfried Floeck's studies on post-modernist Spanish theatre (see 1997, 1999 and 2004). Of course, one could view studies such as Floeck's as justifiably reflective of the theoretical assumptions characteristic of Late Postmodernism (1980s onward).

In positing Francisco Nieva as a postmodernist who began writing plays in the late 1940s, therefore, my study advances the discussion on a wider scale by filling in a conspicuous critical gap, the exclusion of a three-decade span (1950–80) from studies on postmodernism in the Spanish theatre.[6] Further historical con-notations mark this playwright's classification as a major post-modernist. First, in the context of the restrictive cultural politics of the post-Civil War period, the international significance of Nieva's work casts a more positive light on Spain's contributions to the evolution of European theatre. The problematic period in ques-tion is widely seen as having presented little by way of theatrical innovation in Spain. Secondly, the acknowledgement of Nieva as a postmodernist with an entrenched avant-garde foundation mitigates the proliferation of what I call a diluted version of postmodernism that came to characterize much of contemporary Spanish literature. That is, a postmodernism divested of its essential avant-garde attributes, what Jonathan Mayhew aptly describes as 'a vague air of contemporaneity, without any specific intellectual or aesthetic content' (1994, 139). Thirdly, the emphasis on *postismo* as the ideological cornerstone of Nieva's postmodernist

theatre prompts the need to review this Spanish cultural movement's historical consequence in the formulation of literary
postmodernism as a whole. Above all, as a postmodernist whose
work chronologically predates that of several of his celebrated
European contemporaries, Nieva's identity as a postmodernist
presents a broader outlook that transcends the undue dominance
of Anglo-American models, which have moulded the theoretical
and historical contours of postmodernism. If the magnitude of
Nieva's historical role is to be properly assessed, therefore, it is in
this larger, international framework that one must place his work.

One cannot discuss the relationship between postmodernism
and theatre in any extensive manner without first addressing the
resistance of some theatre critics to the theorization of postmodernist theatre. This resistance, which explains the continued
absence of a consolidated theory on postmodernist theatre, has
failed to produce a balanced debate. Instead, what have emerged
are two main categories of criticism: one that keeps harping on
the same old arguments made against the validity of a postmodernist theatre, and another that forges ahead with investiga-
tions of dramatic works within a postmodern framework without
really engaging the polemic. Often, the vast majority of those
who seem to accept the idea of a postmodernist theatre con-
centrate on performance rather than on the dramatic text. In a
study of Antonin Artaud and the Israeli playwright Hanoch Levin,
Erella Brown points out that, in the relatively few instances when
theatre is discussed in books on postmodernism, the tendency has
been to reassess the canon of modernist drama in light of postmodern theory rather than focusing on new postmodern dramatic
works. The implication is that either theatre has not produced
major contemporary playwrights to match the fertility and diversity
of modernism or there has been a lack of recognition within modernist theatre of the advent of postmodernism (Brown 1992, 585).

Since Rodney Simard drew attention to the postmodern tendency
in theatre with the publication of *Postmodern Drama: Contemporary
Playwrights in America and Britain* (1984), most books on the
topic – Simard's included – have not done much by way of
positively affirming or mapping out any theoretical formulations
on postmodernist theatre. A host of studies in the 1990s repeated
this trend through attractive titles that contain the word *postmodernism* or *postmodern* without drawing any conclusions about

what postmodernist theatre signifies. John L. DiGaetani's *A Search for a Postmodern Theater* (1991), Mark Pizzato's *Edges of Loss: From Modern Drama to Postmodern Theory* (1998) and Jeanette R. Malkin's *Memory-Theater and Postmodern Drama* (1999) are only a few of such studies. Stephen Watt's *Postmodern/Drama: Reading the Contemporary Stage* (1998), which methodically exposes the generalizations and superficiality surrounding the topic, surprisingly ends up proposing that one abandon the term 'postmodern drama' altogether as nothing more than 'an empty intellectual marker'. Even Deborah R. Geis's *Postmodern Theatric(k)s: Monologue in Contemporary American Drama* (1993), one of the few studies to define postmodernism on a broad basis and to establish its application to theatre, quickly plunges back into the book's central concern – the proposition that in 'postmodern drama' what pertains is monologue, not dialogue – without expatiating sufficiently on the features laid out by the author.

It is not this introduction's aim to invalidate the claims made against the validity of the conceptual link between postmodernism and theatre but rather to articulate the tenor of what I consider to be the dominant arguments made against that link. An authoritative voice of this resistance is Patrice Pavis. According to this distinguished critic, postmodernist theatre 'suggests as the only inheritance the faculty of replaying the past, rather than pretending to recreate and absorb it' (1992, 72). Contending that 'postmodern theater' is too vague an expression, Pavis puts forward the idea of 'postmodernism in theater'. Pavis's is a sensible proposition indeed, except that he does not go far enough in delineating the features he considers as distinctive of this kind of theatre: de-politicization, coherence and totality and contamination of practice by theory (69–72). In his desire to establish the legitimacy of the connection between theatrical practice and cultural currents such as postmodernism, Pavis creates a notional opposition between *theatre* and *drama*:

> *Drama*, which refers to the written manifestation of theatre (i.e. the dramatic text) does not provide us with a satisfactory means of understanding what is modern about the theatre. The notion of *theatre*, on the other hand, allows us to juxtapose classicism, modernism and postmodernism with respect to the concrete practices of the actor, the stage, the audience – in short, of a specific theatrical enunciation which varies considerably over time. (49)

Now, since Pavis does not show how the concrete practices to which he refers aid us in making the link between performance and postmodernism, it is difficult to embrace his argument wholly, knowing that there is an equal opposition from certain critical quarters to the idea of a postmodernist performance praxis. What is more, because it is in the dynamic interaction between the dramatic text and its stage mechanics where theatre's essence fully comes to light, the kind of schism drawn by Pavis seems to undermine the significance of theatre's verbal and thematic component, which ironically marks the postmodern character of certain plays such as Nieva's. Indeed, as Hans Bertens has shown, a formalist approach – that is, the focus on formal properties to determine a literary work's postmodernness – is outmoded. The major approach to literary postmodernism today, championed by the Linda Hutcheon school of thought, combines form with thematics (Bertens 1997, 8–12). In the case of theatre, this fact implies the need to pay serious attention to textual considerations.

This need, especially the unique relationship between the dramatic text and its performance, constitutes the main focus of Michael Vanden Heuvel's *Performing Drama / Dramatizing Performance: Alternative Theater and the Dramatic Text* (1991). Relegating the often-exalted supremacy of performance, Heuvel makes a strong case for the literary text's role in the contemporary American theatre. Without framing his observations specifically within a postmodern context, Heuvel notes that performance art tends to be viewed as a deconstructive tool that infiltrates and displaces the constraints of textuality. As he sees it, performance became a favourite mode said to differ from literary, textual forms because it 'does not impose a preformed hierarchy of discourses or meaning upon the spectator', or because it does not 'impugn any determinate meaning or interpretation at [the audience]'. Yet, he goes on, performance artists really only succeeded 'in maintaining the dialectical tendencies of Western culture by substituting one authoritarian locus of power for its opposite' (11–12). He explains:

> The power of the performance to induce pleasure, identification, the *jouissance* of deconstructive dispersal, catharsis, or any other spectatorial response still resides within the performer, who has simply displaced the author. The only way such a style of performance art can possibly free itself from such closure and control is for the performance artist to allow himself or herself to be displaced in turn, perhaps by a spectator. (12)

In his study, Heuvel demonstrates how many contemporary theatrical works have grown beyond early attempts at venerating performance 'as the panacea for, or affirmative response to, postmodern consciousness' (233).

No matter how one views it, it seems as if postmodernist theatre were always bound to lose. As Pavis questions the validity of postmodernist theatre on the basis of the literary text, Johannes Birringer and Nick Kaye launch their assault from the angle of performance. In an article, 'Postmodernism and Theatrical Performance', Birringer contends:

> The collapse of the old theatre did not take place, and I think it is misleading to speak of a 'postmodern theatre'. Rather, the movement from the polymorphous theatricalization of everyday life in the 1960s to the nearly total mediatization and technological engineering of culture in the 1990s suggests not only the redundancy of theatre but also a considerable shift in the function of the aesthetic. (1997, 131)

He goes on to say that, whenever modern theatre in all its manifestations questioned its identity and its conventions, the radicalism of subversion is indebted to 'a persistent classical and modern paradigm of mimesis on which it depends even as the emphasis is shifted from text . . . to the performance event or experience as such'. 'Even the shifting . . . discourse of radical theatre theory (Artaud, Brecht)', Birringer maintains, 'does not constitute a postmodern moment for theatre, since the disorienting strategies of Artaud's theatre of cruelty and Brecht's politically didactic *Lehrstücke* (learning plays) were conceived in analogy to other modernist avant-garde projects that sought to destroy theatrical illusion or the illusions of authoritative meaning' (130). Still Birringer:

> While conventional theatre has remained text-based, and is still received today primarily as a representational medium of dramatic fiction, a more recent postmodernist discourse on performance and performance art is partly indebted to this historical avant-garde and its rejection or defamiliarization of narrative, character, acting, authorship and spectatorship. (130)[7]

In *Postmodernism and Performance* (1994), not only is Nick Kaye opposed to the notion of a postmodernist theatre, but he rejects any attempt at defining or categorizing the postmodern. Resistant to any simple circumscription of its means and forms, Kaye argues that postmodernism interrogates its own terms and assumptions and has no stable foundation in art. Because there are *postmodernisms* and 'no "authentic" or "original" postmodernism around which various texts and events position themselves' (1994, 4), it makes no sense to Kaye to talk of aesthetic strategies or devices that one could designate as postmodernist. Similar questions are raised by Roger F. Copeland (1991), who believes that postmodern phenomena in theatre are not recent and do not constitute a full-fledged movement of the sort that one finds in architecture or painting. Delighted that the theatre has not contracted a bad case of what he labels *post-modern syndrome*, Copeland charges that the claims made by postmodernism are all déjà vu. Jane Goodall extends a similar argument when she claims that architecture may be marked by a 'postmodern turn' in aesthetic theory and practice but that it is almost impossible to demarcate an equivalent turn in the theory and practice of theatrical performance (1993, 24). Finally, there has been the tendency on the part of some theatre critics (e.g. Goodall and Wladimir Krysinski) to base their opposition to any theorization of postmodernist theatre on the two-column schema established by Ihab Hassan (1980) in his attempt to distinguish between modernism and postmodernism. But, as will be pointed out in chapter I, Hassan himself later departed from that initial approach to the definition of postmodernism.

One cannot overemphasize the need in today's so-called post-modern world to exercise caution in jumping to conclusions about what is postmodern or postmodernist, especially when it comes to artistic expressions. At the same time, since theatrical practice is shaped by so many variables, one needs to be careful not to dismiss hastily its possible association with the literary culture of postmodernism. Whereas Birringer's affirmations are made on clearly legitimate grounds, I do believe that they are somewhat exaggerated. In the first place, the 1990s mediatization and technological engineering of culture of which he speaks may have reduced the frequency and intensity of theatre-going as a mode of diversion, but these phenomena have not – not yet – rendered the theatre redundant. Well-orchestrated performances of certain types continue to command satisfactory spectatorship in Europe and in the United States. In Spain, the recent boom of audiovisual technology may have boosted the already popular attraction to realistic, everyday-life drama. Even so, contemporary Spanish theatre is largely defined by a multiplicity of genres and aesthetic types, especially works of an experimental nature alongside those framed within naturalistic paradigms.[8] In fact, Erika Fischer-Lichte – one of the few theatre theorists who accept the idea of a postmodernist theatre – even goes to the extent of establishing an oppositional relationship between electronic technology and postmodern theatrical spectatorship.[9]

To focus on the more important point, it is true that the disorienting strategies of Artaud's Theatre of Cruelty and Brecht's politically didactic drama cannot be said to constitute a postmodern moment for the theatre, but it is not because these radical trends or recent performance theory were 'conceived in analogy to other modernist avant-garde projects that sought to destroy theatrical illusion' as Birringer suggests. Equally true is the assertion that the old theatre never collapsed. But the question is, does the old theatre have to collapse in order to generate new radical energies? In this regard, instructive is an observation that Allan Lewis has made in his commentary on August Strindberg's theatre: 'No revolution can be completely new. It must drag along enough of the old to provide comprehensibility and continuity . . . The avant-garde in time becomes part of the Establishment and a new avant-garde comes into being as the artist rejects the sterility of imposed paradigms' (1972, 90–1). The message behind these words, which directly contradict Birringer's argument, is ironically what distinguishes postmodernism: continuity and choice, not rupture and revolution. What Birringer and those who reject the idea of a postmodernist theatre seem not to accept is precisely that which has been emphasized time and again, and which I stress in the present study, namely, that postmodernism is not antithetical to modernism. To employ a commercial jargon, it is modernism-plus. Deriving its livelihood from modernism, postmodernism carefully maintains with modernism a semi-independent relationship akin to separation – but certainly not divorce. If this inherently modernist legacy of postmodernism is so hard to accept, perhaps one should ask if, in the final analysis, there exists any revolutionary quality that bestows an autonomous identity on any of the following cardinal movements in the historical evolution of Western art and literature: the Baroque, Romanticism, Surrealism, Dada, Cubism, Symbolism, Expressionism.

Regarding the argument that it is impossible to apply to theatre that which is applicable to architecture because theatre does not mark a 'postmodern turn', I ask: What precisely constitutes the postmodern moment for other literary types such as poetry and narrative that makes their linkage with postmodernism meaningful but not so with theatre? Why Jorge Luis Borges but not Ramón María del Valle-Inclán? Why the *Novísimos* but not Els Joglars or La Fura dels Baus? Why classify Juan Goytisolo as a postmodernist writer, as Hans Bertens (1997) does, but keep out Francisco Nieva?

I am not arguing against cautious approaches to theorizing post-modernist theatre. Indeed, no matter how one views it, two challenges remain pertinent in any literary application of postmodernism as a concept. First, how does one determine the borders of the post-modernist in any given literary work? In other words, how does one distinguish in each specific case the extent of the new and the old even as both terms cohabit and compete with each other? Secondly, given the difficulty one faces in claiming stable criteria or a common denominator for theatre and for postmodernism as general concepts (a problem raised by Kaye and Krysinski), what criterion does one use in the application of postmodern principles to theatre? Still, these problems are neither exclusive to Postmodernism as a movement, in the first case, nor are they to theatre, in the second. Cognizant of these difficulties, therefore, what I do in the present study is to con-centrate on those attributes of postmodernism that I consider central to any application of the term and whose connotations are in con-sonance with the ethical and aesthetic interstices of Nieva's theatre. In this effort, I do not seek to propose that which is relevant to his work as indiscriminately applicable to all dramatic works legitimately classifiable as postmodernist. Postmodernist theatre is indeed pos-sible, but its conceptualization can only proceed in a tolerant and non-dogmatic fashion, with a focus on postmodernism's core tenets.

As the clouds gradually begin to clear over the erratic turbulence of the dialogue on postmodernism, the benefit of historical perspective makes it compelling for one to become flexible and bold enough to engage past theoretical postures with a revisionist gaze. An en-lightening source for this regenerative critical possibility is Douwe Fokkema's essay, 'The Semiotics of Literary Postmodernism' (1997). In this piece, Fokkema takes advantage of historical perspective to infuse more rationality into the debate, moderating the exaggerated tone of earlier critical discourse on postmodernism. I have taken the liberty to explore briefly his postulations as they bear a direct connection with my own reflections. Fokkema essentially reaffirms old viewpoints and asserts new propositions for postmodern literary criticism. For him, the 'anything goes' ideal is a slogan that belongs to the early days of Postmodernism; textual contexts, made up of signs with conventional meanings, are still valid; there are leftist political connotations undercurrent in the postmodernist work; postmodernism was also motivated by the rise of a new generation (that is, a movement) and by aesthetic needs, hence the validity of examining textual devices that distinguish postmodernist literature. Fokkema continues: one cannot separate texts from the individuals who produce and consume them, since there exist 'pragmatic conventions' partly constituted by authorial intention and readers' acceptance; the competition between modernism and postmodernism is one between groups of people (where older conventions in certain cases may be preferred to newer ones and vice versa); and there are postmodernist tendencies in literature that arose independently of American postmodernism and were later incorporated. Against the common charge that postmodernism is an arbitrary trend, Fokkema responds that 'if all literary conventions were arbitrary, one might as well continue to write in the same way, according to the conventions of realism or modernism' (23).

These perceptive assertions, which have always held true and yet so often been obfuscated in the long struggle to define postmodernism, serve as a positive stimulus for one to review certain critical arguments made in the past, especially those that undermine the literary text's role in the new aesthetic modality. When this is done, one begins to see that strategies and devices identifiable as postmodernist are employed legitimately by some playwrights, many of who continue to be left out of the discussion on the twentieth century's most engaging movement. One such playwright who deploys postmodernist techniques and yet remains sidelined from these discussions is Francisco Nieva. Consequently, whereas this book does not pretend to offer the last word on the bond between postmodernism and theatre, it hopes to legitimize the notion of postmodernist theatre, using as its illustrative point of departure the dramatic universe of this Spanish dramatist.

The first chapter discusses the emergence of *Postismo* in the context of Francoist censorship. I map out the historical and philosophical foundations of the movement, explaining in detail the association of *postismo* with the literary culture of postmodernism. An exposé of Nieva's dramatic postulates, inserted within the aesthetic parameters of *postismo* and postmodernism, creates a theoretical framework for the analysis in the subsequent chapters.

In each of the next three chapters, I discuss what I consider to be the principal characteristics of Nieva's postmodernist theatre. Chapter II is a study of paradox as a postist and a postmodernist device designed to undermine hierarchical structures and unilateral modes of perceiving reality. The analysis establishes the affinity between Nieva's Aesthetics of Crime and Antonin Artaud's Theatre of Cruelty as these relate to the conceptual underpinnings of postmodernist theatre. Chapter III deals with metadrama as a formal technique that Nieva employs to sustain the dualities of his theatre and to generate elasticity in the interpretation of his plays. Metadramatic forms such as the play within the play and ceremony within the play are carefully examined. The complexity of the structural and mechanical components of Nieva's theatre tends to give the impression of an elitist theatre. Chapter IV diffuses this image and discusses Nieva's use of populist dramatic conventions to neutralize the intellectual or poetic undertone of his complex theatre. The discussion also focuses on how Nieva overturns traditional theatrical representations by empowering marginalized voices as commanding players on stage. The study concludes by exploring in chapter V Nieva's role as a director and designer within a postmodernist paradigm. The analysis is framed within performance theory as it relates to the role of the literary text, the actor and the spectator. The chapter also lays out the diverse impediments with which Nieva has been faced in his attempt to stage his plays and how these impediments delayed his standing as a celebrity in the international literary arena.

The study covers the full range of Nieva's work, from the 1940s to the present, with special emphasis on the plays I find most representative of his theatre in general. Throughout the book, my analysis of stage productions of Nieva's plays is based on video recordings, made available to me by Nieva and by Madrid's Centro de Documentación Teatral. Unless otherwise noted, all translations are my own.

I

POSTISMO, POSTMODERNISM, THEATRE

POSTISMO

Founded in January 1945 by Eduardo Chicharro Jr, Carlos Edmundo de Ory and Silvano Sernesi at Madrid's Café Castilla, *Postismo* is a neo-avant-garde movement that places emphasis on imagination, the subconscious and eclecticism as inspiration for literary and art works.[1] The journals that represented the movement's official mouthpiece were *Postismo*, published the same month the movement was formed and suspended after only one issue, and *La Cerbatana*, which was discontinued for lack of funds after its only April 1945 issue. What gave *Postismo* authenticity were its manifestos. The first, signed by Chicharro, was published in the journal *Postismo*; the second, signed by the three, was published in 1946 in *La Estafeta Literaria*; the third, also signed by Chicharro, appeared in 1947 in *El Minuto*, a supplement of the journal *La Hora*; the last one, signed by Ory, appeared between 1947 and 1948 in Chicharro's *Música celestial y otros poemas.*[2] Three other journals were later founded: *Deucalión* (1951–3), directed by Ángel Crespo in Ciudad Real; *Doña Endrina* (1951–5), directed by Antonio Fernández Molina in Guadalajara; and *Trilce* (1952–3), also directed by Fernández Molina in Guadalajara. Besides its founders, the other members of the movement were Francisco Nieva, Gabino-Alejandro Carriedo, Félix Casanova de Ayala, Ángel Crespo and Ignacio Aldecoa. One could also mention Juan Alcaide Sánchez (Nieva's childhood mentor and poet), Ignacio Nieva (the playwright's brother) and Nanda Papiri (an Italian painter married to Chicharro) as persons who were closely associated with the activities organized by the postists. Eugenio D'Ors and the poet Juan Eduardo Cirlot were recognized sympathizers. The main centres of the movement were Madrid, Seville, Cádiz and, after 1946, Ciudad Real. One María del Pilar de Sandoval once carried a report on *Postismo* in Argentina, and in an interview with *Lanza*, Ory relates the repercussions the movement had in Portugal, Italy,

France, the Philippines and the Americas (Pont 1987, 74). The group's major activities consisted of its regular meetings at Chicharro's study, its *tertulias* at the Café Castilla and postist art exhibitions (held three times, in Madrid in 1948, in Zaragoza in 1948 and in Guadalajara in 1953).[3]

Although its leaders insist that *Postismo* is not a movement against any particular philosophical or artistic tendency, its inspiration derives partly from its impatience with the humanist and *falangist* ideological bias that took hold of the literary scene in the early 1940s. Fanny Rubio (1976) has documented how this double agenda – *falangist* propaganda and rehumanization of poetry – was particularly advanced by the journal *Escorial* (1940). It is, however, in the journal *Garcilaso* (1943) and in the activities of the 'Juventud Creadora' where *falangist* lyricism found its most cogent expression (Pont 1987, 24). The postists were provoked by Garcilacists' escapist project in the midst of a society devastated by misery and suffering. Furthermore, the foundation in 1944 of *Espadaña* by the León group of poets, with its strong rehumanizing programme, certainly fuelled the postists' desire to found a journal with a different message. No wonder, they derived much of their inspiration from the most unexpected of places, José Ortega y Gasset's *La deshumanización del arte* (The Dehumanization of Art) (1925), which they embraced enthusiastically, at least until the publication of the Third Manifesto where their rhetoric was laced with a much more humanist undertone. In fact, so disgusted were Ory and Chicharro by the activities of the 'Juventud Creadora' that Félix Casanova de Ayala reports how the two postists (sometimes joined by others) used to march on Café Gijón and other rendezvous of the young *falangist* poets to disrupt their meetings and to irritate them. Gianna Prodan (1989) offers further details, saying that the postists, always opting for the atypical, adopted outlandish and provocative postures in public: they entered art exhibition halls on all fours during inaugurations, they wore their jackets inside out and they dressed outrageously with postist undershirts and blouses painted by Nieva. In the streets, and especially during certain public functions, remarks Prodan, they liked to register their rebellion by adopting distasteful attitudes. She adds that the postists often displayed sexually ambiguous behaviour that greatly scandalized and irritated the society of that time.

But what really is *Postismo*? The best attempt at defining postist theory is offered by one of the movement's representatives in the Radio Seu interview of 15 November 1944, when the movement was first announced:

> *Postismo* is the immediate and inevitable legacy of other movements that we have come to call the *-isms*: Post-structuralism, Post-cubism, Post-ultraism . . . This is why it is called POSTISMO, that is, the *-ism* that succeeds the other *-isms* . . . If one were to define *Postismo* with a single word, it would be this: IMAGINATION. (Pont 1987, 411–12)

Evidently, even this definition is vague and leaves the curious dissatisfied, for it leans heavily on other movements to identify itself. Unable to say clearly what they are, the postists in their Second Manifesto enumerate several objectives in an attempt to define what, at least, they aspire to achieve. It is in the corpus of these goals and objectives where the essence of postist theory is to be found: the desire for pure poetry; a return to the roots of Cubism; exploration of that which is rare and mysterious; the projection of art onto a prophetic, intuitive and subconscious sense of the spirit; the view of language not simply as a tool but as a fountain of poetic inspiration; the desire for total freedom, to the extent of making a cult of Absurdity; the search for beauty in the chaos of forms and values; an inquiry into the messianic and into the artistic universe of children, of savages and of the demented; the need to honour people with kindness, joy and beauty; a return to spontaneity; opposition to cold, poor and academic art as well as an exaltation of the wonders of liberty and imagination; finally, the reciprocal gesture of returning everyone's cordiality with madness. After a citation of Nietzsche's words, the objectives section concludes with the following words of Ory: 'EL POSTISMO ES LA LOCURA INVENTADA' (*POSTISMO* IS INVENTED MADNESS).

Pure poetry, Cubism, mystery, aesthetic liberty, chaos of forms and values, savagery, the world of infancy, spontaneity, imagination, madness. Don't these features resonate with André Breton's notion of surrealism? Indeed they are – but there is a difference. Whereas the surrealists ground their ideology in the importance of the subconscious, the postists insist on logic, on logic within the domain of imagination. The Second Manifesto states that, unlike surrealism, *postismo* does not admit absolute automation, and instead of shunning logic, it turns it into a viable technique. Moreover, unlike Surrealism (known to have some links with the French Communist Party), *Postismo*, say the postists, is an apolitical movement. As María Isabel Navas Ocaña cautions, however, the postists' apolitical stand could be viewed as their defensive mechanism against Francoist censorship (2000, 24), since they were very much aware of the risks they ran with unconventional theories in a conservative political culture.

Postismo's lack of distinction should not be troubling. The postists have repeated time and again that their project is a revisionist one, not a rejectionist aesthetic. That is, instead of being averse to the past, as the historical avant-garde is, theirs is an eagerness to discover, to reactivate, to recycle, as it were, the substance of what they call uncharted territories: 'What we want is to seek out all fortresses of the past in order to put this world of easy decadence on a new course of art and creative possibility' (Front cover of *Postismo*'s first issue, January 1945). As such, like postmodernism, *postismo* grounds itself consciously in Modernism (Dada, *Ultraísmo*, Surrealism, Cubism, etc.) but also seeks to transcend the avant-garde. It is perhaps in this sense that David Castillo Buïls describes the relationship between *Postismo* and the avant-garde as being more fraternal than filial (1989, 12). Gianna Prodan (1989) even goes to the extent of exposing what she calls 'an abyss' between *Postismo* and the avant-garde (she mentions fifteen varieties, from Expressionism to Constructivism), arguing that Chicharro's references in postist texts to these movements do not provide a viable basis for linking *Postismo* with the avant-garde. According to Prodan, this is because Chicharro's avant-garde influence is indiscriminate and his formation in the avant-garde unsystematic. This is to say that, even though *Postismo* is rooted in avant-garde thought, one needs to be careful not to label the Spanish movement simply as another modernist *-ism*; an argument to keep in mind as one compares *postismo* with postmodernism. This eclectic disposition, which allows *Postismo* an unprecedented authority and freedom over other avant-garde movements, unfortunately makes it look like a Jack of all trades and master of none.

Several questions spring to mind: Can one truly call *postismo* an aesthetic even though the postists themselves seem to characterize it as such in their First Manifesto? And with no ambition for novelty, can one really consider it avant-garde as it has been labelled? A theory, maybe, but what kind of literary theory focuses on imagination, when imagination is a given in the production of all literature? When the postists underline the role of imagination in the context of madness – 'la locura inventada' – what they mean is liberty, uninhibited freedom of creativity that nevertheless refuses to become an anti-aesthetic (Third Manifesto). Still, is creative liberty not too broad and too inclusive a category to constitute a theory? Perhaps, but that is precisely the point. Like the semantic uncertainty underlying the definition of postmodernism, *postismo* suffers an identity complex, since it is rooted in other *-isms*. This remarkable resilience prompts Gabino-Alejandro Carriedo to describe *postismo* as a state of mind: '*Postismo* is a state of mind, a way of being, a conjunction of art and nature. Naturally, it has been in existence since the beginning of the world and continues to be the subject of investigation' (1991, 97). Indeed, the element of exaggeration here reminds one of Umberto Eco's meta-historical conceptualization of postmodernism. As is well known, Eco views postmodernism as a spiritual category located in every age and not as a chronologically circumscribed tendency. 'We could say', Eco affirms, 'that every age has its own postmodern, just as every age has its own form of mannerism (in fact, I wonder if postmodern is not simply the modern name for Manierismus as a meta-historical category)' (1983, 2). Let us note, however, that it is possible to trace manifestations of most artistic or cultural phenomena in periods prior to their theorization, a fact that does not necessarily make of such phenomena an a-historical typology. With this lack of specificity, *Postismo* and its advocates came under malicious ridicule. Navas Ocaña reports that, in a 1945 article published in the daily *Baleares*, an anonymous author declared the following in reference to the postists: 'I wish to see those poets and painters rounded up in their hideouts. After catching them, without letting a single one escape, they should be hanged by the master pole. They claim that nothing matters to them. Well then, hit them on the head.' No less aggressive was the outrage hurled by *Satiricón* when it compared *postismo* to previous modernist movements and affirms that, in their search for an aesthetic, the postists have attained little more than what circus clowns do during intermissions in the works of serious artists (Navas Ocaña 2000, 50).

The enthusiastic bid to nip *Postismo* in the bud was the inevitable result of an intolerant and conservative environment created and promoted by Francoism, which was opposed to anything novel and progressive in Spain. With its self-preservative agenda, the regime tended to stifle alternative manifestations on the artistic front. When one scrutinizes the content of the First Manifesto, for example, one finds little basis for the rushed suspension of the journal *Postismo* in which the manifesto was published. Chicharro and his colleagues, aware of the vociferous censors, carefully constructed their manifestos in order not to offend the Francoist hegemonic apparatus. On the basis of the First Manifesto text, one observes that not only did the postists not present themselves as anarchists or even absurdists, but that they went to the extent of embracing the national religion – the source of much repression – and even declared themselves against artistic pornography, a central concern of the Franco censorship. They insisted that they were no iconoclasts and that they respected all religious beliefs. In fact, it appears that the postists often responded in a combative fashion only when they were provoked. Despite these considerations, the movement was so severely castigated that it struggled in vain to find its voice in the literary wasteland of Franco's Spain. Consequently, in 1948, three years after its inception, the movement fell apart, although it continued to function without its principal figures until 1955. Notwithstanding its short-lived history, the rigour of *Postismo*'s cultural and artistic importance remains alive, especially when its theoretical propositions are contemplated in the context of postmodern literary culture.

FROM *POSTISMO* TO POSTMODERNISM

Charles Jencks, a theoretician of Postmodernism from the perspective of architecture, sketches the movement's history by categorizing it into three phases (1996, 14–20). The first period runs from 1870 to 1950 where postmodernism is viewed as the modern period in decline. Jencks indicates that Wolfgang Welsch reports the first use of the term in 1870 by the British artist John Watkins Chapman to announce an art exhibition, which he considered to be more modern than the most advanced at the time. Next was Rudolf Pannwitz's 1917 application of the term to describe the European historical and social crisis that took place from the second half of the nineteenth century to the early 1920s. As Jencks notes, however, it was the Spanish writer Federico de Onís who, in his *Antología de la poesía española e hispano-americana* (1934), made the first, tentative, written use of *Post-Modernism* (1996, 17). The second phase covers the period 1950–80. Postmodernism, which in this instance covers the advent in 1963 of the post-bourgeois ideal up to the publication in 1973 of Daniel Bell's *Post-Industrial Society*, is defined positively as counter culture, double-coding, pluralism and de-creation. The third phase, a period to which Douwe Fokkema refers as Late Postmodernism, goes from 1980 up to the present, a period in which the postmodern condition is attacked and postmodern global morality is defined. It must also be noted that Arthur Kroker and David Cook do locate the beginnings of the post-modern phenomenon as far back as the fourth century, with Augustine's subversion of early expressions of modernism (1986, 8).

Of course, Federico de Onís's work on Modernism, which in José Luis Pinillos's view surpasses in importance all such earlier studies that established the basis of what would later be known as postmodernism (1998, 187–8), places Spain squarely in the historical maelstrom of the postmodern.[4] Yet in all references to the origin and development of postmodernism, the vital link with *Postismo* has not been acknowledged. For sure, before Arnold Toynbee in 1946 coined the neologism 'Post Modern Age' and before North American literary criticism became interested in the topic in the 1960s, Spain had registered the presence of the postmodern in a variety of postist works: Chicharro's book of poetry, *Música celestial* (written 1945–58); Ory's poetry (later published in 1970 by EDHASA as *Poesía: 1945–1969*), his two-act drama, *Historia natural* (1945) and his short stories, *El bosque* (1952) and *Kikirikí-Mangó* (1954); Sirnesi's poems, 'El pigmeo bordonero' and 'Romance del espadín' (1945); Ángel Crespo's own *Música celestial* (1945–48) and, as will be seen, Nieva's drama.[5]

Postismo bears unquestionable resemblances to postmodernism. Semantically, the word *postismo* is synonymous with *post-avant-gardism* (post-surrealism, post-futurism, post-Cubism, etc.)

or, simply, *post-modernism*, since 'avant-gardism' or 'modernism' are truly the terms that correspond with the *-isms* of which the 'post' in 'postismo' is a prefix. The basic difference between *postismo* and postmodernism is that, whereas *Postismo* is officially declared as a literary-artistic movement with manifestos, postmodernism is not organized in such a programmatic manner. Neither is postmodernism limited to literature and art; instead, it covers the broad spectrum of cultural forms, from architecture, through science, to anthropology and religion. Both currents are rooted in the avant-garde and are seen as constitutive of Modernism. That is, they both seek a return to spiritual domains, away from naturalistic, positivistic tendencies. Yet despite their avant-garde orientation, neither of the two currents is bitter or antagonistic; instead, they essentially thrive on ludic sensibilities, employing play as an indispensable artistic technique. This is why in postmodernist theatre what prevail are farce and metatheatre, and not tragedy.

Those who argue that *postismo* is a façade for surrealism should note that postmodernism suffers the same identity problem. As Hans Bertens has pointed out, Ihab Hassan even places the avant-garde – specifically Dada and Surrealism – squarely within postmodernism (1986, 26). Indeed, what sets *postismo* apart from the avant-garde is the same thing that constitutes the mark of distinction between the avant-garde and postmodernism. Linda Hutcheon speaks to this subject matter concisely:

> The avant-garde is . . . seen as critical of the dominant culture and alienated from it in a way that the postmodern is not, largely because of its acknowledgement of its unavoidable implication in that dominant culture. At the same time, of course, it both exploits and critically undermines that dominance. In short, the postmodern is not as negating (of the past) or as Utopic (about the future) as is, at least, the historical or modernist avant-garde. (1988, 47)

Thus, when Pinillos (1998, 200) draws attention to postmodernism's lack of interest in revolution or reform, he strikes a vital chord in *postismo*'s revisionist tenet. According to Pinillos, contrary to the purist and innovative radicalism of the avant-garde, postmodern art opted for pastiche, a play with styles and forms of other periods, and it adopted an ironic and cynical tone that is irritating to the bourgeoisie. Instead of 'dreaming of revolution or reform of the world', Pinillos maintains, postmodernism decided to leave everything as it was and rather enjoy its golden decadence while it lasted. Pinillos's words, in turn, recall Gerald Graff's argument in 'The Myth of the Postmodernist Breakthrough' (1973). Graff contends that the revolutionary claims made for the postmodernist new sensibility are overrated and that, when viewed in the context of the early 1970s social and cultural situation, postmodernism shows itself to be a reactionary tendency, one that reinforces the effects of technocratic, bureaucratic society. In short, he argues that postmodernism should not be seen as breaking with Romantic and modernist assumptions but rather as their logical culmination.[6]

Like *postismo*, postmodernism collapses barriers and thrives on the interconnected fluidity of ideas. This is why Hassan invited severe criticism when he attempted in 1980 to prescribe aesthetic guidelines on postmodernism by tabulating a comparison between postmodernism and modernism. A few years later, Hassan had to come up with a troubling, yet more accurate, characterization of postmodernism. Hassan believes that postmodernism is, at best, 'an equivocal concept, a disjunctive category, doubly modified by the impetus of the phenomenon itself and by the shifting perceptions of its critics'. At worst, he continues, postmodernism 'appears to be a mysterious, if ubiquitous, ingredient – like raspberry vinegar, which instantly turns any recipe into *nouvelle cuisine*' (1986, 508). What this apparently evasive and vague definition teaches us is that, like *postismo*, postmodernism is not about enumerated features, for lists convey a sense of conclusion and closure. Such lists smack of rules which, in Hutcheon's terms (1988, 231), tend to betray the very anti-totalizing ideology on which postmodernism stands.

Still, if one must reduce *postismo* and postmodernism to concrete points of union, here they are: the lack of an absolute definition (that is, the lack of an independent identity without reliance on other -*isms*), the desire for artistic freedom and pluralism, a concerted distinction from the avant-garde through an eclectic reappraisal of the past, reliance on humour and play, fragmentation and an urge toward de-canonization, exaltation of paradox and contradiction and the view of language not simply as a functional tool but as a source of artistic inspiration. Above all, both theories resist the restrictive tendency to make of them another kind of straitjacket ideology: first and foremost, they entail an ethical and aesthetic dynamism that reflects their firm pluralist foundation. Writing about *postismo*'s role in contemporary Spanish poetry, Bernd Díetz affirms back in 1989: 'If during the past half a century there exists in Spain an *-ism*, an organized trend that truly sustains the spirit of experimentation, a concerted rebellion and the artistic renewal that are so badly needed, it is *postismo*' (9). Undoubtedly, had the *Postismo* movement been left alone to negotiate its own treacherous course, it would have gained prominence in the development not only of Spanish literary theory but of postmodernism as a universal phenomenon. Thus, if one is to tell the full story about the history of literary postmodernism, one is obliged to place Spain in the vanguard of that history and, in so doing, begin to reconsider the existing historical boundaries of postmodernism in general. The strong accord between the two currents can no longer be ignored.

Nieva has been *Postismo*'s staunch advocate and he stands today as the most enduring postist of the highest order. The strongest testimony to Nieva's high role in the practice and preservation of postist theory comes from none other than Ory. Ory calls him 'a catechumen of *postismo*', one whose vow of fidelity never weakened and the only witness and authentic participant engaged with the movement's ideals (1970, 277–8). Nieva was introduced to the postist movement by the poet Alcaide Sánchez and it was through him that he met Ory. So strong did the friendship between Nieva and Ory grow that in 1947 the postist poet moved to Nieva's apartment, which he shared at the time with his brother Ignacio. In Ory's company, Nieva frequented the meetings and *tertulias* held in Chicharro's study. In his memoirs, *Las cosas como fueron* (2002), he acknowledges that it was Ory and Chicharro who schooled him in *postismo* and in the literary arts in general. Indeed, it was the camaraderie among the three that truly sustained and sealed this playwright's postist zeal (2002, 54–67). Nieva came to *Postismo* not as a playwright or designer but as a painter; a surrealist painter who would later bring that surrealistic plastic experience to bear on his dramaturgy. The poet has always been in Nieva, and his work always radiates poetry, be it expressed on canvas, in his drama or on stage. His attraction to *Postismo* lies, therefore, in the possibility created by this theory's eclecticism for artistic independence and individual creativity.[7]

In his biography of Nieva, Antonio González (1980) presents a strong case for Francisco Nieva as having preceded the experimental work of some of the very writers whom the playwright would later mention as having inspired him. Carlos Bousoño re-emphasizes this chronological importance of Nieva's drama, saying that, besides a work or two by Italo Calvino, Nieva's symbolist drama predates that of his contemporaries (1990, 74). What is undeniable is that, long before his 1952 trip to France, Nieva had been well schooled in the alternative literary ideas to which *Postismo* gave birth. His theatre's entrenchment in the aesthetic ideals of this Spanish movement ultimately defines its make-up and it is *the* decisive factor in moulding the foundations of his dramatic theory and practice in general. Thus, if one is to place this playwright duly in the chronological evolution of European theatre history, his postist background ought to be taken fully into account.[8]

THE PROBLEMATICS OF SPANISH THEATRE

Before discussing Nieva's dramatic philosophy, let me divert briefly and describe the pertinent historical context in which the uniqueness of his dramaturgy could be assessed. Born on 29 December 1924 in Valdepeñas, Nieva was eleven years old when the Spanish Civil War broke out and fourteen when the Franco dictatorship was imposed. By virtue of his family's republican affiliations (his father was once governor of Toledo and his uncle Cirilo del Río, a minister in the republican government), members of the family were forced to seek refuge in the Sierra Morena where he began to draw, paint and write drama. When Nieva and his family finally moved to Madrid in 1941, this city's predominant theatrical performances were the *astracanada*, an escapist, falsely burlesque drama represented mainly by Adolfo Torrado. At the same time, the innovations of Ramón María del Valle-Inclán and Federico García Lorca were to a large extent eclipsed during and after the war by well-made plays of bourgeois taste popularized by José Echegaray, the Álvarez Quintero brothers (Serafín and Joaquín), Pedro Muñoz Seca and especially Jacinto Benavente (see, for example, *Caperucita asusta al lobo*

(1952) or *Al fin mujer* (1942), a far cry from the high artistic merit of *La malquerida*). Of particular importance was the surge of (mainly rightist) ideological drama featured by writers such as Sotero Otero del Pozo (e.g. *España inmortal*, staged in 1936), José Giménez Arnau (e.g. *Murió hace quince años*, staged in 1953), Joaquín Pérez Madrigal (e.g. *Los que tienen razón* (1939)), Juan Ignacio Luca de Tena (e.g. *El cóndor sin alas* (1951)), Benavente (*Aves y pájaros*, staged in 1940), etc. This evasive and politicized theatre environment came about mainly in response to the kind of biased cultural agenda pursued by the Franco regime, especially through its censorship programme, which was in force from 1938 until 1974.[9]

Almost unanimously, Spanish theatre historians, from Juan Ignacio Ferreras (1988), through José García Templado (1992), to Francisco Ruiz Ramón (1995), have lamented, with varying degrees of emphasis, the deplorable state in which Spanish theatre had been entangled for many years. A debilitating factor underlined by Ruiz Ramón in his comprehensive study *Historia del teatro español* is the general tendency on playwrights' part to superimpose message over drama and technique. Hilde F. Cramsie (1984) has explored the systematic censorship suffered by the Spanish theatre since the reign of Felipe II (sixteenth century), through Gaspar de Jovellanos and Fernández Moratín's Theatrical Reform Plan of 1799, to that infamous Press Decree of 1938. This last-mentioned decree, promulgated in the heat of the Spanish Civil War (1936–9), granted total authority to the ministry charged with the National Press Services to censure and to punish all journalists and writers who challenged the regime and showed signs of disagreement with its ideology. Cramsie shows that, whenever a subsequent decree was declared as if to mitigate the effects of the censorship, the freedom it propagated was always undercoated with heavy conditional precautions to insure the Franco government against criticism. For his part, John London (1997, 9–16) offers an incisive overview of the laughable colour and number classification codes employed by the censors to regulate theatre-going and he underlines the damaging effect of this code system on aesthetic considerations in Spain. He shows that there were instances of press censorship in which actors considered unsympathetic to the Franco regime could not be praised or, in at least one case, even mentioned at all.

During the post-war period, many Spanish playwrights were left to contend with very limited choices: they either had to write in accordance with censorship regulations (e.g. Buero Vallejo or Alejandro Casona after his exile) or write defiantly and be censured (e.g. Alfonso Sastre). If they rejected both of these choices, they either had to go into exile (e.g. Fernando Arrabal, Max Aub) or be compelled to write underground (Jerónimo López Mozo, José Ruibal, José Martínez Ballesteros, Luis Riaza, among many more). This repressive atmosphere led to a rapid decline of the Spanish theatre vis-à-vis the rest of European theatre precisely at the moment – the fifties and the sixties – when European theatre, spearheaded by such writers as Eugène Ionesco, Samuel Beckett and Bertolt Brecht was sweeping the continent with waves of innovation that would change the face of theatre internationally.

Notwithstanding the foregoing assertions, one cannot overlook the qualitative consistencies that marked a certain dimension of the theatre during the Franco period. In a study, *Continuidad y ruptura en el teatro español de la posguerra* (1999), Víctor García Ruiz makes a case for the aesthetic continuities between the theatre of the 1920s and 1930s, on one hand, and, on the other, post-war and contemporary dramatic tendencies. García Ruiz isolates three areas in which this legacy is most evident. First is stage direction, guided by such figures as Felipe Lluch, Luca de Tena, Luis Escobar, José Tamayo and José Luis Alonso, all Lorca specialists whose ideas about theatre and acting were firmly entrenched in the doctrine of La Barraca and of Cipriano Rivas Cherif's Teatro Escuela de Arte. Until the 1960s, when Miguel Narros and Francisco Nieva emerged on the theatrical scene (even though Nieva was then known as a set designer), affirms García Ruiz, it was the good enterprise of these directors to serve the audience and the dramatic work (as against making use of the work) that inspired decades of theatrical production in Spain. The second legacy of the 1920s and 1930s, García Ruiz goes on, is a non-realistic tradition of set design popularized by Spanish National Theatres that took hold of the scene until 1970. This 'avant-garde' tradition (Andrés Peláez's term) was sustained by several designers and painters, including Rafael Barradas, Sigfrido Burmann, Manuel Fontanals, Víctor Cortezo, Emilio Burgos and José Caballero, to mention just a few. A third legacy, a 'popular' theatrical culture, even received the support of the Franco regime,

with enormous repercussions in the 1960s. The initiative, under-
taken by Enrique de la Hoz in 1962, was aimed at making the
theatre more accessible to the rural regions of Spain by means of
Theatre Festivals as an autonomous institution (1999, 147–52).
Above all, García Ruiz underscores Ortega y Gasset's significance
as the foundation for Spanish avant-garde theatre in general and
poetic drama specifically. Ortega y Gasset's aesthetic of escapism
and play became the guiding principles of many a playwright since
the 1920s.[10]

One should not be mistaken by García Ruiz's genuine effort,
however, to believe that 'poetic' or experimental theatre ever
flourished in Spain. Even he concedes that the so-called 'idealist
theatre' never prospered but expressed itself more as a desire,
perhaps an attempt, on the part of a few (68). The question one
faces is not whether or not the Franco period produced any
valuable or innovative theatrical works. The question centres on
the extent to which the ideological or intellectual system framed
by Francoism facilitated or stifled the reception of innovative
drama, whether domestic or foreign. And evidence abounds to
show that the system was largely antagonistic to inventive or
progressive tendencies that echoed the wave blowing across
western Europe at the time. For example, John London has
documented methodically the critical and translation obstacles
faced by several Spanish productions of foreign plays between
1939 and 1963, including Sartre's *No Exit*, Ionesco's *The Lesson*,
The Bald Soprano, *The Chairs* and *Rhinoceros* as well as
Beckett's *Waiting for Godot*. London reports that, apart from
Rhinoceros, all Ionesco productions in Spanish during the period
in question were limited to one- or, rarely, two-night sessions. On
the whole, these works were subjected to overediting in translation
and to heavy misinterpretation and condemnation, if not outright
rejection by theatre critics. Besides the names mentioned above,
London points out, other figures of the avant-garde were all but
absent in Spain until the 1960s (115–40).

This is the prevailing environment in which Nieva's dramaturgy
was formed (he wrote his first major play in 1949), an environment that would ironically propel his experimental proclivity
when he moved to Paris in 1952. Under Franco, alternative projects
in the theatre often encountered resistance from the censorship
apparatus, and many theatre critics seemed to buy into a parochial

mentality consistent with the dictates of that apparatus. No wonder, even though today Nieva has managed to achieve extraordinary success with the stage, he had to wait for almost three decades after he began writing plays in order to realize his first commercial performance, which took place in January 1976, barely two months after General Franco's death. His story, like Arrabal's, is an unfortunate story, one that reflects the damage a nation can do to itself by gagging authentic artistic development.[11]

Toward a Dramatic Theory

Nieva's theatre militates against any absolute definition or classification. It is not easy to establish an internal unity or logical sequence within the universe of his literary production. Nieva himself further complicates the aesthetic categorization of his plays in the 1991 edition of his complete works when he reclassifies them in an ambiguous and sometimes apparently illogical manner.[12] Moreover, his proclivity toward the oneiric, combined with a hermetic diction, produces an extremely complex drama opposed to a unilateral interpretation by readers/critics and spectators/directors alike. What makes Nieva's work more difficult to classify, above all, is the extraordinary heterogeneity of antecedents that inform it. In an interview with José Luis Vicente Mosquete, he enumerates the multiplicity of voices that influence his theatre: Cervantes's *entremeses*, the *Celestina*, Quevedo, Gracián, Artaud, Brecht, Beckett, Ionesco, Jarry and the Surrealists, Bernard Shaw, Pirandello, Valle-Inclán, Lorca, Alberti, Aub, Fellini, Pasolini, Büchner, Ghelderode, Juan Ruiz . . . (Nieva 1987, 15).

Should one insist on identifying Nieva with a specific group of writers, however, that group would have to be the 1960s Generation, internationally composed of writers such as Italo Calvino, Pasolini, García Márquez and Mishima, writers in whose practice of 'magic realism' Nieva (1996h) finds a strong echo of his own dramaturgy.[13] Nieva (1990a, 41) had hinted that he considered the 1960s Generation's break with the avant-garde as having set the stage for post-avant-gardism, a term one can now safely take to mean (literary) postmodernism. Note that the period to which Nieva refers was precisely the moment when literary critics, most notably Harry Levin, Hassan, Howe, Fiedler

and Frank Kermode, began to use the term 'postmodernism' in
reference to the post-World War II experimental fiction of the
Generation with which our playwright identifies himself – Jorge
Luis Borges, Thomas Pynchon, Beckett and others (Groden and
Kreiswirth 1994, 585). In this context, Urszula Aszyk's assertion
(1995, 247) that Nieva's life and work constitute a world apart
may be true, but to insist, as this critic does, that it would be
erroneous to associate him with any movement or group of
writers is to stretch the matter. The question is not whether or
not Nieva's work is classifiable within any aesthetic paradigm at
all; rather, it is whether or not such a classification is absolute.
Nieva's work is classifiable, but the category of writers with which
he is identifiable is notably postmodernist in their adulterated
rooting in avant-garde aesthetics.[14]

The heterogeneity of Nieva's antecedents is not sheer coincidence but stems directly from his artistic philosophy, which
conforms to his own notion of postmodernism:

> The shortcomings of the avant-garde movements lie in the fact that
> they have been very one-sided, very restrictive. Movements such as
> Cubism or Dada – Surrealism not so much – are extremely narrow
> bands. Something similar occurs with what is called postmodernism
> (with which I align myself somehow), which carries a certain aura of
> mannerism in the sense that it has become a kind of unilateral theory
> on collage   But this should not really be the case. *True post-
> modernism* is to ignore the old and past modernity, which established
> very specific fixations that limited the artist's personality. (Nieva
> 1987, 15; emphasis added)

It is clear, then, that for Nieva true postmodernism involves a
symbiotic accommodation of tendencies; it represents for him
what postmodern architecture does for Paolo Portoghesi – 'a
polycentric network of experiences, all deserving to be heard'
(1983, 26). What inspires Nieva's sweeping criticism of modernism, the avant-garde and postmodernism itself is not necessarily a
desire to distance his own theatre from these categories but
to caution against the common propensity to muffle artistic
diversity. Naturally, therefore, in Nieva's vision, no polarity exists
between postmodernism and avant-gardism; on the contrary, he
sees postmodernism as a superstructure bolstered by avant-garde

pillars, especially surrealism, where conflicting elements come to interact freely. It must be recalled that the ideological foundation of the avant-garde itself is heterogeneous, and as a movement, it draws on various systems and combines its borrowings to make up its own doctrine (Szabolcsi 1971, 58). This principle of artistic pluralism, so central in Nieva's notion of postmodernism and reflective of his postist formation, constitutes the philosophical platform on which his dramatic theory and practice are constructed.

Nieva does not have a consolidated body of theoretical formulations. Much of what one makes of his dramatic theory appears dispersed in the form of articles, interviews and introductions to editions of his texts. His most condensed theoretical corpus appears ironically in the form of a poem entitled 'Breve poética teatral' (A Short Dramatic Poetics), which Carlos Gortari calls the boldest, the most forcible and the most original Manifesto of post-War Spanish theatre (1975, 15). The poem reads:

> El teatro es vida alucinada e intensa.
> No es el mundo, ni manifestación a la luz del sol,
> ni comunicación a voces de la realidad práctica.
> 4   Es una ceremonia ilegal,
> un crimen gustoso e impune.
> Es alteración y disfraz:
> Actores y público llevan antifaces,
> 8   maquillajes,
> llevan distintos trajes . . .
> o llevan desnudos.
> Nadie se conoce, todos son distintos,
> 12 todos son 'los otros',
> todos son intérpretes del aquelarre.
> El teatro es tentación siempre renovada,
> cántico, lloro, arrepentimiento, complacencia y martirio.
> 16 Es el gran cercado orgiástico y sin evasión;
> es el otro mundo, la otra vida,
> el más allá de nuestra conciencia;
> es medicina secreta,
> 20 hechicería,
> alquimia del espíritu,
> jubiloso furor sin tregua . . . (BP 94)[15]

[Theatre is a hallucinatory and intense life. / It is neither the world nor a revelation as clear as the sun, / nor is it an instrument of practical reality. / It is an illegal ceremony, / a delightful and unpunished crime. / It is alteration and disguise: / Actors and audience wear masks, / make-up, / they don different costumes . . . / or appear naked. / No one is familiar; everyone is different, / everyone is 'the other', / everyone is an interpreter of the Witches' Sabbath. / Theatre is temptation under constant renewal; / it is a canticle, lamentation, regret, pleasure and martyrdom. / It is a great orgiastic enclosure with no outlet; / it is the other world, the other life, / that which lies beyond consciousness. / It is a secret medicine, / sorcery, / alchemy of the spirit, / a joyful rage without respite . . .]

This poem, or poetics, a cogent synthesis of Nieva's dramatic *Weltanschauung*, resounds multiple voices of the European avant-garde. Latent in the poem's first three lines is the irrational, dream-like echo of Valle-Inclán, Ionesco and Strindberg. The fourth and fifth lines reverberate currents of Jean Genet's criminal and ceremonial drama. The next eight lines recall Greek

1. *Teatro Furioso* (Furious Theatre), drawn by Francisco Nieva. Courtesy of Francisco Nieva.

theatre, bordering on the carnivalesque, grotesque thread of Rabelais's art as formulated by Mikhail Bakhtin. From the fourteenth to the final line, the artistic principles of Artaud, Bataille, Michel de Ghelderode and Alfred Jarry are vividly present in their ritualistic, metaphysical essence. In all, what one cannot miss in the poem is Nieva's presentation of theatre as a non-representational artistic form, which, nevertheless, remains earth-bound, with a peculiar Dionysian splendour.

From an abstract definition of his dramatic vision, Nieva advances a concrete theory of his theatre in general. He calls this theory *Estética del delito*, which evokes Genet's Aesthetics of Crime. Nieva confesses how his reading of *Notre-Dame des Fleurs* shaped the ideological grounding of his theatre and led it toward the nihilistic disposition of Genet's philosophy (1973c, 23). Genet, once a proud editor of the perverted *The Thief's Journal*, consecrates himself as the master of glorified vice. Genet views theatre as the domain of crime, since, for him, artistic beauty has a special poetic power equivalent to what he calls 'the power of crime'. These ideas seem to inform the guiding principle of Nieva's *Estética del delito*, which, above all, exalts liberty, the rebellious desire for freedom from socio-cultural regulation and authority. According to Nieva, social vigilance (conservatism) creates a permanent bond of moral guilt, which society places on its members' path to knowledge. In order for theatre to serve as an instrument of knowledge without feelings of guilt, it ought to be a subversive instrument, a criminal, outlawed religion that undermines self-conservation and all forms of totalizing hierarchies (BP 97).

Nieva also likens the effect of theatrical representation to the fatal consequences produced by indulgence in drugs, recalling Artaud's comparison of the Theatre of Cruelty with the cathartically redemptive power of the plague. Nieva's equation of theatre with drugs is based on his belief that tragic fatality offers multiple possibilities for redemption from guilt and all forms of oppression. For him, tragic theatre is also revolutionary theatre, not in the sense of the radically new, but in the sense of a peculiar reality akin to dream states where total freedom reigns (BP 98). Theatre, then, is a call to rebellion, and the *Estética del delito* becomes the requisite instrument of that rebellion:

> I find it imperative to disobey. I am thus aware of belonging to a
> disobedient class, as much for what I feel as for what others make me
> feel by subjecting my mind to control, particularly in these times of
> tremendous cultural guilt. It should not be surprising, therefore, that,
> from the platform of a guilt-ridden art, an aesthetic of crime has
> spontaneously emerged. (BP 100)

This subversive critique of power and authority – a political act
– accords the *Estética del delito* a strong postmodernist underpinning. The politics, in this case, are not expressed in Nieva's dramatic
universe as a committed, partisan campaign. Rather, residing in
the theatrical act itself, the politics work to subvert cultural values
and to divest them of their rational and moral coating, leaving in
their trail sheer subjectivity and a relativist dialectic of constantly
shifting relationships:

> All values, whether guilt-ridden, perverse, prejudicial or stripped of
> their practical or moral application, remain as a positive-negative
> vital complex within a closed circle and in a perpetual state of
> affirmation-negation, inversion, change and negotiation. *Nothing is
> perfectly bad or good despite what that magnetized needle of guilt
> shows us.* (BP 102; emphasis added)

These words, thoroughly postmodernist in their collective celebration of pluralism and paradox, recall Nietzsche and faithfully connect back to the foundations of postist thought as expressed in the
First Manifesto:

> In an atmosphere of constant transformation and constant movement,
> in that perpetual, repetitive and alternating mechanism of analysis and
> synthesis, in that state of seeing and dreaming, of retaining and losing,
> of releasing and gaining, in that happy and disinterested marriage
> between corporal soul and spiritual soul, of reason and instinct . . . in
> that atmosphere of constant transformation . . . lies the true rationale
> or inevitable effect of the postist 'game'.

This kind of self-contradictory principle lies at the heart of the
postmodern theory advanced by Charles Jencks, who since 1978
has set what I believe to be an essential criterion for the postmodern
in all its manifested forms: double-coding and the 'necessity of

crossing boundaries and mixing genres'. By double-coding, Jencks means 'the continuation of modernity and its transcendence' or 'the combination of modern techniques and something else' or, still, as that which exemplifies itself as opposite pairings in the form of 'elite/popular, accommodating/subversive, new/old', etc. (1996, 30). This concept is the same one that Hassan reconstructs and dubs 'a double view', a principle that, in his view, postmodernism 'demands'. 'Sameness and difference, unity and rupture, filiation and revolt', Hassan proclaims, '. . . must be honored if we are to attend to history [and] apprehend (perceive, understand) change' (1980, 121). In effect, what Chicharro and Ory so vigorously promoted in the 1940s as an essential technique in postist poetry and painting has become a privileged device of postmodernist literature in the form of paradox and irony. It has also become a device of paramount importance in Francisco Nieva's theatre.

By espousing moral relativism, Nieva subverts the basis of human culture whose survival depends on conformity and guilt (the 'aguja imantada' (magnetized needle)). In this way, the playwright situates his dramaturgy in the inner core of the postmodern sensibility, which rebels against monolithic categories that obstruct freedom. In order to create an equilibrium between this ethical relativism and his belief in aesthetic relativism, Nieva inserts his drama within a historicist paradigm that refuses to force a universal appeal: 'The work of art ought to be framed within cultural parameters and based on historical knowledge. It should not claim to be totalizing and arrogantly universalist' (Nieva 1976b, 14). In highlighting the importance of a dramatic work's specific cultural reference, Nieva decentralizes the canonized unity of artistic experience and ensures possibilities for difference, echoing so remarkably Jean-François Lyotard's postmodern model. According to Lyotard,

> [a] postmodern artist or writer is in the position of a philosopher: the text he writes, the work he produces are not in principle governed by pre-established rules and they cannot be judged according to a determining judgment, by applying familiar categories to the text or to the work. Those rules and categories are what the work of art itself is looking for. The artist and the writer, then, are working without rules in order to formulate the rules of what *will have been done.* (1984, 81)

In line with his strategy against ideological fixity, Nieva advocates a dramatic language that is dynamic and in constant evolution. The word, he asserts, is in constant transformation, for language is choice and creativity, something completely resistant to regulation (BP 106). Against linguistic prejudice, he eliminates all division between poetic and conventional language, between linguistic styles associated with commoners and those attributable to nobility. What especially attracts Nieva is the popular basis of linguistic expression, not regulated academic diction. This is why he likes the 'jerga' and the 'caló' spoken by gypsies. For him, these are resilient languages that constantly recreate themselves and sever their bond with cultural heritage. In this sense, Nieva presents language as a key instrument of political power, for in liberating it from regulation, not only does one counteract language's quality as an agent of cultural domination, one also questions the claims of literature to truth and human value, a fundamental postmodern precept. Since he places a premium on the artistic function of language, he is unequivocal in under-scoring the importance of the literary text in theatrical praxis: 'Theatre is dramatic literature' (1996i, 58), he declares. What is more, not only does he trust the referential power of language and of the literary text, he considers these as vital tools of post-modernist theatre. When he was once asked if he considered his 'Teatro de Farsa y Calamidad' (Theatre of Farce and Calamity) as inferior to his 'Teatro Furioso' (Furious Theatre), Nieva res-ponded by saying that it would have been a step backwards if there had not emerged in Western civilization that cultural trend called postmodernism, which exalts the 'return to forms, to textual theatre, to verbal theatre' (1987, 16).

In this connection, it is perhaps worth assessing Ramón Gómez de la Serna's influence on Nieva's theatrical language. Gómez de la Serna (1888–1963), said to be the one who ushered in the Spanish avant-garde, was a major literary figure in the Madrid of the early 1920s. He is best known for his invention in 1910 of the *greguería*, a system of comic metaphors that create false and disjunctive associations between different layers of reality, 'an attempt to define that which cannot be defined', as he aptly puts it himself (1957, 69–70). Among his dramatic works, mostly one-act pieces, are *El palacio deshabitado* and *Beatriz* (1909), *El laberinto* and *La bailarina* (1910), *Los sonámbulos*, *Siempreviva* and *La corona de hierro* (1911), *El lunático* and *Teatro en soledad* (1912) and *Los medios seres* (1929). Some of his most important novels are *La viuda blanca y negra* (1918), *El secreto del acueducto* (1922), *La Quinta de Palmyra* (1923), *La mujer de ámbar* and *El torero Caracho* (1927), *La nardo* (1930) and *El incongruente* (1922), this last-mentioned being one of the most surreal of his novels. A master of verbal dexterity, Gómez de la Serna endows metaphoric language with an enviable creative flexibility comparable only to his Baroque compatriot Luis de Góngora y Argote (1561–1627). Predominant in his artistic universe is the use of imagination to capture the impossible, the subversion of conventional hierarchies, a certain distancing from moral or political concerns, the constant transformation of realities, reliance on intuition, linguistic dynamism and creativeness, and, above all, the use of humour, qualities that would come to mark the identity of Nieva's own artistic repertoire.

No wonder, Pont sees the postists as the group of writers who have benefited the most from the legacy of Gómez de la Serna's poetic language (1987, 229–30). Indeed, Pont cites a case where Gómez de la Serna extols Ory's poems as 'exemplary *greguerías*' (1998, 82). So impressed is Nieva by Gómez de la Serna's text-based drama that, in an article that he wrote for the *ABC* entitled 'La inclemente modernidad de Ramón' (1996e), he passionately defends Gómez de la Serna's modernist theatrical project as a model to which postmodernist theatre owes its strength. He argues that there is nothing in the world that supersedes the historical modernism of Gómez de la Serna's time in terms of radicalism and an 'optical approach' to words, 'the pure textual material'. Something very similar, he adds, occurs with the performance text. This up-beat endorsement of modernism may sound contradictory to Nieva's lukewarm attitude toward the avant-garde, but the contradiction fades when one considers that he is fundamentally a poetic dramatist with strong postist roots. Like the poetic drama of García Lorca or Valle-Inclán (one could add Claudel, Ghelderode or Cocteau), Nieva's plays are designed as much for their reading pleasure as they are for the stage.

Of the poetic dramatists, the one that carries the greatest weight in Nieva's artistic vision, however, is Ramón María del Valle-Inclán (1866–1936), Spain's pre-eminent twentieth-century playwright and novelist who symbolizes a break with the naturalistic

provincialism of Spanish theatre. Although Nieva himself has
been ambivalent about the degree of Valle-Inclán's influence on
him, there is no question that significant ethical and aesthetic
parallels link the two writers.[16] What is more, the reappropriation
of Valle-Inclán in the 1960s in a way serves to condition the
triumph of postmodernism on the Spanish stage. In discussing
Valle-Inclán, it is important to specify to which of the two phases
of his literary career one is referring. The first, a *modernista* phase,
involves the pre-World War I Valle of historical dramas inserted
within Galician folklore, with a decadent appeal to artificialities,
formal beauty and perfection. Some of the dramas of this period
are *Cenizas* (1899) – revised in 1908 as *El yermo de las almas* –,
El Marqués de Bradomín (1906), the trilogy *Comedias bárbaras*
(*Águila de blazón* and *Romance de lobos* (1907) and *Cara de
plata* (1922)), *Cuento de abril* (1909), *Voces de gesta* (1911) and
La Marquesa Rosalinda (1912). The weight of Valle-Inclán's
influence and novelty as a key figure of the European avant-
garde, however, resides in the second evolutionary phase, from
1920 onward, in his elaboration of the *esperpento*, a dramatic sub-
genre that employs grotesque distortion as his mechanism for
presenting Spanish life. This is the surrealist Valle, the cynical
and innovative Valle of *esperpentos* such as *Luces de bohemia*
and *Divinas palabras* (1920), *Los cuernos de don Friolera* (1921),
Las galas del difunto (1926) and *La hija del capitán* (1927).
Perhaps the most defining quality that Valle-Inclán brought to
the Spanish stage is that genuine form of poetic theatre (partly
inspired by the paintings of Goya), expressed through a dramatic
mode and ethic and saturated in mystery, complexity, grotesque
parody and a deformation of conventional values. What attracts
Nieva to Valle-Inclán is that plastic make-up of his literature, what
Nieva calls a 'realismo plástico' (1967, 18). This 'plastic realism'
manifests itself abundantly in the poetic undertone of Valle-
Inclán's stage directions, which tend to be detailed narratives.
Above all, Valle-Inclán expresses a strong attraction to the past –
the 'España negra' or 'España profunda' – where he finds authentic
poetic material in superstition and myth to construct his own
brand of theatre. This reliance on the past as a rhetorical and
aesthetic source for moulding old artistic modes into new ones is
also a postist ideal, which now forms the cornerstone of Nieva's
dramaturgy.[17]

Francisco Nieva's postulates, as elaborated above, do not constitute by themselves a theory of postmodernist drama. What they do offer is a conceptual groundwork on the basis of which the discussion of concrete facets of his work can be understood and the postmodernist character of his theatre as a whole can be appraised. In considering his theatre from a postmodernist perspective, one should not lose sight of the fundamental ingredient that shaped his dramatic theory and practice: his postist ideological formation.

II

CRUELTY AND PARADOX

NIEVA AND ARTAUD

Of the multiple elements that create a bond between the postist identity of Nieva's theatre and postmodern aesthetics, none is as profound and pervasive as paradox. As a dramatic technique, paradox carries an inherent egalitarian principle that collapses dichotomies and hierarchical modes of contemplating reality. An old device particularly popular with writers of the Baroque, paradox (or oxymoron, as it is sometimes known) became one of the principal tropes employed by the postists. The essence of the postist project, indeed, rests upon that notion of field levelling, which paradox firmly upholds. It is a notion expressed by Carlos, a character in José Luis Varela's short postist play *Tornton Wilder en Madrid o un diálogo en recoletos*: 'Un poema postista es bueno o malo. Ni bonito ni feo. O, mejor: ni bueno ni malo, sino todo lo contrario: postista' (A postist poem is good or bad. Neither beautiful nor ugly. Or better put: it's neither good nor bad, but rather the contrary: it is postist).[1]

Nieva's theatre, posited on the pedestal of paradox, finds release and independence by constantly staging and diffusing tension between binary fields to form new artistic possibilities. In his *Estética del delito*, theatre is presented as the revelation of the darker world within, 'the profound truth that everyone fears', 'the human heart's most obscure parts, its most unexplored or inner-most dimensions' (BP 96). Nieva accentuates the ambivalent role of theatre as a destructive and restorative force whose goal is to attain superior existence by way of self-annihilation:

> Theatre – or the world – is the privileged and damned place of orgy where we get to know another world and another life, incubated by orgy, other than that to which we are already accustomed. We participate in the destruction and dilapidation of the self, of ourselves, and this process takes us beyond our conscience. The beyond, so attractive and fatal, is like a superior mixture of pleasure, pain, knowledge and death. (BP 117)

Nieva's commitment to ambivalence and negation is transparent in his equation of pain and death with pleasure and knowledge. He likens the effect of theatrical representation to the fatal consequences produced by indulgence in drugs, since, in his artistic vision, tragic fatality offers multiple possibilities for redemption from guilt and all forms of oppression. No wonder Emil George Signes labels Nieva's as a 'theater of the Marvelous' (1988, 153–7), a concept advanced by Gloria Orenstein that is based on the harmonious coexistence of contradictions. This resilient artistic order, rooted in Nieva's postist orientation, is propelled by the dramatic theory of Artaud, twentieth-century's most radical avant-garde figure who, nevertheless, set the stage for the brand of theatrical praxis one may call postmodernist.

In the Theatre of Cruelty, Artaud invokes the plague as his central dramatic metaphor. He argues that, in the theatre and in the plague, there is something both victorious and vengeful, since the social and organic disaster brought by the plague indicates 'the presence of a state which is nevertheless characterized by extreme strength and in which all the powers of nature are freshly discovered at the moment when something essential is going to be accomplished' (1958, 27). As in the case of the plague, the theatre 'is the time of evil, the triumph of dark powers that are nourished by a power even more profound until extinction' (30). Like the plague, the Theatre of Cruelty is 'the revelation, the bringing forth, the exteriorization of a depth of latent cruelty by means of which all the perverse possibilities of the mind . . . are localized' (30). Artaud views theatre both as 'an avenging scourge' and 'a redeeming epidemic' whose action is beneficial, since it impels human beings to see themselves as they are; 'it causes the mask to fall, [it] reveals the lie, the slackness, baseness, and hypocrisy of our world' (31). The Theatre of Cruelty, the French theorist maintains, must be capable of waking its audience up 'nerves and heart' and acting upon it like 'a spiritual therapeutics whose touch can never be forgotten' (85). In her appraisal of Artaud's theory, Jane Goodall puts it best: 'theater is a counterdemiurgical [*sic*] activity and, as such, it is agonistic and antagonistic in the most extravagant terms' (1994, 64). Nieva's Aesthetic of Crime reveals, therefore, a conceptual correspondence with the Theatre of Cruelty in its celebration of theatre's dualistic energy. But, as will be seen, where Artaud displays a severity bordering on tragedy, Nieva constantly offsets such severity or frustration by intertwining it with playful, even if grotesque, undertones.

Let me hasten to say that Artaud's influence on Nieva is not the case where the latter simply learnt to imitate the former. Rather, Nieva's admiration stems from his eventual discovery of the ideological resemblance that has always existed between the Theatre of Cruelty and his own dramatic principles. Before Colette Allendy called Nieva's attention to Artaud in 1952 in Paris, Nieva had already written a few opera librettos that echoed the French dramatist's ideas and the theatre of the absurd (see Nieva 1973d, 157).[2] At its face value, Nieva's strong pro-language theatre might seem antithetical to the Theatre of Cruelty's aversion to speech. Jacques Derrida even goes to the extent of dismissing as non-Artaudian all theatre that privilege speech. Discussing what he considers to be 'the themes of infidelity' to the Theatre of Cruelty, Derrida lists the following: all non-sacred theatre, all theatre that privilege[s] speech or the word, all abstract theatre, all theatre of alienation, all non-political theatre and all ideological theatre that primarily seek[s] to deliver a message (1978, 243–6). It must, however, be stressed that Artaud's dramatic theory is multidimensional and much more complex than his discourse on speech and language seems to suggest. *The Theater and Its Double*'s stringent essentialism and dogmatic formulation and its unabashed attack on the literary component of the theatrical enterprise are indicative of modernist experimentalism. At the same time, that revolutionary treatise on theatre also served to anticipate and to prepare the grounds for the development of what I call a postmodernist dramatic strategy. Nieva's discovery of Artaud not only authenticated his theatrical postulations but also helped him to overcome his own insecurities and to embolden his rebellious proclivities. Nieva: 'My great discovery when I got to know Artaud's work was to realize that theatre could once again be an orgy: an orgy of blood, of pleasure, of anguish, of confession . . .' (1973c, 24). Two considerations thus emerge as one assesses this Spanish playwright's theatre within the ideological parameters of Cruelty. The first is the concept of theatre as a chaotic and an overwhelming (orgiastic) experience designed to highlight the contradictions intrinsic to that experience. The second is the (important or diminished) role of the literary text in performance praxis. The first consideration forms the genesis of this chapter and the second is explored in chapter V.

THE PARADOX OF EVIL

Nowhere does the notion of paradox and duality express itself more forcefully in Nieva's drama than in his conceptualization of evil. It is also in his subversive approach to evil that his artistic solidarity with the Theatre of Cruelty is most clearly manifested. The one play in which the concept of the double is most effectively deployed is *Nosferatu (Aquelarre y noche roja de)* (Witches' Sabbath and Bloody Night of Nosferatu) (1961), precisely the play that Nieva declares as having most closely united him with Artaud and Bataille (1973b, 163).

Nosferatu is a story about Nosferatu, a vampire who goes about infecting people with evil. Scandal upon scandal follows as the radio announces the end of the world. Meanwhile, the people present Queen Kelly with petitions, but when they realize that the monarchy has betrayed them, they cause a popular uprising. Kelly attempts to escape on the grounded express train, but when she senses danger, she cunningly invites the protesters to get on board. As they mount the train, Mickey Mouse arrives, ordering his armed men to fire. Everyone except the Madrigal chorus and Kelly dies, but Nosferatu later arises from the dead and forcefully takes away the queen in a coach. The goddess Aurora, who appeared at the beginning of the play to rescue a wounded journalist, returns at the end with his skeleton. The play also contains a subplot involving the quarrels between Greta, a vegetable seller, and Azul, a gypsy violinist and prostitute. Systematic though this synopsis may sound, *Nosferatu*'s plot is so diffused and disjointed that it is very difficult to follow the story at first glance.

As if in tribute to Artaud, Nieva (in the 1991 version of *Nosferatu*) sets the philosophical tone for the play by inserting an epigraph containing the French playwright's words:

> Haz vacilar nuestra razón
> en el seno de su propia ciencia
> y arrebátanos la inteligencia
> en las garras de un nuevo tifón. (TC 207)[3]

[Let our reason waver / in the bosom of its own science / and snatch
away our intelligence / in the stranglehold of a new typhoon.]

Aside from alluding to Artaud in the author's notes, Nieva also
highlights *Nosferatu*'s inspiration in García Lorca's avant-garde
literature and declares that his aesthetic mission, like Lorca's, is
anti-Aristotelian. He states his predilection for the director's role
over the author's and affirms the importance of the spectator's
active role in the drama's interpretation. Further, Nieva characterizes
the play as 'apocalyptic', 'millenarian or prophetic' and proclaims
as *Nosferatu*'s ultimate source of inspiration the history of silent
cinema: F. W. Murnau's *Nosferatu* (1922), Erich von Ströheim's
Queen Kelly (1929), G. W. Pabst's *The Street of Sorrow* (1925)
and Walt Disney's Mickey Mouse cartoons. Additionally, the
play is set in what the playwright refers to as the fatal Europe of
Expressionism (TC 209). Evidently, therefore, before embarking
on his theatrical project in *Nosferatu*, Nieva already engages in a
kind of non-mimeticist theatrical tradition that harnesses diverse
modes of artistic expression in order to construct his peculiar
theatrical vision of the vampire myth.

    In the play, a latent evil force seems to control the characters'
conduct and actions. From the opening scene to the closing
moment, the play offers little relief to its audience as it drives
them to encounter the operation of evil in themselves and in
others. One means by which this evil tendency is expressed is the
phenomenon of the apocalypse, a typical postist and postmodernist symbol. I refer here to the meaning of apocalypse as
manifested in the Book of Revelation (New Testament) where it is
proclaimed that there will soon take place a divine intervention in
which hidden realities, known to God alone, will be disclosed and
in which there will be victory over Satan. According to the
Holman Bible Dictionary, the term *apocalypse* is derived from
the Greek verb *apokalupto*, which means 'to uncover', and,
figuratively, 'to disclose, reveal'. What is pertinent and most
vividly captured in *Nosferatu* is the catastrophic process, the
revelatory upheaval associated with the end of time in the form of
war and the plague. The play's atmosphere is invaded by a
cosmic turbulence that is sporadically reported through radio
airwaves: it is said that the world is experiencing a horrible night
of falling stars, that the Caspian Sea is being inundated with bees,

that violent winds are taking over the city and so on. In the 1993 performance of the play, the musician Manuel Balboa inundates the theatre with all sorts of noises typical of horror cinema. These terrifying sounds and the imposing darkness, punctuated by a Dracula-style language and an intense sensation of human agony, all together raise the dramatic dynamics to a level equivalent to what Artaud calls 'cosmic rigour', articulated as the ultimate meaning of Cruelty. A cosmic concept not far distant from what Wole Soyinka designates as 'the cosmic human condition' (1976, 41), whereby human beings and natural forces harmonize themselves as co-participants in the tragic mysteries of the earth.

What accords Nieva's apocalyptic presentation a peculiar postmodernist identity is not simply the sense of an ending so characteristic of such plays as Beckett's *Endgame* or Sam Shepard's *Action*; it is especially the ethical contradiction that underpins the presentation. The restorative dimension of the apocalypse, which gives God a clear victory over Satan, is subverted in *Nosferatu*, making both forces complement each other to victory. In order to project this ambivalent dimension of the apocalypse, Nieva secularizes the phenomenon by dissociating it from its essential moral Judaeo-Christian component, the Judgement. Thus, he labels the apocalypse as 'el sinjuicio final' (TC 231) (the final non-judgement). In so doing, he undermines the final moral account (which he considers as a repressive tool), thus obliterating the division between the Chosen (Good) and the Condemned (Evil). As moral hierarchies are dismantled, the apocalyptic hour becomes at once the gate to Heaven and Hell. It becomes the source of true life, the time when crime and temptation pay and when, for the first time, the powerless have a chance to taste liberty and justice:

LA AURORA – Mira tu calle barrida por la mala suerte. ¿Quiénes son los que aquí viven? Los que de no tener nada quisieran, sin más ni más, comerse la cresta del ave Fénix y sorber la médula del Unicornio, todo por la primera y última vez. Nunca pudo ser posible, pero ahora lo será a las puertas de la muerte. Los pobres abominables vais a pedir y obtener el triunfo de la tentación y el crimen, el gustazo de Nerón y el cachondeo de Agripina. La destrucción y el paraíso. (TC 211)

[Look at your street so overtaken by bad luck. Who are those that live here? Those who, for having nothing and without much ado, wish to eat up Phoenix's crest and suck Unicorn's marrow for the first and last time. This was never possible, but it will now be at the gate of death. You abominable poor shall seek and gain the victory of temptation and crime, the great pleasure of Nero and the banter of Agrippina. Destruction and paradise.]

What is accentuated here is the paradoxical nature of the apoca-lyptic mechanism as producer of Good via Evil. Moral judgement and closure, easy targets of postmodernist assault, here collapse before the pressure of an ethical relativism intended to generate infinite vital possibilities.[4]

This double-edged approach to the apocalypse motif creates a special dramatic atmosphere in which the playwright advances his unorthodox notion of vampirism. In connecting *Nosferatu* with Murnau's film, Nieva reconstructs and situates his play within the vampire world of Bram Stoker's original *Dracula* (1897), which inspired the film. Montague Summers, a renowned authority on witchcraft and vampirism, attests upon opening his seminal work *The Vampire: His Kith and Kin*:

> Throughout the whole vast shadowy world of ghosts and demons there is no figure so terrible, no figure so dreaded and abhorred, yet dight with such fearful fascination, as the vampire, who is himself neither ghost nor demon, but yet who partakes the dark natures and possesses the mysterious and terrible qualities of both. (1960, 1)

In the 1993 performance, the appearance of Nancho Novo, dressed as a vampire, produces electrifying visual effects. His laughter is as frightening as the smile of Milton's Satan, and his nails and canine teeth jut out as if ready to devour. Notwithstanding this demoniac portrayal of Nosferatu, his role in the play radically sets him apart from previous vampires such as Count Dracula of Murnau's film. Nieva's Nosferatu is a subversion of the classic figure: unlike Dracula, whose evil conduct is totally motivated by personal desire, Nieva's Nosferatu is a modern, redemptive vampire whose wicked activities are paradoxically intended to attack evil. The Madrigal chorus acclaims him as a progressive instrument that topples tradition for the common good: 'Dueño

de la ciudad. Suelto pecado progresista, siempre dispuesto a des-
acreditar el pasado . . . Es un enturbiador, unas veces marxista,
otras cubista' (Master of the city. Unbridled sin of progress, ever
ready to discredit the past . . . He is a troublemaker, sometimes a
Marxist, other times a Cubist) (TC 234).

2. *Nosferatu (Aquelarre y noche roja de)* (Witches' Sabbath and Bloody
Night of Nosferatu), directed by Guillermo Heras, with a set designed by
G. Heras and Álvaro Agudo. Sala Olimpia, Madrid, 1993. Photo by Chicho,
courtesy of Centro de Documentación Teatral, Madrid.

The chorus's validation of Nosferatu as a Cubist carries connotations that resonate with the postist tenor of Nieva's theatre.
Nosferatu's mission – to expose and exteriorize 'the depth of latent
cruelty' in human beings as a means to attaining knowledge and
rebirth – reverberates what Georges Lemaitre has suggested as
the defining ideal of the Cubist movement: 'an eager and fervent
desire to penetrate beneath the motley exterior of material ap-
pearances and to grasp something of the fundamental substance
of reality' (1947, 79–80); an unequivocal echo of *Postismo*'s Cubist
legacy as established in the Second Manifesto – '(the movement)
from the exterior into the interior of things'. In *Nosferatu*, the
Cubist web of reality is redefined and invented as a conceived

reality, a non-mimetic order in which the tyranny of logic and guilt is replaced by some sort of cruelty – 'delito' (crime) if you will – as basis for existence. Although utterly avant-gardist, Cubism is nevertheless attractive to the postmodernist: in the Cubist destruction of perspective emerges the postmodern exaltation of multiplicity and indeterminacy, Cubist subjectivity produces postmodernist relativism and Cubist non-differentiation between foreground and background is consonant with postmodernism's quest for the dissolution of hierarchies. As will be seen presently, this Cubist order of things comes to life in the play in more concrete ways.

In the play, Nosferatu's speech is constantly tinged with paradoxical controversy. He defies conventional justice, arguing against punishment for the wicked and advocating hell as the right place for the innocent: 'La práctica del Mal contra el malvado no procura ningún placer, un cincuenta por ciento de inocentes necesita el infierno de verdad' (The practice of evil against the evildoer does not produce any pleasure. Fifty per cent of the innocent truly need hell) (TC 237). So strong is Nosferatu's influence in the play that all who come into contact with him are infected by his ideas. For example, caught in the spell of the vampire's masochistic principle, Celestino and Ottilia, his niece, have come to adopt pain and chaos as a legitimate way of self-expression. In a dramatic move, the Madrigal chorus offers itself in response to Nosferatu's desire to inject virtue into their veins. As Nosferatu bites them one after another, they, like Queen Kelly, twist around in sadomasochistic ecstasy, even as they protest. These instances of self-sacrifice recall Artaud's emphasis on physical pain as a process toward spiritual healing. In her study of this theme in Artaud, Gene A. Plunka has noted that the release of one's conscious drives, which is basically a search from within, cannot be divorced from the physical. 'The purpose of the Theatre of Cruelty', Plunka intimates, 'is to transform the human body, the flesh' (1994, 22–3). To offer oneself to the vampire is to embrace the devil; it is, as the Madrigal chorus declares, to sanction obscenity. But within *Nosferatu*'s dramatic world, the gesture is portrayed as an allegorical act of self-release, because it empowers the victims to expose their concealed inner desires.

In a conversation he holds with his apprentice, this is what Nosferatu says:

Todo ser humano que de algo se precie me llama en secreto para alguna mordedura. Todos se venden y lo venden todo por el éxtasis que no conocen. ¡No habría de ser feliz yo, si en mi diente está el foco más problemático, la bacteria lúbrica por excelencia! Aún se esconden, vergonzosos, para perder el sentido común. Pero el tiempo llegará en que mi necocio prospere. (TC 217)

[Every human being who has something about which to boast calls me aside for a bite. Everybody sells himself or herself and everything else for the sake of the ecstasy they have never experienced. Why wouldn't I be happy, if indeed my teeth possess the most harmful focus, the perfect, salacious bacteria! All these people continue to hide themselves shamefully to avoid common sense. But, surely, the time will come when my business will prosper.]

In uncovering society's inner dark side, Nosferatu shatters the rift between the vampire world (Evil) and the rest of society (Virtue), thereby substantiating Nieva's solidarity with Bataille. In Bataille's view, Evil is not the exclusive dream of the wicked but, to some extent, the dream of Good (1973, 8). So much importance does Bataille accord this concept that he hastens to reaffirm it as the missing element in Breton's own comparable notion of the union of opposites:

'Everything leads us to believe', wrote André Breton, 'that there is a certain point in the mind where life and death, the real and the imaginary, the past and the future, the communicable and the incommunicable, are no longer perceived in contradiction to one another'. I shall add: Good and Evil, pain and joy. This point is indicated both by violent literature and by the violence of a mystical experience: only the point matters. (1973, 15)

On the basis of the foregoing analysis, one is led to conclude that the only difference between Nieva's vampire and the rest of society is this: one attains freedom through self-expression; the other is self-imprisoned by repressing its inner inclinations. They all are children of the devil: '¡Viva el Mal y su hijo preferido que es el Bien!' (Long live Evil and its favourite child, Good!) (TC 243). After everything is stripped of make-up – Nieva points out in a stage direction in *Nosferatu* – all that is left of creation is cruelty:

Muertas algunas virtudes inútiles y a punto de perecer todo lo demás, el mundo es sinceramente malvado . . . (TC 233)

[Once useless virtues are dead and the world comes to the point of losing everything else, the inner perversity of the world truly emerges.]

In his etymological definition of 'cruelty', Clément Rosset explains that the word *cruor*, from which *crudelis* (cruel) and *crudus* (indigestible) are derived,

> designates torn and bloody flesh, that is, the thing itself stripped of all its ornaments and ordinary external accoutrements, in this case skin and thus reduced to its unique reality . . . Thus reality is cruel – and indigestible – as soon as one removes from it everything which is not reality in order to consider it in itself. (1993, 76)

Nosferatu's heroic moment (each time he gains another victim) concurs with the play's ethical triumph – restoration by way of annihilation – because the drama then appears at a point where the victim of agony is 'transformed' – as Goodall would put it – 'into its embodiment' (1994, 53). In other words, through the *theatricalization of suffering*, tragedy reconstructs itself as a blessing by elevating the victim above physical affliction onto the domain of self-discovery. Herein lies the essence of Nieva's Criminal Aesthetic.[5]

The origin of this therapeutic vision, in which adversity appears as the redistilling fountain of cure and redemption, goes beyond Artaud or Bataille. Ironically, it can be found in classical Aristotelian *catharsis* and in modern psychoanalysis. But there is an important difference between Aristotelian *catharsis* – the total effect of fear and pity produced by Tragedy – and Nieva's therapeutic strategy. Whereas *catharsis* is primarily generated by *hamartia* (the tragic flaw attributed to the protagonist), Nieva's principle is linked with a general spirit of transgression and chaos in which the dramatic action is enmeshed. In modern times, various interpretations have been given to *catharsis*, but, as Marvin Carlson points out, all agree that the term is a beneficial, uplifting experience, whether psychological, moral, intellectual or some combination of these (1993, 18–19). In their studies of hysteria, Josef Breuer and Sigmund Freud show that, in order for a patient of psychical trauma to be cured, the origin of the pathological condition needs to be brought into consciousness. Because the abnormality can persist if the patient's reaction is suppressed, Breuer and Freud propose *catharsis* as psychotherapy for hysteria, that is, a state in which the patient relives the cause of his/her condition (1957, 3–17).

The point of appeal in this self-conflictive strategy for Nieva is the subject's self-empowerment against the tyranny of fixture and fate, that is, the subject's ability to rebel against that tyranny by engaging it head-on. This cathartic formula does not always manifest itself in *Nosferatu* through physical affliction; at times it is expressed as a psychological phenomenon intended to produce a paradoxical effect. Nieva dramatizes this situation by making the vampire offer a different kind of antidote to men, since Nosferatu attacks only women. For example, in order to control the Police Chief's corruption and abuse of power, Nosferatu tells him to order his officers to revolt and disobey the law by getting drunk and abandoning the barracks. Similarly, Celestino follows his master's prescription by embracing crime and anarchy as positive signals of regeneration:

> Quisiera dar juego al mundo, vivir la vida, ¡qué carajo! Me gustaría robar y cometer algún crimen pequeño en gato o en perro. Travesuras de revancha. Hacer que tropiece mi padre y llenarme de remordimiento. Sueño que entro en el palacio real sin pantalones y que todos me hacen acatamiento porque me ha bendecido el Diablo. (TC 216)

> [How I wish to play with the world, enjoy life, damn it! I'd love to steal and commit some petty crime. Pranks of revenge. To make my father stumble and then fill myself with remorse. I dream of having entered the royal palace with no pants on and of everyone being amazed because I have been cursed by the devil].

The ethical connotations underlying Celestino's words in the cultural context of vampirism inscribe *Nosferatu* firmly within the rhetorical coordinates of the European avant-garde. What one hears in Celestino is a resounding echo of Jean Genet as especially consecrated by Jean-Paul Sartre in *Saint Genet*.[6] And what the reader or spectator might perceive as Celestino's or Nosferatu's inverted morality parallels Bataille's notion of liberty:

> It is only if liberty, the transgression of laws and sovereign con-
> sumption are envisaged in their true form that the foundations of
> a moral code are revealed for those people who are not entirely
> regulated by necessity and who do not want to renounce the fullness
> which they have glimpsed. (1973, 169)[7]

Like Genet, Jarry or Artaud, Nieva's characters' rebellion and
their sadomasochistic attitude to adversity create paradoxical
premises that project onto the spectator's imagination uncertainties
about ethical codes and order. Remember: 'Nothing is perfectly
bad or good despite what that magnetized needle of guilt shows
us' (BP 102). Still, the Spanish playwright sets himself apart from
these writers in an important way. Instead of being true villains,
Nieva's characters evince dimensions that reflect an attractive
side to their transgressive nature. Rather than educe anger and
horror, as Jarry's Ubu or Artaud's Count Cenci do, the emotion
generally drawn in the audience by Nieva's subversive characters
is bewilderment, if not laughter. For example, Nosferatu does not
attack anyone without his/her consent, he scolds the Gran
Marcial's abuse of power (which he equates with the work of the
devil) on behalf of the oppressed, he criticizes Azul and Greta for
quarrelling and he warns the chorus against its foolish adulation
of the queen. Consequently, what Nieva does is to transform what
would have been a villain of the piece into some sort of perverted
Christ the Saviour, the exemplary instrument of freedom. In this
postmodernist order of things, Nieva adeptly reconstitutes the
vampire as it is known: from the ashes of an old myth (that of
Dracula), a modern myth (that of a benevolent vampire) is born
on the pedestal of Cruelty/Crime and paradox.

In his inquiry into the individual's autonomy in the context of
social domination, Zygmunt Bauman observes in *Postmodern
Ethics*:

> For every social totality bent on uniformity and the soliciting of the
> disciplined, coordinated action, the stubborn and resilient autonomy of
> the moral self is a scandal. From the control desk of society, it is
> viewed as the germ of chaos and anarchy inside order; as the outer
> limit of what reason (or its self-appointed spokesmen and agents) can
> do to design and implement whatever has been proclaimed as the
> 'perfect' arrangement of human cohabitation. (1993, 13)

From the control desk of society, Nieva's recreated, irrational order of transgression may be viewed as anarchy, but from the inner world of his drama, it represents a call to rescue the self from the scandal of cultural control, which this playwright considers as the true problem – a degenerate dictum, once a familiar tune of the avant-garde, has become the postmodernist centrepiece of an *Estética del delito.* The cathartic formula underlying the instances of self-affliction described above injects *Nosferatu* with a postmodernist aura, because the contradictions, if anything, place the drama beyond the confines of fixity by fostering some sort of dialectical resilience.[8]

Beyond characterization and action, the strands of contradiction and paradox witnessed in *Nosferatu* are also transmitted through setting and atmosphere. This visual effect is expressed in the form of a chiaroscuro projection, made especially vivid in Guillermo Heras's production of the piece. The first part of the play opens at dawn, with stucco-embroidered skies, while the second part takes place during an extended dusk, with supposed streetlights of Vienna reflected in its dark waters. Sometimes one sees images of a supposed burning Singer sewing-machine factory that sporadically illuminate the surrounding darkness. As Aurora and El Agonizante exit the stage, they get lost amidst thick clouds. And when Nosferatu prepares to take Kelly to her palace, the stage is suddenly inundated with projections of fog all over the stage. All these indicators of contrast between light and darkness, effected through lighting and the production of fog, connect with Baroque and Cubist theatre. In Cubist theatre, the chiaroscuro represents the mysterious and multifaceted dimension of objects and space, and in Baroque theatre it tends to reveal the tragic sentiment underlying the drama. Like the 1913 Cubist production of the opera *Victory over the Sun* (in St Petersburg), the lighting in Heras's production of *Nosferatu* is designed not so much to enhance atmosphere or to reproduce reality but rather to accentuate form, to blur and confuse in order to homogenize the space between actor and spectator.[9] The composite effect generated by the factory scene, the fire, the pollution, the gases and the clouds is intended to jolt the audience's sensibilities, to impose a choking effect as the spectators observe the characters struggle for freedom. What is more, just as these visual scenic signs are inherently lacking in fixture (the cloud, the fog or the gases evaporate and blend with the surrounding air, darkness disappears at the introduction of light, etc.) so are the rhetorical hierarchies and dichotomies – virtue–vice, life–death, pain–pleasure, order–anarchy, good–evil – annihilated through the drama's actualization.

Nieva's dramatization of paradox and contradiction strikes a resounding chord in the postmodern postulates of Linda Hutcheon. Responding to the distinctions made by Hassan between modernism and postmodernism, Hutcheon affirms: 'postmodernism is the process of making the product; it is absence within presence, it is dispersal that needs centring in order to be dispersed; it is immanence denying yet yearning for transcendence. In other words, the postmodern partakes of a logic of "both/and", not one of "either/or" ' (1988, 49). In Hutcheon's view, the paradoxes of postmodernism (like those of *postismo*) work to instruct us in the inadequacies of totalizing systems and of fixed institutionalized boundaries (224). Drawing on Michel Foucault, Arthur Kroker and David Cook put the matter metaphorically:

> Postmodernism . . . is not a 'gesture of the cut', a permanent refusal, nor (most of all) a division of existence into polarized opposites. The postmodern scene begins and ends with transgression as the 'lightning-flash' which illuminates the sky for an instant only to reveal the immensity of the darkness within: absence as the disappearing sign of the limitlessness of the void within and without . . . (1986, 8–9)

Even Hassan, after tabulating his schematic dichotomy between modernism and postmodernism, acknowledges that, as a philosophical, erotic and social phenomenon, postmodernism veers toward certain forms (open, playful, invocation of silences, disjunctive, etc.) and yet implies their very opposites, 'their antithetical realities' (1980, 125). These ideas, which have now become a distinctive mark of postmodern literature, have always constituted a fundamental part of Nieva's dramatic philosophy and practice since the 1940s. At the hour of composing a piece such as *Nosferatu*, Artaud's ideas certainly energized him, but the significance of his postist background remains fundamentally instrumental in moulding the dualistic disposition of his postmodernist theatre.

In his study of *Nosferatu*, Robert Lima dismisses any affinity between this play and the Theatre of Cruelty, saying that the piece does not follow the premises of Artaud's dramatic theory

(2001, 244). The objective Lima sets for his article reads: 'to show how Nieva's work eschews the traditional concepts of vampirism in order to *play* upon the theme in a surrealistic, absurd manner to make the point that society is so corrupt, decadent, and self-serving that it will accept evil as good' (233–4). This distinguished critic persuasively lays out the differences between the traditional vampire and Nieva's Nosferatu, but his portrayal of the playwright's ethical stance as an attack on evil is questionable. An advocate of amorality, Francisco Nieva is unabashedly decadent. Ample evidence of this assertion is found all over his work – in his essays and commentaries and across his literary production. Nieva's solidarity with Bataille, Genet, Jarry and Artaud is inspired, first and foremost, by these writers' unconventional defence of ethical openness. Even if *Nosferatu*'s strength is seen as deriving from speech and dialogue (and this is not precisely the case), the play connects forcibly with Artaud's theory in other important ways as the foregoing analysis shows.

Indeed, it is really in the play's staging where the interaction between the underlying ideals of Cruelty and Nieva's *Estética del delito* come to life. Lorenzo López Sancho could not have been more accurate in his characterization of *Nosferatu*'s 1993 production as 'a complete spectacle' in which speech comes to light as only one more element in the diverse theatrical resources employed to dramatize the enigma of vampirism (1993, 95). As one watches the play, what one senses is the overwhelming effect of a confusing unravelling of an irrational and turbulent sphere of existence rarely witnessed on the Spanish stage. Little of what takes place before the audience resembles familiar reality. The rest is myth, horror and sheer drama: the monotonous drumbeat of the opening scene, the total darkness, the suspended tramcar in which the goddess Aurora is elevated into the sky, the ceremonial entry and the satanic outlook of Nosferatu, his heroic and emblematic speech pattern, the operatic formation of the Madrigal chorus's movements and of the train scene, the projected image of fire onto the backdrop, the spectacular appearance of the metallic horse, etc. So accomplished is the scenic presentation of *Nosferatu* as a drama of diffusion that, in my view, not even Artaud's own *Les Cenci* – ironically his only piece staged by the Theatre of Cruelty – measures up to the Spanish playwright's rendition.

THE PARADOX OF SELF-TRANSCENDENCE

The dramatization of paradox and contradiction takes on another dimension in *El rayo colgado y peste de loco amor* (Suspended Ray and a Plague of Mad Love) (1952/69), Nieva's second major play. What is expressed in *Nosferatu* as a secular interplay of contradictory terms emerges in *El rayo colgado* as a religious exercise geared toward self-transcendence. This piece is about two nuns, Sor Isena and Sor Prega, who live in an underground convent where they are frequently tortured by a seven-to-eight-year-old child-demon called Porrerito. One day, they become hosts to Sabadeo, a modern civil engineer, who appears at their door seeking aid for a severe stomach ache. Appalled by the nuns' eccentric ways, he beats them up. In revenge, Porrerito nails the engineer's forehead, but in Sabadeo's attempt to charge on him, he is killed in an explosion.[10]

In this play, pain is theatricalized not so much as a measure of ontological relief as it is as a means of spiritual cleansing by way of the body. This therapeutic processing of pain recalls Pedro Calderón de la Barca's exaltation of self-transcendence, as particularly presented by Jerzy Grotowski in his production of *El príncipe constante* (The Constant Prince). As in Grotowski's production, Nieva mitigates the altruistic tenor of the action in *El rayo colgado* by making the nuns indulge freely in self-affliction. For example, as Porrerito hammers Prega's hand to an armchair, she masochistically urges him on, shouting 'Clava, clava, Porrerito' (Come on, nail me, nail me, Porrerito . . .) (TC 400). For her part, Sor Isena prefers to live with a nail Porrerito hammered into her forehead. Consequently, when Sabadeo pulls out the nail against her will, she turns lunatic and begins to speak in a nonsensical language:

> ¡Catafú y malbaratillo! ¡Sálvenos de la justicia siniestraria y téngase por la mano del angélico Bartolo, que en la ígnita facultativa rumorea encapillada! . . . ¡Rajatabla! ¡Rajatabla! (TC 409)

> [Catafú and malbaratillo! May Saint Bartolo rescue and protect us from sinister justice, from those whose inflamed intellect glows like a cathedral! Rajatabla! Rajatabla! . . .][11]

3. *El rayo colgado y peste de loco amor* (Suspended Ray and a Plague of Mad Love), directed by Juan José Granda, with a set designed by the Denok Cooperative. Sala Olimpia, Madrid, 1980. Photographer unknown. Courtesy of Centro de Documentación Teatral, Madrid.

In the end, it is the cultured, believing Sabadeo, the symbol of rationality and order, who perishes; the diabolic Porrerito and the masochistic 'santisbrujas' (holy witches), symbols of irrationality and anarchy, prevail.

Unlikely though it may seem, Nieva's religious references in the play are drawn from the *auto sacramental*, the most authentically original form of Spanish dramaturgy. A one-act allegorical drama often written to support the public celebration of a religious festival, the *auto sacramental* was mastered and popularized in Spain by Calderón de la Barca (1600–81), in *autos* such as *El mayor día de los días*, *El divino Orfeo*, *El mágico prodigioso* and *El príncipe constante*. There were several others who wrote *autos*, three of the most notable being Tirso de Molina (1583–1648), José de Valdivielso (1560?–1638) and Lope de Vega (1562–1635).[12] What is important to note is that, at least for Calderón, the *auto sacramental*, by its glorification of the Eucharist as a sacred symbol, was designed to deepen Christian moral consciousness and devotion

to God, a distant goal from Nieva's complex dramatization (the
auto will be discussed further in chapter IV). Nieva's inspiration
in the *auto* for the dramatization of the flesh's martyrdom as
a paradoxical medium of spiritual liberation finds support in
Christopher Innes's study of *El príncipe constante*. In Innes's
view, the moment of ecstasy in the play emerges at the point
where conscious control over the body is lost and the power of
the spirit returns the human being to his/her animal roots (1993,
155). Like Jesus Christ, the Prince's self-sacrifice is carried out
for the good of others but, as Innes notes, Grotowski's Prince is a
self-willed martyr who controls his own torture and uses his
persecutors to destroy his body in order to purify his spirit.

In Nieva's dramatic reordering of reality, what becomes
evident is a new, primitive religion born out of Christian religious
practice. Latent in Porrerito's brutal act is the image of Christ's
crucifixion, but the inspiration behind the nuns' self-sacrifice is
suspect. At first glance, *El rayo colgado* looks like a well-designed
theological play in Calderón style, that is, a neo-baroque dramatization of redemption from the demon. Inspired by the *auto
sacramental*, Nieva seems to draw upon the historic Golgotha
ordeal, which the nuns' conduct evokes. At the same time, he
undercuts this solemn act by transforming Christ's selfless and
sacred experience into a selfish and mundane ecstasy consummated
under the pretext of religious self-sacrifice. In the end, sanctity is
restored in the play – but not by way of the divine. Instead of the
intervention of God or an angel to forgive the demon, it is Don
Gurrín, an old hunchback, who suddenly arises from a pot-like
structure under the roulette to crown the nuns and to bless the
audience. In effect, what Nieva does is to recycle local dramatic
traditions (Calderonian theology) and transform them into a
modern subversive mechanism in order to construct a peculiar
theatrical order, one based on the union of incompatible realities.
That is, he makes use of the *auto* format but inverts its moral
attribute to serve his amoral project.

AESTHETIC COMPOSITION AND DOUBLING IN SPEECH

The dynamic of contradiction and paradox thus far discussed
sometimes expresses itself in the very aesthetic composition of

Nieva's plays. Between plays and within them, an artistic pendulum swings between the polarities of tradition and innovation. No single piece follows perfectly the aesthetic rubrics of any one category; even the 'Teatro en clave de brevedad' (Short Plays), which is generally clearly written, with psychological more complex characters, still carries significant poetic undertones. A case in point is *El baile de los ardientes o poderoso cabriconde* (The Dance of the Passionate or the Powerful Horned Count) (1975), a play performed by the Francisco Nieva Theatre Company in March 1990 at Madrid's Albéñiz Theatre. This piece is perfectly constructed along the lines of traditional, Aristotelian plot development. Even though it is not divided into acts and scenes, stage directions clearly mark the end of each scene. The plot is even divided into two parts, each of which contains subheadings that show different phases of the plot. The piece is written clearly and free of Nieva's usual metaphoric language, hence, unlike plays such as *Nosferatu* or *Los españoles bajo tierra* (Spaniards Underground) (1973), one follows the plot with little effort.

El baile's logical representation, however, contradicts the mythical discord witnessed in characterization, action and setting. When the young poet Cambicio begins his adventure to Naples to marry one of the daughters of the noble Orla family, everything seems transparent and real. As the plot unfolds, however, not only does the atmosphere become grotesque but also increasingly oneiric and theatrical. Cambicio is greeted with death-tolling bells, and when he urinates in front of Imperia Gavrotti, she embraces the behaviour as courteous. Astounded by the hallucinatory ambience, Cambicio faints twice, and instead of a beautiful fiancée, the Cabriconde himself appears as his betrothed. Cambicio's satanic audacity before the horrors, driven only by the desire to surpass his limits into the mysterious, recalls the rebellious passion of such Romantic protagonists as José de Espronceda's (1808–42) Pirata (in the famous poem 'La canción del pirata' (The Pirate's Song)) or Don Félix de Montemar (in the dramatic poem *El estudiante de Salamanca*). In the play's 1990 staging, this Romantic ambition is enhanced by an atmosphere invaded by typical Romantic (and Surrealist) imagery: signs of thunder and lightning, representations of a torrential rainfall, the gloomy image of a family cemetery in the middle of the hall, the display of a coffin, court ladies clothed in mourning gestures, a hellish, impounding darkness in which crazy flames dance to illuminate the human figures there present, etc.[13] What pertains to Nieva's drama is a striking combination of representation (derived from his allegiance to the *género chico* tradition) and theatricality (born out of his postist orientation), but the poetic atmosphere overshadows the rational arrangement, almost as if to transcend and parody it. Herein lies a distinguishing factor between Nieva and the playwrights of the 'Generation of 1982': whereas the postmodernism of the younger writers (e.g. José Luis Alonso de Santos or Fermín Cabal) is derived from a realism connected with daily life and social experience, Nieva's theatre is, first and foremost, operated within a conceived world, according to its own rules, with a gaze that shocks, teases and belies sociocultural reality.

Delirio del amor hostil o el barrio de Doña Benita (Delirium of Hostile Love or the Neighbourhood of Lady Benita) (1977) is an ideal example of a play constructed along traditional lines and interlaced with psychological depth, but one that is also accompanied with a considerable level of linguistic contortion. As Jesús María Barrajón rightly points out, this play's structure and theme belong to the Theatre of Farce and Calamity (TFC) whereas its exercise of linguistic contortion resembles the Furious Theatre (FT) (1991, 590). Pointedly, Nieva even classifies *Delirio* as a 'furious' drama. Similarly, *Los españoles bajo tierra* (TFC) is perfectly structured along three acts, with the first act further divided into two parts. Yet even though the action evolves systematically toward a resolution, principal characters such as Dondeno and Cambicio remain static and lack any clear psychological development. Moreover, both language and style appear to be more consistent with the characteristics of the FT than of the TFC under which Nieva classifies it. That is, *Los españoles bajo tierra*'s hermetic and surrealist undertone is inconsistent with the kind of realistic dialogue often associated with the TFC. Thus, in the 1991 edition of his complete works, Nieva had to reclassify this play as part of his Furious Theatre.

On another plane, the dualistic vision of Nieva's theatre expresses itself cogently in speech and dialogue. In his plays, dialogue is often wrapped in a complex of contradictory enunciations bordering on what Joseph Bristow, in reference to Oscar Wilde, calls 'wittiest phrases [that] turn conventional wisdom on its head' (1992, 6). Suffice a few examples from *The Importance of Being Earnest.* Algernon – '. . . I love hearing my relations abused. It is the only thing that makes me put up with them at all' (I); Lady Bracknell – 'I dislike arguments of any kind. They are always vulgar, and often convincing' (III); Gwendolen – 'This suspense is terrible. I hope it will last' (III). In Nieva's drama, such witty phrases are most commonly evidenced in the paradoxical pronouncements of La Reposada in *Las aventuras de Tirante el Blanco* (The Adventures of Tirant Le Blanc) (1978/86). Upon entering the stage, this character's first words are:

> Me siguen . . . Ya no me siguen. Sí, me siguen. ¡Al fin escapo con vida! Pero me matan, me hacen trizas. No, no me hacen. Ya estoy tranquila. ¡Yo me muero! Aquí caigo. Me levanto . . . (TC 1063)

> [Someone is following me . . . I am no longer being followed. Yes, I am being followed. Finally, I have escaped with my life! But I am being killed. I am being torn to pieces. No, I am not being killed. I am now calm. I am dying! Here I fall. Actually, I am up . . .]

La Reposada equates horror with wonder; she finds Tirante's wicked heart very generous; she will avenge Tirante if he rescues her; she expects her deceased husband El Gran Podrido to trust her because she is so insincere; she is unable to find the key to Constantinople gates because it is so large; she finds Tirante so handsome that she feels like killing him. And as El Gran Podrido beats her up, she screams:

> Oh, qué placer . . . qué martirio . . . tus golpes me dan la vida. No te perdono si no me matas, malhombre' (TC 1077)

> [Oh, what a pleasure . . . what martyrdom . . . your blows give me life. I will not forgive you if you don't kill me, evil man.]

The total effect on the audience of this kind of paradoxical speech pattern, in which Nieva's theatre as a whole is steeped, can be profoundly penetrating. Not only is this kind of speech entertaining, it also creates a peculiar coherence in the drama's movement, for the paradoxical speech is actualized as a way of life in a manner consistent with the unstable foundations on which the drama rests overall.[14]

On the whole, the disparate combination of styles and the inherent paradoxes that characterize Nieva's drama share a common ground with the aesthetic norms of postmodern literature in general. In a review article, 'Writing about Postmodern Writing', Brian McHale notes that 'despite everything that has been written by apologists both for and against postmodernism about its abandonment of mimesis, the mimetic commitment apparently still persists, albeit transformed'. He then asks, '. . . is it even possible to write fiction that has no mimetic commitment whatsoever? Or to write about fiction in such a way that no mimetic commitment emerges?' (1982, 226). As Hal Foster has suggested, postmodernism should be best perceived as 'a conflict of new and old modes', whether cultural, economic, or artistic (1983, xi); a position later reiterated by José Luis Pinillos in his characterization of postmodernism not as a force of revolutionary transformation, but (like *postismo*, I may add) as a mesh of pastiche, the interplay of old styles and forms (1998, 200). Nieva's version of post-modernism derives its strength precisely from the insertion of new (poetic) artistic values in juxtaposition to traditional (representational) forms. It involves an intricate *interplay* of mimeticism and theatricality, not a *replacement*.

A Celebration of Open Theatre

For Nieva's drama to uphold this spirit of instability and subject-ivity, it must necessarily be an open drama. This is to say, it must not only rely on varied aesthetic resources to construct itself, but it must also empower the spectator or the reader to participate in the drama's signifying process by avoiding easy resolution. Nieva's drama, ever resilient and non-totalitarian, offers little resolution to the problems it generates through plot. In the plays, nothing stays irrevocable, and as the final curtain drops, the spectator, dis-illusioned, struggles to decipher the spectacle's *raison d'être*. Even death's conclusive quality is often challenged. Insurgent characters who die arise from the dead, thus perpetuating their resistance as if to force upon the audience the drama's troubling repercussions beyond the theatre hall.

Nosferatu expresses better than any other play Nieva's com-mitment to open theatre, for this piece represents one of two (the other piece is *Pelo de tormenta* (Tresses of Turmoil)) created deliberately as an open drama that Nieva calls *reópera*. The *reópera* is a short script written with a compressed plot that is totally open to the director's interpretation. Its central concerns as described by Nieva are flexibility, improvisation and accommodation in rendition:

> Open theatre is intended to introduce forms and reforms of a visual nature: dances, processions and a versatile setting charged with special effects. Open theatre, then, is about a conduit, a concise script on the basis of which other motives and concepts can be consolidated. The text can be musicalized, converted into a song or a melopoeia and it can equally be improvised or constructed as supplementary marginal notes. (Author's notes, TC 173)

In a sense, therefore, one can say that the *reópera* expresses Nieva's desire to move the theatre away from 'performance' (the representation of the playwright's intent) toward 'interpretation', thus transforming the director into what Ignacio Amestoy calls 'the postmodern author' (1997, 5).

Neither *Nosferatu* nor *Pelo de tormenta* offers any plot resolution. Nosferatu's assassination by Mickey Mouse's men toward the play's end as a restorative act to remove the devil is neutralized by the vampire's resurrection from the dead to reaffirm his power over Queen Kelly, whom he takes away. When Mickey Mouse appears at the end, unmasks himself and declares the play ended, the playwright metatheatrically exposes the character's own awareness of his dramatic role. In other words, Mickey as actor steps out of the dramatic universe into the audience's universe and by so doing reaffirms the non-mimetic principle behind the play: the gesture reminds the audience that the performance is after all a defiant piece of art operated within a conceived world and not a faithful copy of nature. This reaffirmation of life by way of death, a constant motif in Nieva, echoes Alfred Jarry's pataphysics, his theory of imaginary science, which glorifies the equality of opposites and the indissoluble double.

When a character in Nieva's play arises from the dead, he/she symbolically reasserts that fundamental paradox of beneficial destruction, for the destructive instrument (death, in this case) engenders a new order out of an old one that nevertheless persists.

Action-packed as it is, *El rayo colgado* ends meaninglessly, with
the characters awaiting answers to be delivered by one Don
Gurrín who died several years before. As if waiting for a Godot
that might never appear, Prega and Isena hope against hope,
since no one knows when the turning roulette wheel will ever stop
to enable the answer to be delivered. It is not even clear what sort
of answer is expected, nor does one know why there is a need for
one. In *El fandango asombroso* (The Amazing Fandango) (1961),
time serves only to wait, and the characters, although submerged
in the *fandango* (a Spanish regional dance), continue anxiously to
await its beginning. The sinister forced burial of Coronada and
her supporters in *Coronada y el toro* (Coronada and the Bull)
(1974) to bring to a definitive close the tension between the forces of
conservatism and change is overturned when Coronada astoundingly
arises from the dead, as if to perpetuate the ongoing tug-of-war.
In short, at the end of every performance of Nieva's play, the
spectator is left with more questions than answers. Indeed, the
audience may feel mocked as it becomes disoriented, but what is
important is that the disorientation impels and empowers the
audience to participate more actively in the drama's interpretation. Like the director, the spectators are enabled to supply what
Umberto Eco calls 'a free, inventive response' (1989, 4), so
fundamental in making the postmodernist work complete. In this
sense, Nieva remains faithful to the postist project, which exalts
the creative capacity of the reader as a complementary force to
authorial power.

The open-ended disposition and the ambiguous underpinning
of Nieva's drama bring into play a core characteristic underlined
by Linda Hutcheon in her theorization of postmodernism, namely,
the need to sustain contradictions. In Hutcheon's view, the contradictions of postmodernism are not really meant to be resolved
but are to be held in what she calls 'an ironic tension' (1988, 47).
Invoking Foucault, Hutcheon contends that irreconcilable in-
compatibilities are the very basis upon which the problematized
discourses of postmodernism become apparent. 'While unre-
solved paradoxes may be unsatisfying to those in need of absolute
and final answers,' she intimates, 'to postmodern thinkers and
artists they have been the source of intellectual energy that has
provoked new articulations of the postmodern condition' (21).
She concludes that if postmodern art is to avoid betraying its anti-

totalizing ideology, then it cannot offer answers to the problems and questions it raises. What needs to be stressed is that, by the late 1980s when Hutcheon was making such theoretical pronouncements, Nieva had long been promoting the same principles through his dramatic practice on the basis of lessons learned in the 1940s from Chicharro and Ory, lessons that became revitalized through his connection with Artaud's work.

The theatre critic David George (1989) has written about how theatre essentially thrives on ambiguity, not as a dialectic driven toward resolution but as a condition that accepts its contradiction. Speaking about Hegel's dialectics, George describes how all ambiguities create temporary states in which two forces are not reduced to one but coexist, purged of antagonism but preserved in difference; a situation especially associated with Japanese Noh theatre. As old as this basic fact about the theatre is, not all playwrights have worked against unitary ambitions. For various ideological reasons, neoclassical or agitprop theatre tend to lack the kind of dynamism and balance that George describes. At least, in the immediate Spanish historical context in which Nieva wrote plays such as *Nosferatu* or *El rayo colgado*, many playwrights and theatre artists, in composing their works, chose to ignore that fundamental need for dynamism. As a postmodernist, Nieva studiedly replays that primary drive toward doubling and ambiguity throughout his drama. To be postmodernist is to be ambivalent; it is to refuse to collapse dualisms into unitary solutions irrespective of fashionable ideological pressures. For Francisco Nieva, the principles behind the Theatre of Cruelty serve as a catalyst in moving his theatre toward achieving that goal.

III

METATHEATRICALITY

METADRAMA AS DRAMATIC METHOD

There is nothing new about metadrama (or metatheatre, as some prefer to call it). Long before Luigi Pirandello, Shakespeare and Calderón used this dramatic technique as an effective mechanism to highlight the theatrical contention between art and life, with *Hamlet* and *La vida es sueño* (Life is a Dream) as its enduring models. It was, however, in the 1980s and 1990s that critical interest in metafictional works became fashionable. The source of this new energy is Lionel Abel's *Metatheatre: A New View of Dramatic Form*, published in 1963 at the outset of the postmodern debate. The publication of Abel's book and the upsurge of postmodernist literature and criticism were not mere coincidence. The greatest achievement of Abel's theorization is that it justifies metadrama as a bona fide genre that transcends the traditional tragedy–comedy dichotomy. Inspired by Shakespeare and Calderón, Abel isolates two basic characteristics of metadrama: the representation of the world as a stage and the representation of life as a dream. Abel lays special emphasis on the power of imagination, that is, the power to create a partnership between illusion and objective reality on the basis of stage-specific experiences. He could not have been more accurate, therefore, in his appraisal of Calderón's dramaturgy when he affirms that the paradigm for this Spanish playwright of a real event was a 'true thought' (71). It is worth noting that Nieva's attraction to Calderón and his inspiration in the *auto sacramental* as a model for his own brand of poetic theatre are grounded precisely in the supreme importance that this Baroque playwright accords the power of imagination in the construction of his drama.

Abel actually identifies only the play within the play as the specific form in which metadrama is consciously constructed. Thirteen years after he published his seminal work, Richard Hornby came out with his own study of metadrama in *Drama, Metadrama, and Perception* (1986), where he establishes metadrama's varieties and offers a more concrete definition of the term.[1]

Having defined metadrama as 'drama about drama', Hornby goes on to identify its forms as the play within the play, ceremony within the play, role-playing within the role, literary and real-life reference within the play and self-reference. Besides identifying concrete metadramatic forms, Hornby contributes significantly to our understanding of this formal device by laying emphasis on its effect on the spectator: a jumbled sensation of unease, dislocation of perception, estrangement and what he calls 'seeing double' (32). To the extent that metadramatic effect operates upon the intricate relationship between fiction and actuality, it enforces Brecht's non-representational principle, which, as Martin Esslin believes, admits openly the fact that 'theatre is a theatre and not the world itself' (1971, 133). As one well knows, Brecht's central dramatic concept, *Verfremdungseffekt* or *distantiation effect*, derived from the Russian formalist Victor Shklovsky's *ostrannenie*, proposes that theatre should destroy any illusion of reality and create an emotional distance between the audience and the stage spectacle.

Now, in what way does metadrama serve as a requisite tool of postmodernist theatre? To address this question, it is necessary, once again, to turn to Abel, for the functions he attributes to metadrama profoundly echo cardinal postulates of the postmodern (1963, 113). The functions are the following: a strong sense that the world is a projection of human consciousness; the ability to make human existence more dreamlike by showing that fate can be overcome; the assumption that there is no world except that created by human striving and human imagination; the mutability of order as something continually improvised by human beings; above all, the falsity of all implacable values and glorification of the unwillingness of the imagination to regard any image of the world as ultimate. What ties together these characteristics is an underlying sense of subjectivity and relativism, which June Schlueter identifies as typical of the world of modern humanity (1979, 5). If indeed double vision is the true source of metadrama's underlying significance, as Hornby contends, and if ambivalence or double-coding define the postmodernist work of art, as Charles Jencks and others argue, then it makes sense to posit metadrama as a key formal resource upon which postmodernist theatre thrives.

Francisco Nieva uses metadrama consistently as his most reliable formal technique. In discussing his use of this technique, one needs to keep in mind that some of his metaplays were

written over half a century ago, even before such plays as Genet's
The Balcony (1956) and long before critical interest in metafictional
works became fashionable. Indeed, Nieva's use of the metadramatic
device dates back to the 1940s when he wrote several short plays
collectively classified as *Centón de teatro* (A Collection of Plays).[2]
Because the various forms of metadrama are interconnected, it is
not appropriate to draw a dividing line when analysing their
presence in given texts. For the sake of clarity, however, I have
created in this chapter two broad sections, one focused on the
play within the play and another on ceremony within the play.
Within each of these categories, I also discuss self-reference and
role-playing within the role.[3]

THE PLAY WITHIN THE PLAY

A play in which this metadramatic form is best employed is
Tórtolas, crepúsculo y . . . telón (Turtledoves, Twilight and . . .
Final Curtain) (1953), one of Nieva's most imaginative plays that
has yet to be staged. Set in the 1920s, this piece is about a theatre
company that finds itself quarantined in an old theatre by the city
authorities because of an epidemic. The actors soon find that the
theatre boxes are inhabited by several individuals who watch and
unduly interact with the actors as they experience their predica-
ment. A giant metallic curtain unexpectedly descends amidst
tormenting sounds and a black-out to close the first part of the
play. In the hullabaloo, the actors become dazed and collapse one
after another. When they later regain consciousness, a fight ensues
between two brothers, the Barrabás, that stirs a violent row among
the entire group. A scandalous actress called Zemira, whose arch-
enemy is Trapezzia, the theatre company's leader, steps in to
order their release and to close what she considers to be a well-
executed performance. When the final curtain refuses to come
down, the actors laugh spitefully to ridicule Zemira. Frustrated,
Zemira commands Senedian, the porter, to kill Trapezzia. He
refuses and instead shoots down the curtain, which mysteriously
gathers itself and wraps up all the actors in the midst of a cloud of
dust from which they struggle to free themselves.

The play is constructed on the basis of a very complex structure.
Such is the complexity of the spatial configuration and role-playing

in *Tórtolas* that it probably explains why this excellent piece has not been staged since it was written over fifty years ago. Besides considerations for the potential high cost of the décor, any director of this piece needs to exercise maximum precaution in order not to confuse the audience about the direction of the main plot. The frame play is the piece entitled *Tórtolas*. Unlike *Sombra y quimera de Larra* (Shadow and Chimera of Larra) (1976), the frame play is not independent of the inner play, and the reader gets to know this only as he/she reads on. The very theatrical space is designed to enhance a fluid exchange between real-life experiences and the theatrical universe. The piece is set in a decadent classical Italian theatre with three proscenium boxes on each side. Inspired by E. T. A. Hoffman's *Don Juan* (a story in which allusion is made to a hostel bedroom that has an outer chamber with a small door connected to an opera box), Nieva recreates the classical proscenium theatre by converting the boxes into inhabited units, thus giving the theatre the look of an apartment complex. The dramatization of the actors' lives and of acting companies also provokes reminiscences of Ramón de la Cruz's *sainetes de costumbres teatrales*.[4] It is told that the same theatre used to serve as gallows where brutal executions of criminals took place. The theatrical space was also once used as a hospital, then as a cemetery during a cholera outbreak. Moreover, the sets and props used for the inner performance are supposedly gathered from the ruins scattered all over the stage by the Barrabás brothers. Even though this structural arrangement takes place within the spectacle itself and does not actually involve the external audience, the idea is as brilliant as it is innovative. The arrangement is intended to promote the notion of a fluid role exchange that transcends the dichotomy between art and life. In this sense, even if on a theoretical level, Nieva undermines the avant-garde's injunction against the proscenium stage as a restrictive theatrical space that prohibits actor–spectator interaction.[5]

The inner play has its own set of spectators who watch the performance either from their respective box seats or from the very stage. The performance they watch, therefore, is the development of the frame play's plot. But that which the inner audience considers to be a theatrical performance is confusedly viewed by the external audience as an accidental event. The characters of

the frame play are also actors of the inner play, but since the
inner play is closely identified with the frame play, the characters
do not need to switch roles in order to assume new identities. All
the boxes' occupants play at least a triple role, two of which correspond with the double-pronged space within which they constantly move: they appear simultaneously as ordinary citizens in
their living spaces and as spectators occupying a theatrical space.
Additionally, by intervening in the stage action, they function as
actors. One of the boxes houses two old snoopy spinsters who
constantly cross the boundaries of their role as passive spectators
by hurling garbage and waste onto the stage during performances.
Similarly, the professor's sons force their way into the action from
their box turned into a charcoal bunker. As actors of the unfolding
drama, they play the part of typical unruly children but, at the
same time, they behave as critics who, when dissatisfied, attack
the performers physically. In Zemira's case, one sees her act simultaneously as the inner play's director, as a spectator, as an actress
and as an ordinary citizen who likes to invite her lovers into her
box/home. This constant shift between real-life roles and stage
assignment rhetorically serves to blur the borderline between fact and
fiction. For example, in vesting Zemira with the responsibility of
director and in portraying her role-playing as a fluid experience,
Nieva distances his own authority as the drama's creator and
thereby decentralizes its interpretation. In this sense, the metadramatic format presents itself as an effective mode by which
the drama's very composition is used to generate plasticity in
the play's interpretation. Because of their disruptive behaviour,
the inner spectators tend to provoke uneasiness in the external
audience. At the same time, their rebellious conduct demonstrates
that role and identity are not fixed or compartmentalized but
rather a matter of negotiation, adaptability and exchange.

Another metadramatic form that Nieva uses effectively throughout the play is self-reference. For example, referring to Opal who
has been taken for dead, Zemira exclaims:

> ¡Desgraciados! ¡Presuntuosos! . . . Volved la vista y mirad a esa
> criatura desmayada, olvidada, acaso muerta . . . ¿No la veis? Ella ha
> representado la muerte con la mayor exactitud. Ella lo ha hecho
> mejor que todos . . . Hermanos, hacedla saludar. (TC 165)

[You mean lot! You conceited bunch! . . . Turn and look at that fainted creature who is forgotten and perhaps dead . . . Don't you see her? She has impersonated death with supreme accuracy. She has performed her part better than all of you . . . Brothers, make her greet us.]

Suddenly up from her fainting spell, Opal enthusiastically responds:

No se molesten. ¿Eh? ¿Qué tal? Visto que no hay final me incorporo. Señora Zemira, en previsión de lo que pudiera ocurrirnos, me he pasado todo el tiempo fingiendo. Tan sólo estoy convaleciente de un venial catarro, pero soy una joven y ambiciosa actriz que no deja, ni en peligro de muerte, escapar la menor oportunidad. (TC 165)

[Don't trouble yourselves. All right? How's it going? Seeing that there is no end (to this spectacle), I decided to sit up. Madam Zemira, in view of what could happen to us, I've spent all this time pretending. I have just recovered from a minor catarrh, but I am a young and ambitious actress who doesn't let the least opportunity pass by, even at the risk of death.]

These kinds of auto-reflexive pronouncements, so typical of Nieva's drama in general, create a special metadramatic effect on the audience. Spectators hardly need a reminder that what they are watching is made up. Instead, what they expect from the actor is credible pretext. In an essay, 'The Shock of the Actual: Disrupting the Theatrical Illusion', Theodore Shank argues that what spectators go to see in the theatre is not the paint and the light nor the actor, but an orchard and characters. According to Shank, so accustomed have audiences become to this way of perceiving in the theatre that theatrical illusions tend to coincide with their expectations. In his view, one way of presenting something startling or fantastic in the theatre is to direct the audience to focus on actuality, which is something one does not expect to see on stage. He adds that this explains why in experimental theatre, actuality is framed as art and made to seem fantastic in contrast with the expected theatrical illusion.

The *Tórtolas* spectator, placing sufficient trust in the actor as a good pretender, pretends along too in the hope of being entertained. For this kind of spectator, any wake-up call from that stream of illusion creates a metadramatic impact, for the self-reflexivity undermines the escapist diversion that he/she has been enjoying in the drama's fictional space. It is a sensation akin to that provoked in Genet's *The Blacks* by Archibald, who, in his role as Master of Ceremonies, addresses the audience in metadramatic modes. Unlike Genet and most experimental playwrights, however, Nieva often designs the self-referential technique to offer the audience some emotional relief from the intensity of the play's unorthodox action and rhetoric. That is, instead of startling the audience by drawing its attention to actuality, hence paradoxically reinforcing the drama's illusionism – as Shank says about experimental theatre – Nieva resorts to self-reference in order that the audience, reminded that what it has been watching is all made up, receives the dramatic rhetoric without being completely alienated. This motive of Nieva's is often underlined by the unnecessarily lengthy explanation that his main characters, perhaps concerned about being misunderstood by the audience, tend to offer at the end of his dramas about the piece's ethical principles.

If *Tórtolas* exemplifies Nieva's use of metadrama to stage the fluid interconnection between art and life, *No es verdad* (It Is Not True) stands as a complex testimony to the question of truth and identity.[6] Written in 1987, this short piece is about a young aristocrat called Blanche de Bressac who is abandoned by her father and left in the care of Pippon, a maid and governess of the estate. Blanche falls in love with Eric de Villemont, a savage who claims to be the chief of a herd of wolves. Meanwhile, Elin de Saint Clarc, who is courting Blanche, adamantly rejects the stories about the wolves. One morning, Pippon is found dead and Elin wounded, an incident that invites the police's intervention. Blanche confesses the truth to the police, saying that the whole thing is a game that she and Eric have been playing. The three are placed in a rehabilitation home, where Eric dies. Elin is later set free, and Blanche, who disappeared, later comes back accompanied by Ixión, a female wolf, to inform Elin that she and Eric were the ones who released the wolves to attack him and Pippon.

No es verdad is driven by a single purpose: to question and confuse that which is upheld as truth. Thus, this piece ends up raising questions rather than answers: How does one determine the truth? By appealing to one's imagination or to that which is visible? If the story is made up as Blanche confesses to the police, how does one explain Pippon's death and the violent attack on Elin? Secondly, how does one explain the presence of Ixión, which threatens to attack Elin? Furthermore, how can one reconcile Blanche's confession with her later statement that she and Eric were the ones who made the wolves attack Elin and Pippon? The fact is that, although Blanche has maintained the wolf story as an invention, Pippon, who knows the family well, tells Elin all sorts of things that make the story seem credible within the dramatic context. For the play to produce the requisite metadramatic effect, there must be a balance in the audience's perception of both versions of the story. The audience needs to go along with the playwright in confusing fact with fiction by accepting the wolf story, even if hesitatingly. That is, one must at least accept as plausible Blanche's second confession, namely, that she and Eric released the wolves to kill Pippon. Yet even at the point of real danger, as he looks for an escape from Ixión, Elin continues to insist on the falsity of the story. This ultimate disbelief in the face of open danger confuses the audience even more and upsets any level of certainty it might have previously reached about the story's truth. No one can be sure any more whether or not Pippon is actually dead.

As one reads the play, one cannot miss the striking resemblance it bears to Pirandello's *Six Characters in Search of an Author,* whose beauty and novelty lie in its ability to stage persuasively life and theatre as coexisting realms.[7] Note, for example, the parallel between the wonderful ending of *No es verdad* and Pirandello's piece, where a debate ensues as to whether or not the moribund son is really dead:

Some Actors: He's dead! He's dead!
Other Actors: No, no, it's only make believe, it's only pretence!
The Father (*with a terrible cry*):
                       Pretence? Reality, sir, reality!
The Manager: Pretence? Reality? To hell with it all! Never in my life has
                       such a thing happened to me. I've lost a whole day over
                       these people, a whole day! (1998, 52)

Nieva's dramatized fusion of fact and fiction in *No es verdad* resonates with what Herbet Blau has said in 'Letting Be Be Finale of Seem: The Future of an Illusion'. In this essay, Blau observes:

'The truth is it takes just as much truth to play credibly false as it does to appear indubitably true; and sometimes to convince others (and even ourselves) that we are true we have to play at being true. The illusions by which we live are the illusions by means of which we sustain the fiction.' Blau adds that if the theatre were real one would not brother with it, and when it is not real, one complains (1977, 61). Like Calderón's *La vida es sueño*, Genet's *The Maids* or even Pirandello's *Day and Night*, *No es verdad* leaves it to the spectator to separate fact from myth. It presents no definitive answers to the overdetermined ambiguities in which the play is enmeshed. Instead of presenting an ultimate truth, it paints truth as that which evades us like fantasy. Put concisely, to believe is to doubt, to affirm is to question and wonder. This is a legitimate postmodern slogan made perfect by Nieva through the mechanism of metatheatricality.

In his review of the 1988 performance of *No es verdad*, Eduardo Haro Tecglen faults the show for representing what he considers to be nothing more than the author's own diversion (1988, 34). Undoubtedly a strange drama with little bearing on the audience's reality, *No es verdad* nevertheless radiates an artistic complexity that should not be overlooked. The play is a pastiche of old and modern traditions. A melodrama of French leaning, this piece draws on mid- to late nineteenth-century Romantic drama and is interlaced with Gothic qualities. At the same time, elements of surrealist cinema and expressionism colour its atmosphere. The story itself goes deep into the mythological past and evokes myths about wolves and semi-humans. In her study of the play, Rosette C. Lamont establishes an intertextual connection between Eric, on one hand, and, on the other, Victor Hugo's Ruy Blas and Alfred de Vigny's wolf in the famous poem, 'La Mort du Loup'. Lamont recalls Hugo's fascination with Spain and his use of Spanish to set down his private sexual emotions (1995, 39). Where Nieva's play distinguishes itself is its ability to rely on a complex formal device to modernize a legendary theme in the context of a Spanish theatrical culture that has been slow to embrace alternative dramatic styles and strategies. To ignore the sophistication of the play's metadramatic method is to ignore its underlying poetic rhetoric, which transcends the calculated, familiar message of didactic value that many Spanish audiences have come to expect.

CEREMONY WITHIN THE PLAY

The most common form of metadramatic technique employed by Nieva is ceremony within the play. As a metadramatic device, ceremony within the play is a self-conscious attempt on the playwright's part to create a peculiar reality out of the stage experience, and, like the play within the play, it operates on the Brechtian distantiation principle.[8] In formulating his dramatic philosophy, Nieva accords the ceremonial a prominent place:

> Theatre is a hallucinatory and intense life.
> It is neither the world nor a revelation as clear as the sun,
> nor is it an instrument of practical reality.
> It is an illegal ceremony,
> a delightful and unpunished crime. (BP 94)

In affirming theatre as a ceremony and a hallucinatory experience, Nieva underscores theatre's spiritual, ritualistic essence, an integral component of theatre since its inception. At the same time, however, he subverts theatre's ceremonial quality by modelling it as an illegal act, as an outrageous transgression of the established order. If ceremony is to undermine the status quo and to wake the audience up 'nerves and heart' – to borrow Artaud's expression – then it must concern itself with what Anne Ubersfeld calls the unthinkable, that which is logically, morally or socially scandalous (1989, 39). Yet when ceremony annihilates social taboos, it loses its function as an instrument of social cohesion; strictly speaking, it becomes a *counter-ceremony*. In the context of the pervasive censorship of Franco's Spain, the unequivocal taboo is sex. Consequently, it is not surprising that, in his conceptualization of the ceremonial, it is precisely the sensual element in Greek theatre to which Nieva finds recourse. This is because the original (Greek) dramatic form produces a passionate metaphysical relief, just like the ceremonies of the Roman Saturnalia (BP 95). It must also be recalled that, in his essay 'Posología y uso', Eduardo Chicharro mentions Greek mythology as an important source from which *postismo* derives its inspiration.

Several of Nieva's plays incorporate ceremonial elements (*Pelo de tormenta*, *Coronada y el toro* and *El baile de los ardientes* are outstanding examples). I focus on *La carroza de plomo candente*

(The Carriage of White-Hot Lead) (1969/71) because, although a one-act play, it epitomizes Nieva's ceremonial theatre in terms of technical sophistication and thematic wealth. It is the only piece in which ceremony within the play is constructed in a full-fledged fashion. Not only does this drama contain several ceremonies, it is framed within a ceremony; it is subtitled 'Ceremonia negra en un acto' (A One-Act Black Ceremony). For this reason, I consider any formally constructed ceremony in *La carroza* as already a ceremony within the ceremony, even though the inner ceremony may hardly be distinguishable from the frame ceremony, that is, the frame play.

First, a brief synopsis. La Garrafona, Prince Luis III's wet-nurse and witch, arranges a ceremonial wedding in the prince's bedroom between Saturno, a bullfighter, and Liliana, a he/she goat. The purpose is to excite the prince so that he marries the daughter of the European king in order to produce an heir. Although the goat soon turns into the goddess Venus Calipigia, Luis remains unexcited. Venus Calipigia disappears and, in her place, Liliana reappears with Luis on its back and with Saturno holding on to its rear legs. Garrafona goes on to organize another ceremony in which Luis produces the heir himself with Saturno's help. Luis soon disappears, leaving in his place a twelve-year-old Tomás whose only utterance is an irritating 'na'. Impatient and infuriated, the ceremonial gang suffocates him with pillows.

Like *Tórtolas*, the frame play does not have an independent plot; it is almost totally composed of the inner ceremonies. The shock value that the wedding ceremony produces resides not so much in the *idea* of a bullfighter having a sexual experience with a goat; it lies in the subversive unconventionality of the action graphically transmitted through what Anthony S. Abbott calls 'the theatrical act itself' (1989, 204). What *La carroza* actualizes is in fact the systematic desecration of the sanctity of a Catholic-style wedding through the allegorical conversion of a sacrament of love into a loveless, animal desire. Note the strong invocation of religious symbols: the procession to the altar (the pedestal), the Paschal offering (the goat laid back on the pedestal), the candle, the seraphim's singing (the cats' meowing), the solemn benediction, etc.[9] More importantly, the visual effect of the wedding ceremony is as provocative as it is metadramatic. This is because the ceremony creates an estranging effect by staging a grotesque spectacle to which the audience's store of experiences bears little correspondence. At the same time, the ceremony's shock value, its point of alienation, is rooted paradoxically in the carefully orchestrated revelatory sensuality of which the same spectators are invited to partake. That is, because the sensual activity is scandalous and funny, it synchronously attracts and repels. The ceremony's overall impact on the audience is comparable to what Ubersfeld terms a Brechtian paradox. In a close reading of Brecht's theory of distantiation effect, this drama semiotician observes: 'It is precisely at the moment of highest identification by the spectator with the spectacle that the distance between them becomes greater. At this moment, the "distance" between the spectator and his/her own action in the world also widens' (1989, 35). Put

4. *La carroza de plomo candente* (The Carriage of White-Hot Lead), directed by José Luis Alonso, with a set designed by the Grupo Escuela A. D. Fígaro Theatre, Madrid, 1976. Photographer unknown. Courtesy of Centro de Documentación Teatral, Madrid.

differently, Ubersfeld is saying that Brecht's so-called alienation phenomenon is impossible without the prerequisite of some sort of spectators' emotional solidarity with the show.

The mysterious transformation of Liliana into Venus Calipigia sets the stage for yet another ceremony: Calipigia's body exhibition. Although this spectacle contains essential ceremonial features, it is constructed totally within – and functions as an extension of – the wedding ceremony. Further, since the body exhibition is an integral part of the frame ceremony, the Calipigia show becomes a ceremony within the ceremony (the wedding) within the ceremony (the frame ceremony). One cannot miss here the parallel between the body show and Coronada's ceremonial masturbation in *Coronada y el toro*. In the Calipigia body show, the metadramatic effect, created by means of the interplay of objective and subjective realities, is expressed not so much through setting and action as through dialogue and the characters' emotions. When intense lighting is directed on Calipigia's buttocks, the scene becomes transformed into a sensual magical show as the characters begin to act as if possessed and capable of speaking only incantatory and metaphoric language. When Garrafona asks Saturno to relate what he sees, this is what takes place:

> SATURNO–Veo . . ., veo . . ., veo . . . una compañía de abejas picando todas en el mismo punto. ¡Ay, qué picor, qué picor! . . .
> LUIS–Qué estrañas alucinaciones.
> GARRAFONA–Sigue, sigue. ¿Qué más ves?
> SATURNO–Veo el mar por primera vez. Lo veo entero. Todo por fuera y por dentro, y la luna bañándose en él, y a todas las ostras con la boca abierta . . .
> FRASQUITO–Yo veo un tiburón sin dientes, color de rosa, masticando pañuelos de encaje, almohadones de terciopelo y angelitos marinos, gordos como cochinillos. (TC 308–9)

> [SATURNO–I see . . ., I see . . ., I see . . . a cluster of bees, all stinging the same spot. Alas, what a sting, what a sting! . . .
> LUIS–What strange hallucinations you've got.
> GARRAFONA–Go on, go on. What else do you see?
> SATURNO–I see the sea for the first time. I can see it all. Completely inside out, the moon bathing in it, and all the oysters with their mouth open . . .
> FRASQUITO–I see a rosy toothless shark chewing laced handkerchiefs, velvet cushions and little sea angels as fat as suckling pigs.]

Through the magical power of language, Nieva adroitly turns the dramatic stage into an arena of quasi-religious and mystic experience, echoing so remarkably Artaud's metaphysical formula. Indeed, the Calipigia scene may look obscene, but the playwright effectively ritualizes the obscenity by portraying the spectacle as a sacred ceremony in which various individuals gather to venerate Venus as their deity. It is precisely the combination of the metaphysical charm of drama with its possibilities for sensual freedom that draws Nieva to the original *ceremonia saturnal*, from which he creates his own *ceremonia negra*. It is in the obscure balance between carnal pleasure and the operative force of the unconscious where this playwright metadramatically dismantles the Spanish taboo of eroticism, for the ceremonial mechanism facilitates the process of self-liberation through its emphasis on myth and illusion.

Unlike *Tórtolas*, where the characters unconsciously play different roles synchronically, in *La carroza* the characters consciously assume new identities within their bigger role as characters of the frame play. In charge of the wedding ceremony is Garrafona as Master of Ceremonies. Saturno and Liliana are contracted by Garrafona to play the bridegroom and bride respectively. She appoints her arch-enemy, El Padre Camaleón, as the official who marries the betrothed. Frasquito plays the bridesmaid and midwife, since it is expected that a baby will be delivered at the end. Luis, representing the witness, performs his part faithfully by applauding as the ceremony proceeds. The theatrical space, which is Luis's bedroom, represents the church. In the body exhibition, these roles are all switched. Luis steps into Saturno's role as the passionate bridegroom; Saturno now plays the passive onlooker, while Camaleón and Frasquito become guards charged with the duty of keeping Saturno's aggressiveness under control. This multiple assumption of roles, so reminiscent of the metamorphosed role-playing in Ionesco's ceremonial plays *The Chairs* and *Victims of Duty*, generates a special metadramatic effect in the context of the play's vacillating double vision (illusion–reality). Whenever a character assumes a new role, he/she loses his/her identity twice, first as an ordinary person outside the drama and then as a character with an original role. With this double loss of identity, the character's role becomes more theatrical – hence more fantastic – as he/she penetrates the drama's inner world. The further the character escapes his/her identity as a member of society and the closer

he/she approaches the centre of theatrical illusion, the more he/
she ironically resembles the audience's real selves.

In *Metafictional Characters in Modern Drama,* June Schlueter
argues that, in the modern, industrialized world, collectivism and
its consequences have progressed to the point where an 'essential
self' no longer exists. Basing herself on Robert Corrigan, Schlueter
affirms:

> If identity is defined in life in terms of actions or roles and modern
> man's essential self is denied then the traditional dramatic character,
> itself no more than the sum of its actions, is closer to being an exact
> representation of its real-life counterpart than it ever has been. (1979,
> 12)

Umberto Eco puts the matter even more explicitly: 'It is not
theatre that is able to imitate life; it is social life that is designed as
a continuous performance and, because of this, there is a link
between theatre and life' (1977, 113). To the extent that ceremony
within the play, like the play within the play, stresses role-playing
within the role as a fundamental feature, it registers the interconnection between art and life, between the real and the role. In
La carroza, the 'aberrations' that come to mark the various
characters' identity are, after all, assigned roles, which recall the
constant role-playing that takes place in life.

The spiral of illusion and mirage that underpins the dramatic
action produces a disorienting effect on characters and spectators
alike. When all attempts to gain access to Calipigia as a sexual
partner fail and she disappears, the Master of Ceremonies shows
that not even she understands the basis of the interruption:
'¡Maldición! ¿Qué sucede ahora? Esto no entraba en el programa'
(Damn it! What now? This was not part of the programme) (TC
310), she hurls. When Liliana suddenly reappears with Luis on its
back and Saturno holding on to its hind legs, Garrafona's further
declaration exacerbates the confusion: '*Nada* ha salido a derechas.
¡Ha vuelto la esposa sucia! La Calipigia se nos ha evaporado'
(TC 311) [Nothing has come out right. The dirty wife has
returned! Calipigia has vanished on us.] Garrafona's comments
are laden with metadramatic force. But for the self-reference, the
audience would not be able to tell whether or not the interruption
and the subsequent transformations are of the sorceress's design.

By declaring that nothing came out right as planned, Garrafona suggests that the ceremony has all along been out of control without the awareness of the characters and the audience. In other words, it can be argued that Garrafona's role as director of the magical spectacle and transmutations is fraught with uncertainty. This uncertainty reveals the extent to which the playwright has successfully compelled the audience to lose itself in the depths of the spectacle without the ability to decipher any more the line between fantasy and reality. The spell cast by Garrafona over the characters has apparently affected the audience too, for, like the characters, the audience must depend on the sorceress – not the playwright or director – to wake it up from the ongoing 'dream'. In a way, the playwright (or director) has surrendered his authority to Garrafona as director-within-the-play, who, in conducting the inner ceremonies, determines the general direction of the drama. Yet one comes to see that, despite her authority, the director-within-the-play stands on the same shaky ground as the spectators and other participants of the ceremony.

This inherently unstable direction of the plot serves to illuminate the underpinnings of the play's thematic core. If ceremony within the play is indeed a way in which society examines the eternal, unchanging aspects of life, as Hornby suggests (1986, 55), then *La carroza*'s shifting, disintegrative orientation is consistent with the tenor of the relativist ideological foundations of Nieva's art in general: to obscure moral divisions and break down monolithic structures of cultural domination. This fundamentally post-modernist vision is further manifested in diverse ways in the play: Saturno's sexual activity with an animal, Luis's intimate relationship with cats, the fusion of witchcraft with familiar 'logical' reality, Luis's homosexual relationship with Frasquito, Camaleón's androgyny, Liliana's bisexuality and androgyny and so on. What all these examples have in common is that, by their unusual nature, they serve as alternative possibilities to fixed cultural impositions; they open up a more complete dimension of humanity by exteriorizing its potential for the unfamiliar. What is more, they enhance the play's metadramatic effect as they impel the audience to disregard any image of the world as ultimate and instead see it as that created by human imagination. The seemingly estranged ceremonies of *La carroza* may alienate the conservative spectator, but it is precisely in their alienating yet liberating power where this dramatic piece's postmodernist quality glows. This is because the ceremony establishes the basis for a peculiar theatrical framework – not necessarily consistent with the external audience's reality – in which cultural values are questioned and reconstructed. This tendency toward cultural dislocation by way of subversion and non-conformity is the driving energy behind the action and plot in *La carroza*. It is what increasingly creates the need for ceremonies, even as the ceremonies fall apart. Thus, if this drama is to accomplish its thematic objective – to verify eternal truths – Garrafona's ceremonial project as an instrument of subversion must succeed. No wonder, despite the insults and the threats with which she is faced upon the ceremony's collapse, Garrafona manages to invent yet a fourth tier in the labyrinth of ceremonies, leading to the suffocation by the other characters of the recalcitrant child.

In analysing the play, Anje C. Van der Naald provides the following interpretation:

> Tomás's physical death, his disappearance, expresses the Spaniard's spiritual death. He has been exterminated by the Inquisition, by the people's attitude to sensuality and by an unhealthy upbringing. (1981, 64)

Let me advance Van der Naald's analysis a step further by offering two interpretations of the murder. I begin with the murder's significance in the context of Nieva's subversive conceptualization of ceremony. The instinctive, heinous act shocks the audience intellectually, because it nullifies the effort put into the long, complicated process of the prince's making. In other words, the wicked irrationality of the murder makes one question the *raison d'être* of the ceremonies, especially since Garrafona herself participates in the murder. As an absurd negating act, the murder serves to reveal the true essence of the 'ceremonia negra': it is indeed 'un crimen gustoso e impune', in short, a *counter-ceremony*. A more compelling factor still makes *La carroza* a counter-ceremony. Instead of functioning as a tool of cultural reaffirmation, the ceremonial process undermines social tradition (sexual discipline) by engendering an alternative norm. The alternative norm is presented as synthesis of the multifaceted sexual formulations that characterize the elaboration of the play's ceremonies. The inaugural ceremony, arranged as a wedding between Saturno and Liliana, ends up in casual, individual acts metamorphosed in the form of a sexual union between the least expected of partners: Luis and Saturno, on the one hand, and Calipigia and Liliana, on the other.

What Nieva does is to effect a double demystification from different angles of an ideological platform: he is unequivocally defending homosexuality, lesbianism, but especially bisexuality, as alternatives to heterosexuality. By creating an asexual/homo-sexual king who is unable to marry conventionally, the playwright has subverted the reality of heterosexuality as the ordained quality upon which royalty thrives. Moreover, by uniting Calipigia and Liliana sexually, it is clear that not only does the playwright challenge the idealized Romantic image of woman (beauty = virtue) as man's ultimate desire, but he transcends conventionality in introducing animal bisexuality into human (heterosexual) culture. In being animal(istic), bisexual and androgynous, Liliana emerges as a paragon of the complete sexual creature. Thus, in a subversive spirit, Nieva has jubilantly reinvented the terms of reality, echoing what Robert H. Deming has said about Robert Herrick's use of ceremony in his poetry. Deming notes that, for Herrick, ceremony is the artistic means of discovering the order of the 'real' in the 'unreal', of 'arriving at the ground of being, for it allows him his fullest play, his fullest art, and his fullest freedom, as an artist and, we assume, as a man' (1974, 19). The resounding message in Herrick's use of ceremony strikes a chord in the underlying melody of *La carroza*'s chaotic ceremonies: the quest for liberty in the twilight zone of familiar reality and invented reality.

My second interpretation of the effect produced by Tomás's murder is that it transforms into some sort of grotesque tragedy a piece that would otherwise have ended simply as a farce. I am using the term *tragedy* here in the pragmatic sense in which Hornby uses it, namely, as a certain emotional effect on the audience and not as the Aristotelian tenet of character flaw.[10] Let it be stressed: it is impossible, in any case, for Nieva as a post-modernist to write tragedy in its Aristotelian sense, for *hamartia* implies a tacit acceptance of a certain moral standard, which when breached invites punishment for the culprit. Neither is comedy his cup of tea, because in its ultimate exaltation of dramatic resolution and order, comedy tends to deflect the anarchic liberty that the postmodernist work so much upholds. Thus, the ultimate artistic genre through which Nieva most comfortably expresses himself is the grotesque. By its humorous repulsiveness (that is, the mixture of horror and comedy), the grotesque severely mocks the refined, the well-ordered, the cultured, and in theatre it displaces the audience's sense of order by hyperbolically staging unorthodox behaviours that cultural regulation often suppresses. In Nieva's theatre, the stronghold of such unorthodoxy resides in what Philip Thomson, in his definition of the grotesque, perceptively calls 'the ambivalently abnormal' (1972, 27), made especially vivid in the paintings of Goya and Diego Velázquez.

In the end, what makes *La carroza* tragic is not so much the actual killing of Tomás; it is the sequential sensation of evil and horror that marks the rest of the play from the moment of the murder, when suddenly the sensual ceremony of enchanted, even burlesque, transformations turns diabolic. Tomás, after all, is a helpless child, an innocent victim of delirious adults whose delirium is replayed through the boy's idiosyncratic manners. What makes the play avert total tragedy, however, is that the prince's mysterious resurrection in the final scene restores to the drama some degree of emotional integration. That is, at the close of the performance, the audience does not remain bitter, with the smell of death; rather, it is left with a renewed yet bizarre sense of relief. To the extent that the overall emotional impact of the ceremony is alienating but not necessarily tragic or comic, it is metadramatic. This admixture of emotions in the audience is a quality that Nieva's postmodernist theatre generally aspires to achieve. It is fully accomplished in *La carroza de plomo candente*, whose historical significance in the development of Spanish theatre cannot be denied. A *tour de force*, *La carroza*'s stage production (along with *El combate de Ópalos y Tasia* (The Battle of Ópalos and Tasia) (1953), catapulted Nieva into wide recognition as an innovative playwright who broke ranks with the prevailing traditional theatre in Spain, just as Valle-Inclán had done earlier in the twentieth century. In an artistically effective display of nudity and homosexuality on the Fígaro stage for the first time ever (on 27 April 1976), barely five months after General Franco had died, *La carroza* (and *El combate*) gained immediate critical applause. In winning the prestigious Mayte Theatre Prize with this performance, Nieva transformed 'scandal' into acceptable theatrical practice, perhaps permanently, thus asserting his non-conformist theatre as a pioneer in a new, post-Franco era.

IV

SEXUAL POLITICS, GENDER POLITICS AND THE POPULAR

Nieva and the Popular

At first glance, the rhetorical and structural complexity of Nieva's works gives the impression of an elitist theatre. But were this indeed the case, it would be hard to reconcile that elitist quality with the egalitarian principle that underpins his theatre as a whole. In reality, his poetic and intellectual adventure has a firm grounding in popular theatre, especially that promoted by Carlos Arniches y Barrera (1866–1943) and Ramón de la Cruz. A prolific writer and master of idiomatic language, Arniches represents the best of the *género chico* tradition, which marks the initial phase of his literary production (a good example is his work *El santo de la Isidra* of 1898). The second phase, from about 1916 onward, presents what is known as grotesque tragedy, profoundly expressed in such works as *La señorita de Trevélez* (1916) and *Que viene mi marido* (1918).[1] Nieva's could very well be viewed as an intellectual theatre, but, following in the footsteps of these writers, the intellectual tone is systematically mitigated by a fundamental tendency to exalt the popular, to erase the borderline between the powerful and the marginalized, between high and mass cultures. This systematic bridging of gaps by means of populist artistic resources is what this chapter seeks to examine.

In his poetic treatise, Nieva defines the *pueblo*, the lower classes, as a jubilant and selfless category, as authentic creators of tragedy who have a special faculty for understanding symbols. In his scheme of things, the bourgeois class comprises all who regulate social morality and free will, what he calls the vigilante class (BP 110). When once asked about his notion of popular theatre, Nieva responded that anything could be popular once it is well entrenched in local roots. In popular theatre, he adds, imagery and symbolism are never constructed as abstract artistic resources but are embedded in the historical context of local traditions (1976a, 62).

Thus, he refers to Valle-Inclán's *esperpento* as '*género chico* in big style' (1978, 28); the reason being that, although a surrealistic mode of expression, the *esperpento* is rooted in Spanish cultural tradition. Naturally, therefore, Nieva's artistic vision goes against the drive to posit the popular as base and mimeticist and the poetic or the abstract as intellectual or elitist.[2] Indeed, in his 1990 induction address to the Spanish Royal Academy entitled 'Esencia y paradigma del Género Chico', he divests the popular of all naturalistic connotation and instead accords it emblematic and ceremonial qualities. Theatre, especially popular theatre, Nieva contends, is not a calculated and faithful reflection of reality but rather a reality stylized through instinct (see TC 1343).

Nieva's observations connect with an important dimension of the popular: the festive and the libertine, as particularly expressed in the *género chico* (literally, little genre).[3] In an interview (1973c, 25), he laments the absence in contemporary times of authentic *verbenas*, the *género chico* sub-genre that he exploits the most.[4] The principal characteristics of the *género chico* as a dramatic genre are its short duration, its musical accompaniment (in *zarzuela* fashion), the direct and informal nature of its perfor-mance style, its humoristic critique and its low cost, which makes it easily accessible to the lower classes. José María Rodríguez Méndez accentuates this genre's popular character, saying that the small librettos of the comic Spanish operetta are tinged with irony, subtlety and jeers designed to celebrate great national themes (1972, 18). He insists, however, that all this happened without solemnities, without pretension, without any kind of didactic motives; instead, what always stood out was the air of freedom with which the masses celebrated. This festive notion of the *género chico* resonates with that espoused by Domingo Piga in his theorization of the popular. In an essay, 'Problemas del teatro popular', Piga notes that, linked with folklore, popular tradition always reflects a cultural reality that serves as basis for a popular theatre. He laments that the popular feast, the feast that unites a whole community in song, dance and chorus, has not been ex-ploited and is not perceived as a people's way of expressing themselves theatrically. He then asks, 'How did theatre originate? From a popular feast that served to unite the Greeks in the Dionysian festivities. In it were mixed song, dance, poetry and wine. It was a feast for all, a truly popular spectacle' (1979, 71).

Nieva's political agenda is not motivated by an agitation for political action against a specific target, say, Francoism. It entails a parodic yet playful mechanism to critique and to question the sources of repressive cultural domination in his society. The surest route he plies into the heart of his theatre's political project is that which leads to sex and gender.[5] As Bataille notes, when uncoerced, eroticism is one of the highest personal modes by which self-independence and power are manifested. When officially regulated, continues the French philosopher, agitation for sexual liberation becomes one of the most violent attacks on the establishment (1962, 273). By Nieva's sexual politics, then, I refer to his manoeuvring and conceptualization of art as a subversive device against the tyranny of institutional control over his characters' sexuality, their wholeness as human beings. Where power relations are implied, they are located between both sexes, on the one hand, and the patriarchal establishment, on the other. The second part of the chapter examines Nieva's gender politics, what in Kate Millett's terms one designates as *sexual politics*, that is, the representation of power-structured relationships whereby one group of persons (females) is controlled by another (males).

THE POLITICS OF SEX

In Western society, the attitude to human sexuality has historically been characterized by extreme ambivalence and evasion. As Michel Foucault has shown, until the eighteenth century the topic of sex and sexuality was condemned as a taboo. This negative attitude emerged primarily as a legacy of Greek dualism. With its emphasis on spiritual love, Platonism denounced interpersonal, heterosexual love based on physical pleasure, privileging what it terms Heavenly Eros (the pursuit of intellectual love, the Absolute) over Common Eros (the pursuit of physical love) (Foucault 1978, 181). Later, this division was transformed into what Demosthenes Savramis calls 'genitocentric theology' (1974, 50) – the total opposition of religion to sex – championed by the most influential figure of Christian theology, Augustine. Savramis enumerates as central characteristics of this theology: dualism, sexual anxiety, the demonization of women, the portrayal of sex as satanic and sinful, antagonism toward the sexual, confinement of sex to marital monogamy and

the justification of sex exclusively for the purpose of procreation
(44). For his part, the American theologian Lewis B. Smedes
observes that Augustine interpreted Christians' calling to struggle
against evil as a calling to struggle against their sexuality. He adds
that 'Augustine could not imagine an innocent person in Paradise
turned on sexually: a sinless Adam could never have been sexually
aroused by a pure Eve; Adam and Eve could not have walked with
God in the day and made spontaneous love at night' (1984, 17).
Not even Freud in his theorization of sexuality escapes the dualism.[6]

In Spain, where for centuries Catholicism thrived not only as a
national religion but as an accepted fact of life, ecclesiastical interference in sexual matters reached proportions equivalent to what
Joaquín Latorre refers to as 'terrorism' (1969, 24). Besides direct
political criticism, the single most important targets of the Franco
censorship (which lasted officially until 1974) were sex and sexuality.
Ricardo Landeira reports that 'El Reglamento de Espectáculos', a
1935 Act that contained guidelines for the censorship of literary
works, prohibited sexual material with such severity that neither
female nudity nor kisses, no matter how innocent, were permitted
in the cinema and theatre halls (1987, 6). In a 1953 Concordat he
signed with the Vatican, General Franco officially joined the apparatus of Church and State and attracted the Church's support by
making the regime's laws consistent with Catholic dogma (1987,
150). For his part, John London calls attention to José Manuel
Vivanco's *Moral y pedagogía del cine* (1952), an important document with severe implications for the Spanish theatre, in which
Vivanco is opposed to any expressions of 'overt sexuality, obscenity,
anti-clericalism, and anything deemed unpatriotic' (1997, 13).
Relying on Antonio Beneyto's findings, London cites a ridiculous
case where the censors once removed the adverb from José María
Pemán's stage direction: 'Se besan apasionadamente' (They kissed
passionately) (14). Efigenio Amezúa presents the problem metaphorically, saying that in Spain love and sexuality are like a frail
body whose better members have been amputated by strong
defensive breastplates made up of moralists, nobles and ecclesi-
astics (1974, 214). In emphasizing the Judaeo-Christian basis of
Spanish sexual repression, it is important not to lose sight of the
historical role played by Arabic culture, whose long-standing *amor
árabe 'udri* rhetoric largely complemented Christian ascetic
principles, at least until Juan Ruiz restored in the fourteenth

century acceptance of women's humanity through his concept of *loco amor*.[7]

Today, Spanish attitudes to sex and sexuality may be considered liberal, but it is in the specific historical context of taboos and stern intolerance that Nieva's sexual politics is to be comprehended. Nieva declares his defiant opposition to the prevailing atmosphere of sexual repression, saying that he accords Eros great importance because in Spain sexual matters have always been subjected to patriarchal vigilance. The forbidden, he adds, animates him precisely because it is very tempting (Nieva 1973c, 24). No single play brings into play Nieva's sexual politics more cogently than *Pelo de tormenta* (Tresses of Turmoil) (1961), which, in his own words, represents the maximum expression of his spirit of subversive resistance (BP 102).[8] In effect, even though *Pelo de tormenta* by no means represents a 'realistic' effort to record the Spanish experience, it draws forcibly on its operative cultural codes – the culture of the Inquisition and the Crusades – not simply to reflect, or even reinforce, that experience, but, as in Brechtian theatre, to examine it, to call it into question.

The action in *Pelo de tormenta* is dramatized as a battle between Mal-Rodrigo, the catalyst of desire, on one hand, and the institutions of Church and State, on the other. The very physical space, the setting, is designed to highlight this opposition. The well in which Mal-Rodrigo, the sexual beast, lives is flanked by a convent on one side and the king's palace on the other. As a symbol of Catholicism, the well is represented by La Abadesa, the sacristan El Raboso, Sor Juana de la Coz and the chorus of nuns called Las Sublimitas. The palace, which symbolizes the State, is represented by King Dieciocho, La Duquesa, El Alcalde Oficiante, El Alguacil Más Gordo and the quartet of bailiffs. In Nieva's terms, these characters could be considered as constituting the bourgeois class. The Ciego, the general chorus and Ceferina belong to Mal-Rodrigo's popular band.

The State launches its attack on Mal-Rodrigo with the backing of King Dieciocho, and, like the police officers in *Nosferatu* who scrutinize the vampire's every move, the bailiffs constantly surround the well to spy on the monster's activities and to harass those who come close to the well. When El Ciego challenges the bailiffs' abuse of power, El Alguacil Más Gordo quickly legitimizes their action by invoking the king's authority, but it is said that King Dieciocho rules by the law of the Inquisition (TC 174). In other words, the political campaign sanctioned by the king against Mal-Rodrigo is tantamount to an inquisitional assault against the Devil – in this case, sex and sexuality – in the name of God and King. To fulfil the religious facet of this inquisitional warfare, the Church declares its own *Cruzada* (Crusade) against the dragon. During his visit to the convent, El Santo Obispo launches the holy Crusade by literally arming the abbess with a spear. Like the bailiffs, who legitimize their harassment of the ordinary citizenry by invoking royal authority, the abbess regains her confidence during her confrontation with Mal-Rodrigo by alluding to the pope as the bona fide command behind her offensive (TC 202). The bishop's crusade establishes a tragic connection between the past (the Spanish Inquisition of 1237–1834) and *Pelo*'s immediate historical context (the 1960s), when Franco's ruthless crusade against communism and all forms of opposition to his regime were in force.

The ecclesiastical and political phobia for Mal-Rodrigo, however, is presented as only surface manifestation of a deeper struggle within the self. In his study of Victorian sexual repression, Jeffrey Weeks has shown that bourgeois concerns about working-class 'immorality' always revealed middle-class anxieties. 'Even when the moralising concern was directed to other individuals or classes', he intimates, 'the issues were mainly those germane to the respectable middle class' (1989, 38). In the play, although the characters representative of the Church and the State antagonize the sexual beast, their actions show that they privately adore it. The convent, where most of the action takes place, is portrayed as an institution of double standards where its residents use the protective secrecy it offers to express their concealed desires. The hypocrisy is particularly expressed in the strange yet imaginative construction of Sor Juana de la Coz as a character. This nun has gained a reputation as the paragon of purity because of her un-compromising objection to the amorous advances of a man whom she kicked in the groin. Yet she lives in a cell-incubator where, like a hen, she incubates eggs. Her passion for this activity apparently stems from the fact that the heat produced by the incubation agitates her sexual sensibilities. When she breaks one of the eggs in order to hatch it faster, it produces a viper instead of a chick. The appearance of the snake is metaphoric of the unravelling of

her prohibited attraction to sexual temptation, which is represented by the viper, another phallic symbol.

Furthermore, when the sexual monster offers gifts to the tailed
sacristan, the nuns enthusiastically express their admiration and
ask to taste the cigar. Cigar in this case could be viewed as metaphoric
of the penis, and the in-and-out penetration as the image of
copulation.[9] In short, what the playwright does is to undermine
the convent as symbol of chastity and to portray it as a prison where
nuns indulge in aberrations to rediscover their lost maternity. On
a more general level, the playwright seems to be questioning the
very theological foundation of the Catholic value system that
equates sexuality with evil. As is well known, modern theological
studies have abundantly demonstrated that Christ's teachings are
at variance with the circumstantial interpretations advanced by
his followers about sexuality. Thus, when the abbess, with a spear
in hand, mounts the sacristan as a horse in a show of force against
the monster, the audience cannot escape the humour. The audience,
in a privileged position, sees the sexual politics in operation: it
sees that the spear being brandished by the abbess is a phallic
symbol and that the horse she mounts is a sign of virility. In this
symbolic expression of free will, the abbess overturns her ascetic
order and, like the duchess, shatters the divisionist notions about
sex and sexuality that perpetuate artificial tensions between the
pueblo and the bourgeoisie. If there is any wonder about the
severity of the social connotations of Nieva's mockery of Christian
values in the context of Francoist Spain, one should pay close
attention to the words of the nuns' prayer, which Harold Mark
Larson (1993, 164) correctly interprets as their Lord's Prayer:

> Santo plato de verduras que adornas las escaleras del altar, ahuyenta
> de nos la carne con sus despellejados estremecimientos, danos la salud
> del brecol y el pudor de la alcachofa, que viva nuestro espíritu en
> cuaresma y nuestro cuerpo en verde letargo . . .

> [Holy vegetable plate, who adorn the stairways of the altar, drive
> away from us the flesh with its flayed trembling. Shower upon us the
> health of broccoli and the purity of artichoke. May our spirit live in
> Lent and our body in green lethargy . . .]

'La carne con sus despellejados estremecimientos' is obviously an
indirect allusion to the vibrating quality of the penis, whose

rejection is betrayed by a deep appetite for food. Food, in this context, is inevitably a sexual symbol; the hunger for it is sexual desire, and the act of eating or devouring is metaphoric of sexual intercourse. This is why in depicting the duchess as more sexually appealing to Mal-Rodrigo, Ceferina compares herself with the duchess in gastronomic terms: whereas *she* is a mere 'plato del día' (the day's special), the duchess is 'delicatessen' (TC 181).

5. *Pelo de tormenta* (Tresses of Turmoil), directed by Juan Carlos Pérez de la Fuente, with a set designed by José Hernández. María Guerrero Theatre, Madrid, 1997. Photo by Chicho.

Like the religious order, those characters representative of the State display a special attraction to Mal-Rodrigo, a revelation that stands in sharp contrast to their simultaneous declaration of war on the sexual beast. The dramatization of the duchess's concealed attraction to the beast particularly recalls Marie Antoinette. In her study of Marie Antoinette and the French Revolution, Lynn Hunt argues that the queen's body was of great public interest not because it was sacred and divine but because it represented the opposite principle, namely, 'the possible profanation of everything that the nation held sacred'. Hunt underscores aristocratic dissimulation – acting one way in public and another in private – as the central cause of public denunciation of court life (1991, 111–12). Although Nieva's duchess is not a queen and is not about to face execution like Antoinette, she perfectly exemplifies the aristocracy in her insincerity about her sexual feelings. Thanks to her refuge in the convent (where she is able to 'confess' her true desires), the audience is able to see the contradictions that underlie her public condemnation of Mal-Rodrigo. In this context, one can safely explain the monster's choice of the duchess's body over Ceferina's as his attempt to expose bourgeois hypocrisy and to free it from guilt, a panacea that Ceferina and the *pueblo* do not need.

This exposure of aristocratic hypocrisy carries implicit political undertones, which most pertinently recall Richard Bolton's 'instrumental postmodernism'. Like Linda Hutcheon, Bolton postulates that any systematic critique of knowledge (which leads to a critique of power) is a political act, since it demystifies the authority that representative bodies and institutions have over society's members (41). Inspired by Brechtian dramaturgy, Bolton remarks:

> [The practice of instrumental postmodernism] aims for the removal of all authoritarian systems that oversimplify experience and deform human potentiality. It attempts to stimulate discourse, with the assumption that reality is always changing. And it attempts to enlist history as a *tool* (not as a ruin), presuming that history can be changed, and that a vital bond with the world can be formed. Thus instrumental postmodernism supports the participant over the spectator, and it forms its knowledge from engagement instead of detachment. (1986, 43)

What takes place in *Pelo de tormenta* is a systematic critique of the institutional powers that have long controlled Spanish society. If Mal-Rodrigo is indeed evil as the Church and the State depict it, the duchess and the nuns have shown by their hidden sexual inclinations that they are competitive partners in an evil order shared by the monster.

In a highly perceptive essay, Paul Ricoeur affirms the following:

[T]he true evil, the evil of evil, shows itself in false syntheses, i.e., in the contemporary falsifications of the great undertakings of totalization of cultural experience, that is, in *political and ecclesiastical institutions.* In this way, evil shows its true face – the evil of evil is the lie of premature syntheses, of violent totalizations. (1981, 439; emphasis added)

A close observation of Ricoeur's words greatly aids the *Pelo* spectator to capture the essence of the philosophical connotations that underlie the issues raised in the play. Rather than being the devil, the Evil-Rodrigo emerges as a source of unity that transcends social categories; the sexual beast bridges the gap between the high and the low, the religious and the unbeliever, the powerful and the marginalized. As the 'bourgeois' characters in the play learn to accept the monster-devil, they make a monumental move away from the grip of guilt toward liberty; they collapse social borders through solidarity with the *pueblo* in their collective celebration of Eros.

Spiritual friction with sexuality, especially within the Spanish context, is not a modern problem; it is an old, Baroque tradition particularly elaborated by Francisco de Quevedo y Villegas (1580–1645). Quevedo, the pre-eminent Baroque poet and novelist and master of metaphoric language, was ever torn between Christian faith and the bitter realities of humanity. In *Virtud militante*, Quevedo cogently captures the issue:

El Apóstol dijo que el espíritu militaba contra la carne y la carne contra el espíritu. Luego tú, que eres compuesto destas dos cosas, eres una perpetua milicia y tu combate continuo: campo de batallas, eres dichoso, si en ti vence la mejor parte. (1932, 932)

[The Apostle said that the spirit militated against the flesh and the flesh against the spirit. And you, who are made up of these things, are at perpetual war, and your combat is endless: a battlefield, you are fortunate if the better part wins in you.]

Yet the Baroque never idealized love or woman; instead, it glorified sexuality in its most vividly carnal terms. Consider the exaltation of eroticism in Luis de Góngora's sonnet 'Mientras por competir con tu cabello' (While Competing with Your Hair):

goza cuello, cabello, labio y frente,
antes que lo que fué en tu edad dorada
oro, lilio, clavel, cristal luciente,

no sólo en plata o víola troncada
se vuelva, mas tú y ello juntamente
en tierra, en humo, en polvo, en sombra, en nada. (1939, 16)

[enjoy the neck, the hair, the lips and the forehead, / before that which in
your golden years / was gold, lily, carnation, shining crystal, / not only
into silver or truncated violet / does it turn, but you too, along with it, /
into earth, smoke, dust, shadow, nothing.]

Nieva's return to the Baroque through a masterful command of
sharp antitheses is meant precisely to dislodge guilt, the neo-
Platonic basis of moral dualism, and to restore to Eros its natural
turbulence, its flesh-inspired *tormenta*. It is imperative, nevertheless, not to interpret this playwright's opposition to social control
as a plea for a return to primitivism, for Nieva equally finds primitivism problematic (1973c, 24). As Bronislaw Malinowski has
shown, even in so-called 'primitive societies', morals have always
been present and acquired habit has always been important
(1949, 182 and 191). Nieva's reaction is aimed at what Herbert
Marcuse in his sexual theory designates as 'surplus repression'
(1955, 37), that is, excessive social domination of sexuality. The
difference is that, whereas Marcuse blames capitalist exploitation
in general for the unnecessary regulation, Nieva faults the Spanish
patriarchal establishment for its extraordinary assault on sexual
freedom. For both, the victim remains the same: the *pueblo*, the
masses.[10]

In the play, it is the common people who celebrate the positive
vision of Eros as a vital conductor of life. This liberal attitude is
seen, for example, in the chorus, which collectively represents the
commoners as a social group. The chorus's role in the play recalls
Greek drama, where the chorus – composed only of humble,
attendant beings (Nietzsche 1964, 525) – often functions as the
people's representative voice, helping 'to bridge the distance between
the characters on the stage and the average audience in the
theatre' (Burton 1980, 3). For Nieva, however, the chorus signifies
much more. He insists on its humility as a quality of strength and
how it transforms that humility into an irrepressible will to survive

and to prevail (BP 111). Rather than play the victim, the chorus transforms oppression into a source of empowerment by adamantly parading its loyalty to Mal-Rodrigo. Still, Ceferina's sacrifice exemplifies best the golden moment of the *pueblo*'s determination to resist patriarchal domination. The sacrificial act, which the State condemns, is unequivocally exalted by the ordinary people as Eros's triumphant moment. Ceferina's positive attitude to the ceremonial sacrifice raises moral questions about sex in the play's religious context. Not only is the sacrifice staged as a public show of illicit sex, but the procedures leading to the ceremony desecrate Catholicism by consecrating Ceferina in the image of the Virgin Mary. The ceremony begins with a procession in which Ceferina is carried in a litter through the streets of Madrid, just as in the popular Spanish Easter procession in which effigies of Mary are carried on shoulders. By likening Ceferina's virginity, which is about to be violated, to Mary's purity, the playwright subtly demystifies the Mother of God's image as icon and epitome of holiness and restores sex and sexuality as nature's gift.

The action is interlaced with popular devices throughout the play. In his rhetorical campaign against bourgeois control of sex and sexuality, Nieva draws on the liturgical value of the *auto sacramental* while transgressing its moral coating. Ironically, the mechanism he employs to undermine the *auto*'s didactic value is the same mechanism Calderón stresses as the defining characteristic of the *auto*, namely, merriment.[11] Like Calderón's *El mayor día de los días*, *Pelo de tormenta* is sumptuous and saturated in music and dance. The Ciego's opening speech is greeted with music, and with his own guitar music, which is reminiscent of the 'romance de ciegos' (romance of the blind), he then leads the guards in a free-style, hedonistic song and dance. Thus, the spiritual upliftment, inspired in the *auto* by the Eucharist, is portrayed in Nieva's play as the resulting energy from some sort of ceremonial exercise in honour of Dionysus. Note that Dionysus' symbols are the growing ivy and the phallus, of which Mal-Rodrigo is emblematic. It is also worth noting that Nieva himself characterizes *Pelo* as a 'bacanalia popular' (BP 103), which calls to mind the Greek bacchanal (as portrayed by Euripides), a popular feast notorious for its amoral anarchy. Moreover, the women who cheer up Mal-Rodrigo could be said to represent the Bacchantes or Maenads, the Greek god's female followers who perform his ritual. Even

Ceferina's sacrificial procession vividly recalls the procession in which the bull is led in sacrifice to Dionysus. And without stretching the matter, one wonders if it was sheer coincidence that *Pelo*'s première was in March, the official time when the City Dionysia used to be performed.

Indeed, the play's up-beat rhythm – the music, the dance, the processions, the picnic, the excited emotions – coupled with the grotesque sexual energy it exudes, makes it a genuine carnivalesque piece of art. Writing about Mikhail Bakhtin, Christopher Innes notes that '[a]rtistic forms qualify as carnivalesque if they release imaginative and sexual energies by subverting social, moral and aesthetic categories, norms and prohibitions' (1993, 8). Let me add that the undercurrent subversive quality of the carnival carries a special postmodernist appeal. In his classic work *Rabelais and His World*, Bakhtin spells out the function of the carnival this way:

> . . . to consecrate inventive freedom, to permit the combination of a variety of different elements and their rapprochement, to liberate from the prevailing point of view of the world, from conventions and established truths, from clichés, from all that is humdrum and universally accepted. This carnival spirit offers the chance to have a new outlook on the world, to realize the relative nature of all that exists and to enter a completely new order of things. (1984, 34)

Bakhtin's assertions coincide with David D. Gilmore's extensive study of the February carnival, the *locura de febrero*, in the Andalusian region. Gilmore describes the Andalusian celebration (which invariably reflects other forms of Spanish carnivals) as a form of socio-political protest, 'a license for the expression of powerful feelings and impulses normally kept in check by a repressive moral code' (1998, 3). In constructing his version of the carnival – the *verbena* – on the basis of a quasi-religious practice, Nieva proposes to reinstate the original attribute of the medieval festival amidst what he considers to be gloomy *verbenas* that were being staged at the time by his socio-realist contemporaries (1973c, 25). As Julio Caro Baroja (1979) has shown, contrary to its historical link with the *currus navalis*, the carnival is a child of Christianity. Its practice has been historically linked with the Cuaresma, the advent of fasting (the carnival is celebrated on the Tuesday that precedes Ash Wednesday, which initiates the fasting).

In *Pelo*, the inversion of the mass, of devotional prayer and liturgical songs, all conform to the spirit of the 'viejas aleluyas españolas' (old Spanish alleluias), which Baroja highlights as a subversive ingredient fundamental to the Spanish carnival.[12] In its campaign in honour of Mal-Rodrigo, therefore, *Pelo de tormenta* replays the classic carnival in multiple ways: by pillorying the edicts on which Catholic religious practice is founded; by shattering the Platonic chasm between *carnalitas* and *spiritualitas*; by transcending the divisions between social categories; by demystifying sex and sexuality. These instances of subversive acts are deployed in the play in a peculiarly postmodernist or postist fashion. The systematic deconstruction of repressive mores and practices, in the context of a modern Spain, is effected through the theatrical act itself by drawing on and recycling traditional, popular conventions on a modern stage. Indeed, it is the critique of authority and of the status quo that compels Linda Hutcheon to declare that postmodernism cannot but be political. 'While the postmodern has no effective theory of agency that enables a move into political action,' she argues, 'it does work to turn its inevitable ideological grounding into a site of de-naturalizing critique' (1989, 3).

Pelo's very make-up as a *reópera* underscores the significance of its populist orientation in the deconstruction of sex and sexuality. Besides the *reópera*'s compressed script, which allows improvisation and ample interpretation on the director's part, a fundamental feature of this dramatic genre is its emphasis on visual power (dance, processions and special effects). As a dramatic form, the *reópera* bears significant resemblance to, and is indeed rooted in, the *género chico* tradition: both genres are distinguished by their short duration, they incorporate the *zarzuela* (Spanish musical operetta) as a principal element and their primary target is the *pueblo*. Moreover, like a typical *género chico* play, *Pelo* is set in the most popular of places, the central plaza. In the 1997 performance directed by Pérez de la Fuente, the action is brought directly to the spectators, who sit next to the reconfigured thrust stage, as if invited to partake of the ongoing spectacle. Because of this open stage design, the audience was obliged to feel the full impact of the sheer number of actors (thirty-one of them) and their merrymaking. Reviews of the performance did not fail to stress the overall effect of the popular strategies that went into making the play a resounding success. Juan Ignacio García Garzón compares the María Guerrero Theatre that night to Madrid's Plaza Mayor (1997, 91) and Eduardo Haro Tecglen dubs the playhouse a bullfighting ring (1997, 32).

One should not be misled, however, into thinking that *Pelo*'s populist composition makes it a naturalistic play, for this is by no means the case. From the voodoo-like *fandango* in which the *pueblo* seems entranced, through the horror of a deceased bishop who remains standing on his feet, to the sun's unconventional movements (rising from where it sets), *Pelo* emphasizes mystical and symbolic elements bordering on the Spanish Romantic play, which, in turn, draws on the eighteenth-century oneiric universe of Goya. These grotesque presentations are intended to expose Nieva's unconventional view of Spain, the Spain he refers to as 'paradoxically dragon-like and real' (1997c, 23); a direct echo of Valle-Inclán's *esperpento*, which, as seen earlier, Nieva upholds as a popular aesthetic. In effect, by creating a *verbena-reópera* in which multiple art forms converge, Nieva once again shows that art is capable of crossing boundaries, of juxtaposing and merging diverse techniques to compose a new whole without any ambition for originality. 'There is nothing new in this world, for everything is combined with various elements that proceed from the past', he boldly admits (1997c, 25); an unambiguous lesson in *postismo* that reaffirms a playwright's postmodernist stance.

DENATURALIZING TIME

In order to maintain this fluid dialogue with the past as vital energy for his theatre, Nieva sets his works free of the confines of conventional time. He constantly interjects or transcends the chronological flow of his plays' temporal setting. This temporal mode is evidenced in the stage directions of several plays. In *La señora Tártara* (Madam Tártara) (1970), the action is set in eternity, when '*todo sucede entonces, siempre y antes de siempre*' (everything takes place then, always and before all time) (TC 675). Although *Tórtolas, crepúsculo y . . . telón* is set in the 1920s, the playwright describes the decade confusingly as 'un próximo pasado' (an approaching past) (TC 119). In *Coronada y el toro* (Coronada and the Bull) (1974), the action takes place during 'tiempo de

España en conserva' (the era of a Spain caught in conservatism) (TC 419). *Pelo de tormenta*'s plot is set in Madrid, but the action is situated vaguely outside of time: '*Hace mucho tiempo, poco antes del fin del mundo*' (It was a long time ago, just before the end of the world) (TC 174). The apocalyptic aura that dots this a-temporal frame of references is reinforced in *Pelo* by an oblique stillness that circumscribes the impounding atmosphere: '*Es un día desastroso y sin hora, ni claro ni oscuro. El sol se va por donde quiere y los vientos se disputan*' (It is a timeless, disastrous day, neither clear nor dark. The sun sets wherever it wants and the winds are in dispute) (TC 174). In this dramatic context, not only does time release itself from the tyrannical monotony of the human-made clock, nature itself breaks the lineal regularity in which its movement is imprisoned. Note that this use of the *didascalia* is a clear evidence of Nieva's inspiration in Valle-Inclán, who uses this technique extensively not so much to aid the director as to advance the drama's own narrative. Nieva often relies on this device to reinforce the play's poetic atmosphere and to intensify its psychological effect on the audience; quite a challenging resource for any director to translate into a visual reality on stage.

In some important ways, Nieva's dramatic conceptualization of time reminds one of the postulations of certain postmodern theorists. Writing from an architectural viewpoint, Paolo Portoghesi affirms:

> Those who are amazed that, among the most apparent results of the new [postmodern] culture in its infancy, there is also a certain superficial feeling for a 'return to the antique', seem to forget that in every serious mixture, the artificial order of chronology is one of the first structures to be discussed and then dismissed. (1983, 13)

As Ihab Hassan has shown, a period must be perceived in terms of both continuity *and* discontinuity. Postmodernism, he argues, requires both a chronological *and* typological, a historical *and* theoretical definition (1980, 120–1). For his part, Wallace Martin sees postmodernism as a phenomenon in an apocalyptic zone where 'the concepts of linear time and traditional thought simply do not apply' (1980, 145). These assertions in turn coincide with Armand Gatti's 'time-possibility' concept, which, in Marvin Carlson's view, is opposed to a fixed and fallacious system of past, present and future and instead enables the theatre to show 'an action from many perspectives and without a sense of closure, encouraging its audience to see the world as open to change' (1993, 472–3).[13]

In bridging the gap between the past and the present, Nieva inserts his drama within the inner core of the postmodernist sensibility, for he enables himself to crystallize hybrid models freely without the rigidity of artificial chronological boundaries. Still, his stance regarding periodization does not wholly conform to that propounded by the majority of postmodern theorists. For example, Linda Hutcheon insists that in postmodernism '[t]he past is always placed critically – and not nostalgically – in relation with the present' (1988, 45). In order to interrogate the present, she contends, one needs to explore its vital historical parameters, but not desire it. Nieva sets himself apart from such theorists by adopting a dualistic approach in which he subverts the past – the 'España negra' (the Spain of darkness) – and at the same time longs for it. His position is shaped by a love–hate attitude. The 'España negra' is the Spain of cultural immobility and ignorance, the Spain of the civil guard that pursues its citizens, the Spain of rigid norms and superstitious traditions that recall the past and also cut across time. On the occasion of *Pelo*'s 1997 staging, Nieva affirms his ambivalence about the Spanish past: 'For me, Spain was dark and yet romantic; a black jewel, to put it better . . . In this work, everything was meant to be theatrical and false but, at the same time, shockingly true and Spanish, without hope or shame' (1997a, n.p.). If indeed postmodernism thrives on inclusion and paradox, as Hutcheon has abundantly shown, then it seems to me that Nieva's position is more logical than the prohibitive pose adopted by some postmodern theorists. The 'España negra' that he questions manifests itself variously, among other things, in the form of sexual repression, opposition to homosexuality, chauvinism, sexism and blind obedience to religious and political authority. Still, this conservative culture evinces another, more attractive quality. It represents a magical and spiritual universe inhabited by old customs, village feasts and processions, witchcraft and sorcery, irrationality and primitivism. Nieva nostalgically invokes this supernatural component of his cultural universe because it offers him a non-realistic arena where, like Artaud, he is able to imprison actor and spectator in the ceremonial rites of the theatrical experience.

The Politics of Gender

In contemporary Spanish theatre, with few exceptions, it is female playwrights who arose to write against the current, to break down some of the conventional writing modes by reorganizing – or simply reversing – the terms of what Nancy Reinhardt calls 'the central male space and the peripheral female space' (1983, 44). Nieva is one of those exceptions. He stands out as a male Spanish playwright who advances the empowerment of women on the stage through sophisticated dramatic techniques. At the foundation of his dramatic adventure lies an unabashed determination to project the female character as a 'víctima superior' in the face of patriarchal control:

> Sometimes women appear in my theatre endowed with an arrogant disposition that adversity is unable to conquer . . . Thus, it can be said that, for me, the female principle, the secret world of children and the subversive energy of the ordinary people have a positive value, one that is tenacious, regenerative, germinal, creational and rebellious. On the other hand, the male principle, which is passive, worn out, propitiatory and subject to temptation, is engrossed in an alienation that is difficult to overcome. (BP 113)

Besides women, ordinary people and homosexuals, Nieva's glorification of the marginalized involves children. From Óscar's recalcitrance in *El maravilloso catarro de Lord Bashaville* (The Marvellous Catarrh of Lord Bashaville) (1967), through Tomas's irritating manners in *La carroza de plomo candente* (The Carriage of White-Hot Lead), to Gustavo's rebellious behaviour in *Los mismos* (The Same Ones) (2005), one witnesses a world in which children, divested of innocence, follow a moral code that runs counter to the oppressive obsession of adults.

In Nieva's drama, women take the centre stage. They are strong, defiant, triumphant. In their audacious eloquence and laissez-faire conduct, these female characters display the full glow of their humanity, questioning the validity of standard stereotypes about their sex. Instead of submission to male domination, they bully and ridicule men (Garrafona, Otilia, Azul and Coronada of *Malditas sean Coronada y sus hijas* (Damned Be Coronada and Her Daughters) (1949/68) serve as good examples); in place of representing paragons of finesse and gentility, they can be as grotesque as they are profane (Imperia Gavrotti, Ópalos and Tasia, Sor Isena and Sor Praga); rather than embodying insecurity and weakness, they are bold, arrogant and they fervently guard their independence (Lady Whitelady, Blanche de Bressac, Dama Vinagre); in lieu of playing motherly roles, they are manipulative and aggressive (Kelly, Zemira, La Coconito); instead of being exemplars of kindness, they can be wicked and evil (Cósima Wagner, Catalina, La Reposada); and, as Coronada (of *Coronada y el toro*) proves, they break down the chains of conformity where there is injustice.

Nieva's theatre ardently works against the marginalized representation of women on the stage, against what Jill Dolan calls traditional theatrical representations. Basing herself on Teresa de Lauretis's film studies, Dolan notes that, in traditional theatrical representations, there is a tendency to 'objectify women performers and female spectators as passive, invisible, unspoken subjects' (1991, 2). Dolan goes on to say that, in this kind of scenario, women emerge as mothers and are relegated to supporting roles that enable the more important action of the male protagonist; attractive women performers appear made up and dressed to seduce or be seduced by the male lead; and while the men are generally active and involved, the women seem marginal and curiously irrelevant, 'except as a tacit support system or as decoration that enhances and directs the pleasure of the male spectator's gaze' (2). Nancy Reinhardt earlier made similar observations in her own study of classical tragedies. For Reinhardt,

> rarely does the proper (normal) female character of classical tragedies or of traditional serious plays take the centre stage as the initiator of the public action . . . Most female challenges to the male will are kept within the domestic interiors – the private comic niches, wings, bedchambers and romantic gardens. (1983, 43)

This lamentable situation, by no means the reserve of the classical past, is even more vividly expressed in the contemporary cinema, a fertile ground for the film theories advanced by de Lauretis that have influenced major contemporary feminist critical approaches to theatre.

To discuss Nieva's gender politics within the parameters of the popular, it is most appropriate to concentrate on *Coronada y el*

toro (Coronada and the Bull) (1974), a play that bears salient
ethical and formal similarities with *Pelo de tormenta*. Moreover,
Nieva himself claims this piece as the most representative of his
dramas and as best defining the essence of his dramaturgy in general
(1976b, 6–7).[14]

Coronada y el toro dramatizes the story of the confrontation
between Coronada and her brother Zebedeo, the mayor of a
provincial town. One day, during the celebrations in honour of
San Blas, the town's patron saint, Coronada interrupts the
acclaimed bullfighting feast just inaugurated by her brother. With
the support of two feminists, La Melga and La Dalga, she condemns the bullfighting and pleads for Marauña's release from
prison. Marauña has been held a prisoner for years by the mayor,
who releases him annually to fight the bull in public. Zebedeo
puts her under house arrest, but when the bullfight begins, a male
nun, Hombre-Monja, emerges from the bull-chute instead of the
long-awaited bull. Zebedeo calls for an immediate search for the
lost bull, and when the animal is traced to Coronada's house, an
infuriated Zebedeo orders her band buried alive, a command each
obeys by carrying his or her own coffin in a procession to the grave.
In a supernatural mood, Hombre-Monja commands Coronada
to rise from the dead; she responds, along with the rest, all mounted
on a white horse that takes them away.

In the play, everything spins around the supreme Spanish symbol
of tragedy and virility: the *toro bravo* (the fighting bull). The most
popular traditional Spanish diversion, the bullfight has ironically
invited much love and hatred, registering remarkable protests
and prohibitions along its history, particularly in the sixteenth
century. José María de Cossío, the pre-eminent authority on bull-
fights, tracks the jagged history of anti-bullfight protests and
prohibitions, most notably the 1555 petition by the Valladolid court
and its subsequent repetition in 1567 by the Madrid court that
called on the king to ban the feast (1931, 91–8). An important
protest document to this effect is Francisco Núñez de Velasco's
Diálogos de contención entre la milicia y la ciencia (1614), which
Cossío aptly cites in his own study. The fact remains that the
fiesta brava has resisted a long registry of protests and managed
to thrive. As Lidia Falcón said in a public lecture at the College of
Wooster (Ohio) a few years ago, in Spain today, you could oppose
or defend whatever you want, from football through lesbianism

to fascism, but when you touch the bullfight, you are bound to meet with fierce opposition. The reason being that, despite its horrifying imagery, the number one ritual is an original cultural practice that distinguishes the authentically Spanish; a popular art form with a supposedly artistic quality that inspired Ernest Hemingway to write *Death in the Afternoon* and *The Dangerous Summer*. In this context, Coronada's confrontation with the bullfight is to be seen as a powerful mechanism designed to raise the stakes in her battle as a woman. Her unique rebellion, then, becomes an allegorical act intended to question a protected patriarchal institutional practice and to shift the established power models and gender gaps. On a personal level, her protest before the patriarchal powers signals her resolution to overturn the power relations that define her identity and to make a move from her marginalized social status into the position of the commanding subject.

In an essay, 'Pluralism in Postmodern Perspective', Hassan argues that derision and revision are versions of subversion – terrorism, for example – but that ' "subversion" may take other, more benevolent, forms such as minority movements or the feminization of culture, which also require de-canonization' (1986, 505). Let me add that the representation of minority movements and the feminization of culture are principles of affirmative action that thoroughly capture the spirit of the postmodern. Any engagement in the redress of social injustice, any manoeuvre at levelling the playing field for all, depict an exercise in postmodernism at its practical best, because such an effort works against hierarchical structures and detrimental power imbalances that tend to muffle minority voices. In *Coronada y el toro*, the unflinching support shown by Melga and Delga for Coronada's cause is to be seen as an organized political strategy, even if on a minor scale. When Zebedeo sarcastically refers to these women as 'el partido de las Martas' (the party of Marthas) (TC 432), he means to pose their activist conduct against the passive, conservative stature of Mary, an image he sees as more appropriate for women. But the playwright sabotages this chauvinist mindset by way of irony and parody. In Coronada's agitation for justice, it is the *macho* himself whom she serves to liberate. Despite the public demonstration of bravery that Marauña is expected to stage, he is shaky and swiftly escapes when Coronada and Hombre-Monja cause confusion in the arena. Coronada's intervention not only redresses the personal injustice committed against Marauña, but she also reveals the potential brutality to which all bullfighters are subjected. Most importantly, by reducing the bull to submission without arms, unlike the way men do, Coronada, in a benevolent yet truly heroic style, exposes the ontological fallacies that underpin enshrined male valour. As she reminds Zebedeo, 'El heroísmo y el miedo siempre han ido de la mano' (Heroism and fear always go hand in hand) (TC 461). This is why she calls the 'fiesta brava' (a bullfighting feast) a 'fiesta de miedo' (a feast of fear), which indeed captures more aptly the true essence of the Spanish popular pastime.[15]

In an important way, Nieva's project in *Coronada y el toro* sustains García Lorca's legacy. Firmly positioned behind the feminist cause, Lorca effectively employs theatrical devices to call attention to the plight of Spanish provincial women. But Nieva's feminist posture, I submit, is much more aggressive. Whereas Lorca's approach tends to uncover the exploitation of women by portraying them as victims of patriarchy, Nieva empowers the female sex, assigning women roles that create new gender authority relations altogether. As the voice of rebellion (in *La casa de Bernarda Alba*), Adela would never have committed suicide in a Nieva play, and if she did, she would be brought back to life to immortalize her effort and to reclaim victory over tyranny. Similarly, La Novia of *Bodas de sangre* would probably have defended her escape with Leonardo as the ultimate sign of her innermost desire and not beg for punishment. This kind of firm resistance is what Nieva means by 'víctima superior'. Call it utopia if you will, but keep in mind that the didactic value of Nieva's drama does not derive necessarily from logical reality but from that which allows actor and spectator to dream of possibilities. When Zebedeo's officers charge and drag Coronada away, she does not play victim but relies on her womanhood – her self-independence – as her sole legitimate source of strength: 'Soy mujer y tengo fe y me sé hacer muy bien el moño yo sola sin ayuda de nadie . . .' (TC 422) (I am a woman of faith, and I know perfectly well how to make a fist alone with no one's help . . .). Indeed, when Zebedeo condemns her to death, she does not panic but instead reaffirms her pride and dignity as a woman before descending into her grave, just as Antigone does in Sophocles' famous play:

Lo haré. No tengas cuidado . . . Pueblo consagrado, hermano alcalde, don Cerezo, pastor en baldío: yo soy Coronada, heroína, que entra en la tumba por su propio pie . . . Soy más mujer que delincuente y, por lo mismo, llevo el corazón lleno de novedades, más que un almacén de capital imperio. Soy española y sencilla, pero incomprendida por el tumulto y malfamada por el populacho fidelón. Por esto vuelvo a la tierra, madre de libres gusanos, desnudos como Adán y Eva, donde todos volveremos a encontrarnos poniendo huevos a granel y aliment-ándonos de balde en comunidad apelotada de paraíso. (TC 463–4)[16]

[I will do it. Don't worry . . . Honourable commoners, brother mayor, Don Cerezo, worthless pastor: I am Coronada, a heroine who willingly enters the tomb on her own feet . . . I am a woman, not a criminal, and so my heart is filled with more novelties than a warehouse of imperial capital. I am Spanish and simple but misunderstood by the crowd and demonized by this sycophantic rabble. For this reason, I am returning to the earth, mother of self-independent worms, as naked as Adam and Eve, where we shall all meet again laying eggs in abundance and feeding ourselves freely in the crowded community of paradise.]

The power politics in play here cannot be overlooked. Whereas the condemned woman employs intellectual power to make her case, the autocrat uses physical force as a way to punish those who defy his authority. When Zebedeo orders Melga and Delga to be raped, he breaks the same honour code that he uses as an excuse to kill Coronada's boyfriends. As a crime against woman-hood, rape, especially when mandated as it is by Zebedeo, trans-forms coitus as a source of mutual pleasure into supreme example of male control. Even uncoerced coitus, Kate Millett contends,

> can scarcely be said to take place in a vacuum; although of itself it appears a biological and physical activity, it is set so deeply within the larger context of human affairs that it serves as a charged microcosm of the variety of attitudes and values to which culture subscribes. Among other things, it may serve as a model of sexual politics on an individual or personal plane. (1970, 23)

Indeed, what Zebedeo wants is to subjugate 'rebellious' women through the power of the phallus, the ultimate sign of patriarchy. But his creator, the playwright, frustrates his ambition and foils his efforts by allowing Melga and Delga to escape mysteriously.

In this context, one may view Coronada's masturbation scene, a perverse taboo in the cultural context of 'España negra', as a subversion of the power of the phallus (that is, female sexual satisfaction without a man), proof of her ability to transform domination into self-autonomy and liberation. In Marcusean psychoanalytic terms, the masturbation exercise could be viewed as 'a rebellion against the hegemony of procreative, genital sexuality' (Weeks 1986, 166), which patriarchal systems adamantly defend.

The question of procreative sexuality leads me to another perspective from which Nieva reinforces his gender politics: his subversion of fixed social representations of sexual identity. In his drama, homosexuality, bisexuality and androgyny are posited as accepted alternatives to the male–female and heterosexual–homosexual dichotomy. Even the distinction between human beings and animals is obscured. As shown in *La carroza de plomo candente*, a bullfighter engages in a sexual act with a goat (itself both a he- and she-goat), he expresses lust for a goddess (Venus Calipigia) and, at the same time, he is attracted to the king. In *Te quiero, zorra* (I Love You, Bitch), Villier's passionate love for Zoé is propelled by his

6. *Coronada y el toro* (Coronada and the Bull*)*, directed, with a set designed by Francisco Nieva. María Guerrero Theatre, Madrid, 1982. Photographer unknown. Courtesy of Centro de Documentación Teatral, Madrid.

attraction to the latter's tail, which Villier views as a mark of (animal) sincerity (TC 1250); an anthropomorphism that also forms the thematic core of such works as *Caperucita y el otro* (Red Riding Hood and the Other), *No es verdad* and his 2005 play *¡Viva el estupor!* (Long Live the Wonder!), where Mady is slowly conquered by the erotic advances of the sea monster Capitán Cap.

In *Coronada y el toro*, Nieva creates an androgynous character, Hombre-Monja, who, endowed with divine powers, firmly defends Coronada's cause. Moisés Pérez Coterillo calls him the synthesis of conflicts, the transcendence of antagonisms, the embodiment of a mysticism without dogmas and excommunications (1982, 95).[17] Carlos Bousoño foregrounds this double sexual identity in his enumeration of the appellatives Nieva uses in the play in reference to the man-nun:

> 'Reverendo padre y madre', 'Doctora caminante y Magdaleno selvático', 'hombre abadesa de confianza', 'madre con barba', 'padre materno', 'madre cura', 'madre y muy señor mío', 'padre amadrado', 'santa madre barbuda', 'padre amantísima', 'santo de los pajares y santa de los mitones', 'padre monja', 'beato entreverado', 'madre fraile', 'padre femenino', 'hijo entrecruzado' . . . (1991, 265)

> ['Reverend father-mother', 'travelling physician and wild male Magdalene', 'a trusted man abbess', 'bearded mother', 'maternal father', 'priest-mother', 'mother and dear Lord', 'mothered father', 'holy bearded mother', 'beloved father-mother', 'male saint of barns and female saint of gloves', 'nun-father', 'androgynous Blessed', 'friar-mother', 'female father', 'male-female son' . . .]

Clearly, Nieva is using verbal dexterity to deregulate the undercurrent canon in conventional sexual categorization. From the platform of linguistic distortion (the marriage of incompatible elements), he collapses the idea of a stable identity, thus questioning the gender polarities between male and female, between the masculine and the feminine. Even if this non-conformity impels verbal chaos, the resulting air of liberty unmistakably captures the essence of what the playwright wishes to communicate.

The inspiration behind Nieva's alternative proposition calls to mind a central postmodernist principle, which Jean-François Lyotard underlines, namely, that postmodernism 'refines our sensitivity to differences and reinforces our ability to tolerate the incommensurable' (1984, xxv). Indeed, in his/her dual essence, Hombre-Monja illustrates what many feminists and modern theorists – Foucault, Juliet Mitchell, Kenneth Plummer, Jacques Lacan – have taught us, namely, that sexuality is not given, but that 'it is a product of negotiation, struggle and human agency' (Weeks 1986, 25). As Elin Diamond suitably puts it in her brilliant theorization of a 'gestic feminist criticism',

> [w]hen spectators 'see' gender they are seeing (and reproducing) the cultural signs of gender, and by implication the gender ideology of a culture. Gender in fact provides a perfect illustration of ideology at work since 'feminine' or 'masculine' behavior usually appears to be a 'natural' – and thus fixed and unalterable – extension of biological sex. (1996, 123)

Through Hombre-Monja, Nieva takes his gender politics a step further by questioning the idea of a stable-gendered subject, thereby forging an alternative, third way.[18]

Hombre-Monja's role introduces into *Coronada y el toro* a religious dimension that, once again, relays back to the *auto sacramental*. Mysterious and divine-spirited, the man-nun appears in the drama with an allegorical role, a *deus ex machina* of sorts prepared with a prophetic message to restore order and justice. Once again, however, Nieva cleverly avails himself of the structures and symbols of an artistic canon and then derails its moral foundation. Despite the divine quality he personifies, Hombre-Monja's immediate motive upon entering the bullring is to find a fox that stole his/her bread. The apparently mundane bread he is chasing could be viewed metaphorically as the bread of life, the Eucharist, the *auto sacramental*'s locus of inspiration. What is more, during Coronada's masturbatory ceremony, the image of the Eucharist solemnly appears in the form of a musical disc, which she sanctifies and plays to grace her erotic act. This is the way the playwright describes the scene in the stage direction:

> Abrujada por los instintos encarcelados, Coronada hace de aquel disco un pan viático de todos sus demonios, una especie sacramental y comulgante de misa nigromántica. (TC 441)

> [Bewitched by her controlled instincts, Coronada turns that disc into

a viaticum bread of all her demons, a kind of sacrament and a
communion of black-magic mass.]

Note too that when she eventually initiates the erotic act, it is a
religious icon upon whom Coronada calls: '¡Vamos ahora a la
función solemne y a la adoración de la Santísima Caraba!' (Let's
begin the solemn ceremony and adoration of the Holy Caraba!)
(TC 441); of course, the saint's name is invented. In this mystical
fusion of the sacred with the mundane, Nieva transforms the devotional basis of the *auto sacramental* into an ecstatic *auto sexual* in
which carnal pleasure serves as basis for spiritual stimulation. In a
thoroughly postist spirit, he has realized theatrically what Mario
J. Valdés has identified as the pivotal inspiration behind the postmodernist work: the 'critical remaking' of the past to 'bring about
a subversion of authority' (1994, 455).[19]

On the whole, Nieva's feminist posture as a male writer follows
the legacy of Juan Ruiz's poetic corpus, *Libro de buen amor* (1343),
and Fernando de Rojas's pre-eminently influential dramatic novel,
La Celestina (1519), both texts known for their reversal of an
exhausted culture of Platonic romance.[20] Still, it was Tirso de
Molina (his pseudonym, Gabriel Téllez) (1583–1648) who in the
seventeenth century most systematically laid out the grounds for
the creation of a genuine autonomous space in the theatre for
Spanish women. The author of the legendary protagonist Don
Juan Tenorio of *El burlador de Sevilla* and of plays such as *La
venganza de Tamar*, *El amor médico*, *El celoso prudente*, *El
vergonzoso en palacio* and *El condenado por desconfiado*, Tirso
promoted anti-clericalism and the eschatological, spearheading the
dramatic subversion of patriarchal authority (this is most notably
expressed in his critique of fathers who marry their daughters to
old men). More than any Spanish playwright of his time, Tirso is
the one who raised anti-Platonism to its high pedestal, persistently
making a mockery of the *ens et unum et verum et pulchrum con-
vertuntur* (Being = Unity = Truth = Beauty) ideal, which in no
small measure propelled the flame of anti-feminism.

What does Coronada's powerful presence imply for the production
of meaning and interpretation on the stage? What positive effect,
if any, can this presentation of the female character produce on
the feminist spectator? Writing back in 1977, Hélène Cixous
explains why she considers theatre-going as tantamount to going

to her own funeral and why she stopped going to the theatre altogether:

> It is always necessary for a woman to die in order for the play to begin. Only when she has disappeared can the curtain go up; she is relegated to repression, to the grave, the asylum, oblivion and silence. When she does make an appearance, she is doomed, ostracized or in a waiting-room. She is loved only when absent or abused, a phantom or a fascinating abyss. Outside and also beside herself. (1984, 546)

For her part, Dolan shows that, in performances that represent the male spectator as an active subject, the feminist spectator is pushed into the outsider's critical position. This is because, whereas the male spectator is encouraged to identify with the male hero in the narrative, the female spectator is placed in an untenable relationship to representation. Dolan adds:

> [The feminist spectator] cannot find a comfortable way into the representation, since she finds herself, as a woman (and even more so, as a member of the working class, a lesbian or a woman of color), excluded from its address. She sees in the performance frame representatives of her gender class with whom she might identify – if women are represented at all – acting passively before the specter of male authority. (1991, 2)

It cannot be denied that in some ways *Coronada y el toro* alters the traditional Spanish gender paradigm of its spectator-ship, at least theoretically, for as Nieva empowers the female character and grants her control over the dramatic action, he synchronically subjectifies the feminist spectator. I do not know what to suggest of the play's chauvinist spectator, except that he has no hero with whom to identify here. If he insists on identifying with one, it can be none other than Hombre-Monja, but that process of identification would evidently require a radical trans-formation on his part. On the other hand, just as Coronada draws inspiration from her own list of female heroines – Isabel (la Católica), Agustina (de Aragón), María Pita (who defended La Coruña against English attack in 1589) and Antonia Mercé (a famous flamenco dancer) (TC 421–2) – the feminist spectator is offered a formidable sisterhood to embrace in Nieva's lead character. Along with any open-minded audience watching *Coronada y el toro* on stage, the feminist spectator is likely to be encouraged by Coronada's systematic de-canonization of the Romantic, idealized image of woman and by her displacement of the prejudices associated with patriarchal systems. Above all, when Coronada and her rebellious party arise from the dead and are carried away on the white horse, she symbolically challenges death's conclusive quality, as if to perpetuate her resistance, thus forcing upon the audience the victory of her empowerment.

Now, how does one reconcile Nieva's strong humanist posture, as evidenced in his presentation of Coronada, with postmodernism's negation of the human subject as a coherent agent capable of shaping history? Does the inconsistency reside within postmodernism itself, that is, does postmodernism contradict itself in its rejection of an essential unified self and its simultaneous will to centre the marginalized subject? Patricia Waugh wrestles with this problem in *Feminine Fictions: Revisiting the Postmodern*. In this study, Waugh argues that feminist fictional writers seem to be writing against the postmodernist current by 'pursuing the sort of definition of identity and relationship to history which postmodernists have rejected' (1989, 10). She is referring to these writers' accommodation of 'humanist beliefs in individual agency and the necessity and possibility of self-reflection and historical continuity as the basis of personal identity' (13). Waugh apparently resolves the puzzle, however, when she affirms that many of these contemporary feminist texts have modified the traditional form of such beliefs in order to emphasize the provisional and shifting disposition of identity. Thus, what such texts suggest is that 'it is possible to experience oneself as a strong and coherent agent in the world, *at the same time* as understanding the extent to which identity and gender are socially constructed and represented' (13). Waugh's contention guides the Nieva reader or spectator a great deal in comprehending his defence of the feminist principle. In order to empower and to subjectify the marginalized in his/her relationship to history, the subject's identity cannot remain fragmented and dispersed. In fact, so much have theorists and critics abused and exaggerated this particular facet of postmodernism that it sounds as if postmodernist literature were populated with robots. What is important is that the literary subject question the fixed representations that underlie what he/she is supposed to be and that he/she kick against the power structures that oppress his/her well-being. This, I believe, is a legitimate goal of the post-modernist at the hour of constructing his/her characters; a goal resoundingly achieved in *Coronada y el toro*.

Nieva's greatness derives from the extraordinary amusement that his dramas exude, but the playfulness often carries an undeniable political underpinning. Surprisingly, this playwright sees no politics but sheer diversion, referring to his rhetorical project in *Pelo de tormenta*, for example, as nothing more than 'sacristy jokes' (1997c, 20). Nevertheless, in the context of Francoist censorship, scenic representations of a convent nun who lays eggs that hatch snakes, or of a phallus worshipped publicly by nuns, duchesses and mayors, carry much more loaded implications than 'sacristy jokes'. For a dramatic piece to be political, it does not necessarily have to present a concrete political situation as often witnessed in the works of, say, Erwin Piscator, Edward Bond, Dario Fo, or in Rafael Alberti's *Noche de guerra en el Museo del Prado*. Neither does the drama have to degenerate into a partisan, ideological spectacle such as Jacinto Benavente's *Aves y pájaros* or Sotero Otero del Pozo's *España inmortal*. In his quest to shatter sex taboos and to destabilize essentialist gender categor-izations, Nieva effectively engages *Pelo de tormenta* and *Coronada y el toro* to question the authority and the powers that shape such cultural modalities and phenomena. This subtle yet parodic mechanism of rearranging power relations onstage is a peculiarly postmodernist political act, for the systematic critique breaks down inequities among social categories and creates a central space for those who tend to be heard from the margins.

V

PERFORMANCE

A SISYPHEAN TRAJECTORY

Before delving into Nieva's stage praxis, let me first lay out the impediments with which he has been faced in his protracted attempt to get his works performed. In this way, some of the reasons behind the limited recognition of his standing as a major European dramatist will have become clearer. It is a widely accepted fact that, for a dramatic piece of work to gain full artistic realization, it must be performed before a live audience. After all, as described in the *Greek–English Lexicon*, the etymological definition of the word 'theatre', derived from the Greek *theatron*, means 'a place for seeing'. Notwithstanding the importance of theatre's histrionic make-up, performance involves a complex and risky process that often has little to do with the intrinsic merit of the dramatic text. Yet although playwrights have little control over the outcome of a performance event, it is such productions that ultimately earn them the necessary exposure and public recognition. The complicated process to which I refer is the hydra-headed enterprise of stage production, whose needs are not limited to material resources but, as is especially the case in Spain, are often determined by the cultural and ideological framework within which the industry as a whole functions. This intertwined dynamic – funding necessity and political manipulation – lies at the core of Nieva's long struggle to bring his plays to the stage.

With the compendium of innovative works that Nieva has, one would expect that these would have attracted the attention of Spanish directors, but in reality their interest has been lukewarm. His dependence on subsidies from public institutions such as the Ministry of Education and Culture or the Madrid City Hall has been detrimental to his career, for this reliance was instrumental in determining when and which of his works could be staged. Public funding in Spain has been notoriously designed to constrain the work of writers, especially during the Franco regime. Such policies particularly affected playwrights whose ideological positions were not in tandem with those in charge of regulating the artistic industry. With this kind of censorship, it is no surprise that Nieva's first commercial performance was delayed until January 1976, after the general's death.[1] The staging of *Sombra y quimera de Larra*, directed by José María Morera at Valencia's Teatro Nacional de la Princesa, was quickly followed in April of that year by the remarkably successful production at Madrid's María Guerrero Theatre of *El combate de Ópalos y Tasia* and *La carroza de plomo candente* under the direction of José Luis Alonso. That this last performance, an utterly subversive infraction of the nation's ultimate taboos, received so wide an acclaim as to be awarded the Mayte Prize speaks volumes about the air of liberation that the novelty of Nieva's appearance injected into the suffocating atmosphere of the theatre in Madrid. As testified unanimously by several newspaper reviews at the time, Nieva became a star in the eyes of the general public with only two productions, after almost thirty years since he wrote his first major play.

This enthusiastic applause for Nieva's inauguration into the public arena of Spanish theatre during the transitional period (from dictatorship to democracy, 1976–82) was short-lived, however; it was rapidly met with half-hearted support. With little scrutiny, one can see that, of his first five performances, which took place between January 1976 and December 1979, three were adaptations and not original works. (The other original piece was *Delirio del amor hostil* (Delirium of Hostile Love), staged in January 1978 at Madrid's Bellas Artes Theatre.) All three adaptations were solicited and written specifically for national theatres and festivals. A request for a performance based on Mariano José de Larra as a classic figure led to the production of *Sombra y quimera de Larra*, an adaptation of Larra's *No más mostrador*. Another request was for a version of Aristophanes' work, which led to the production of *La paz* (Peace) (1977) in July 1977 at Mérida's Roman Theatre. Finally, *Los baños de Argel* (The Baths of Algiers) (1979) is a version of Cervantes's piece, which was staged in December 1979 at the María Guerrero. The point is that all these offers for adaptations were made enthusiastically while Nieva's original works were being ignored.

This awkward situation of Nieva's reveals a broader systemic problem related to Spanish experimental theatre in general. In an essay on what she calls the Symbolist Generation, María

Francisca Vilches de Frutos (1999) portrays precisely the period between 1976 and 1986 as the most fruitful for Spanish symbolist or experimental theatre. And yet a scrutiny of the performance record of this group of writers as mapped out by Vilches de Frutos evinces not a cheerful story but a gloomy one: Nieva (eight productions from 1976 to 1982; Vilches de Frutos wrongly mentions seven), Luis Riaza (four), Jerónimo López Mozo (three), Miguel Romero Esteo (three), Martínez Mediero (three), Alberto Miralles (three) and García Pintado (two). With Franco's demise, one would expect that the advent of democracy would have changed matters drastically for the better. In reality, exactly the opposite occurred: democracy produced a setback for experimental theatre as a whole. Indeed, the relatively positive performance track initiated in 1976 by the Symbolist Generation continued when the socialist government came into power in 1983. As Vilches de Frutos shows, however, that track began a rapid decline from 1986 on, so rapidly that, except for Alberto Miralles, who staged six works between 1986 and 1990, thanks to his own independent group, Cátaro, the growing experimental presence was by 1990 almost totally eclipsed by what Spanish theatre officialdom preferred to promote – naturalistic theatre galore. With the penchant to project concerns about urbanization and its attendant social problems in the 1990s, experimental or alternative drama was almost completely sidelined. The notable exception to this disappointing scenario was the independent theatre movement (which includes such groups as Els Joglars, Els Comediants, La Cubana, Dagoll-Dagom, Tábano, Ditirambo, La Cuadra and La Fura dels Baus, just to mention a few), which has been registering success with its experimental campaign in the theatre centres of Catalonia since the 1960s. The relative success of these groups lies precisely in their attraction of wide social support, hence the flow of financial assistance from certain institutions, corporations and the media.

For Nieva in particular, the severity of Francoist censorship never ended but was passed on to the socialist officials of the Partido Socialista Obrero Español (PSOE). Notwithstanding his struggles, he could boast of eight productions before the advent of the socialist government in 1983, and four of those events were almost unanimously acclaimed as *tours de force*. I am referring to *Sombra de quimera de Larra*, *El combate de Ópalos y Tasia* and *La carroza*

de plomo candente, Los baños de argel and *La señora Tártara,*
this last piece directed in December 1980 by William Layton and
Arnold Taraborrelli at Madrid's Marquina Theatre. The other
plays performed during the same period were *El rayo colgado* in
July 1980 and *Coronada y el otro* in 1982. Moreover, his work
had been staged in official and commercial theatres, including
three features at the María Guerrero. So what happened after the
socialists came into power? Unlike some experimental playwrights
who continued to stage their plays well into the democratic era,
Nieva's work attracted no interest, absolutely none. For five years,
from May 1982 to June 1987, he experienced the driest period in
his artistic career, staging not a single work. Unsurprisingly, he
lays the ultimate blame on the biased misconduct of the socialist
officials who controlled financial support for the arts (see Galán
1989, 36). Eleven years of democratic indifference leads a
frustrated playwright to become even more explicitly bitter in his
attack on the PSOE:

> In terms of its achievements, the PSOE has not played any leading or
> corrective role toward theatrical culture. They have obviously failed;
> this is a fact. During eleven years of rule, we have seen many genuine
> playwrights withdraw from the scene. This does not speak well of a
> political party that wanted to change Spain and, rightly so, put it on
> an equal footing with European culture. (1996i, 61)

If one considers, for instance, the venues of Nieva's shows of those
years, one notices that not a single one of them was an official or
commercial house. The advent of socialist rule did not change
Nieva's luck; he was simply denied access to commercial theatres,
and, as a result, he had to take whatever space was available,
playhouses such as the inadequate Albéñiz or the so-called beginners'
stage, as the Olimpia was viewed at the time. The point is that,
even though Nieva's theatre presents its own peculiar challenges
for staging, it continued to suffer well into socialist democracy
some of the fatal maladies it inherited from the Francoist censorship.

One may wonder why Nieva has depended so much on public
sponsorship in the first place, when, as in the United States,
private sponsorship, fairly freed from political interference, plays
an instrumental role in supporting the theatre. Of all the public
performances of Nieva's plays, only three have received any

significant private sponsorship: *Los españoles bajo tierra, El baile de los ardientes* and Juan José Granda Marín's *Lobas y zorras* (She-Wolves and Bitches). Indeed, as is the case in the United States, besides protecting the director against political manipulation, private sponsorship in Spain also employs mechanisms to guard against box-office fiasco. When private enterprises undertake a production, they obtain a limited amount of official financial support. With this limited assistance, these private corporations are able to cover basic production costs. Additionally, they often support theatre companies whose casts ensure that the public will be attracted and the event will be sold. These conditions, however, expose an inherent difficulty embedded in the production of Nieva's theatre in particular: it is an expensive theatre. Performance undertakings of Nieva's plays are costly and demanding, for the tasks are always much more complex and challenging than the average theatrical production. Most of the elements that enrich the productions' quality, especially music, décor and costume design, tend to be much more complex. His theatre especially requires spacious stages with considerable technical support. In light of such financial considerations, Nieva's is often seen as a risky business, since, in the theatrical enterprise, the success of a production is hard to predict. In part, this risk factor is what has dissuaded a lot of producers and directors from undertaking the staging of his work, thus exacerbating an already fragile situation.[2]

Among the factors responsible for the jagged performance history of Nieva's works, one must also bear in mind a series of problems that Vilches de Frutos associates with Spanish symbolist theatre as a whole since the mid-1980s, namely, audiences' lack of preparedness for non-conventional language and directors' preference for classic texts, foreign contemporary authors and new Spanish playwrights (1999, 131).

To forestall the lack of professional interest in his work, Nieva in 1987 formed his own company, the Francisco Nieva Theatre Company, with the help of his ex-student and friend, Juan José Granda.[3] The other co-founders of the company, Juan Antonio Cidrón and Manuel Gijón, regularly served as designer and artistic director respectively. Drawn from the cinema, television and other theatrical productions, the actors were individually contracted, although a few later became constant features in performances of Nieva's work, actors such as Francisco Maestre, Ana María

Ventura, Julia Trujillo, José María Pedreira, Manuel de Blas and Francisco Vidal. For their productions, the company depended on the usual public sources of support in addition to box-office sales. Unfortunately, since Nieva's is not, strictly speaking, a popular, commercial theatre, the company found itself preoccupied with finances. Of the five shows that the company staged, Nieva himself served as director and designer in four. He even collaborated with the musicians he contracted. Despite these attempts to minimize cost, lack of resources often forced the group to improvise and to simplify the setting much beyond Nieva's desire. After barely five productive years, the Francisco Nieva Theatre Company, incapable of sustaining itself, had no other choice than to fold up. It would take ten years (since the staging of *Los españoles bajo tierra*) before Nieva approached the stage again as director of his own play. Between these dates, only two of his major original works were staged in Spain – *Nosferatu* in May 1993 and *Pelo de tormenta* in March 1999.

Today, the performance record of Nieva's drama looks impressive compared with that of his contemporaries, but, besides a few generous gestures from friends and admirers, this success has been the direct result of his foresight and of his resolve to take matters into his own hands amidst competing odds. Who knows what would have happened had he not set up his own company? Those five years (1982–7) of institutional and professional indifference and silence would most probably have been well extended. Over 75 per cent of Nieva's works have been staged to date, if one sets apart the short pieces that compose *Centón de teatro*. It is, however, a success story truncated and unjustifiably delayed by an absurd system of controls that has still not embraced symbolist or poetic drama, especially in Madrid. As I have suggested at the beginning of this chapter, since it is performance (rather than dramatic texts) that typically accords playwrights exposure and acclaim, this delay has not only stifled the timely recognition of Nieva's place in the evolution of European theatre, it has also caused Spanish theatre to shoot itself in the foot, as it were, by unduly suppressing the contributions of an adept writer and director such as he is.

PERFORMANCE AND THE DRAMATIC TEXT

A clear distinction between conventional or naturalistic theatre and modern, avant-garde theatre is the relative role of the literary text in performance. Interestingly, the fundamental difference between avant-garde theatre and postmodernist theatre has also come to rest precisely on the degree of the dramatic text's importance in the process of stage production. With the advent of the avant-garde, the age-old tradition of textual reliance became assailed, generating a polemic that has yet to disappear. This dramatic turn of events, generally associated with Artaud's influential call for a theatre of gestures devoid of speech, signalled the so-called death of the theatre of the author. 'Dialogue – a thing written and spoken –', Artaud contends, 'does not belong specifically to the stage, it belongs to books . . .' (1958, 37). Pronouncements such as this inspired and shaped the experimental productions of the gamut of avant-garde theatre practitioners that came to dominate European and North American stages since the 1960s (the Becks' Living Theatre, Bread and Puppet, Beckett, Grotowski, Chaikin, Kaprow, even French political theatre groups of the 1970s such as the *Théâtre du Soleil* and *Le Folidrome*).

Since European drama of the second half of the twentieth century became dominated by experimentalism, it makes sense to claim, as Fred McGlynn (1990, 37) and others have done, that the theoretical roots of a postmodernist theatre were planted in *The Theater and Its Double*. If this is so, as I believe it is, how does one explain the fact that performance-based productions have lost steam precisely in the midst of the postmodern cultural heat? In this regard, it is worth noting that a postmodern theorist – John Barth – was one of the earliest to recognize the failure of the performance-based productions of the 1960s experimental theatre.[4] Barth notes that 'it might be conceivable to rediscover validly the artifices of language and literature – such far-out notions as grammar, punctuation . . . even characterization! Even plot! – if one goes about it the right way, aware of what one's predecessors have been up to' (1977, 74). In his study, McGlynn also alludes to Julia Kristeva, who echoes Barth's argument in reference to French political theatre groups of the late 1960s and early 1970s that were inspired by the European version of the Becks' Living Theatre. In 'Modern Theater Does Not Take (A) Place', Kristeva affirms:

As its only remaining locus of interplay is the space of language, modern theater no longer exists outside of the text. This is not a failure of representation (as is often said), because nothing represents better than language (*la langue*) – that privileged fabric of identification and fantasy. Rather, it is a failure of de-monstration, of the theater as de-monstration. Severed from its intra-linguistic production (*le langage*), this de-monstration can do nothing but chain itself to the normative ideologies to which the failure of contemporary social sets, and perhaps, even the failure of the human race, affixes itself. (1977, 131)

This defence of the text, frequently made in criticism of Artaudian dramaturgy or of early experimental theatre in general, has steadily become commonplace: June Schlueter (1985, 221), Fred McGlynn (1990, 141–54), Masakuni Kitazawa (1992, 169–72), Erika Fischer-Lichte (1996), Douwe Fokkema (1997, 21–4), Gay McAuley (1999, 210–34), among others. The argument invariably raised by these critics is that, for (Artaud-style) ritual theatre to work, there must be a community of observers who share in and value the spiritual connections among members outside the theatre. This kind of bonding, the critics maintain, is lacking in modern Western society where individualism and materialism are the order of the day.

Let me stress that Artaud-inspired theatrical praxis that undermines the literary component of the performance experience does not – and cannot – represent a postmodern modus operandi. The undeniable contribution of the Theatre of Cruelty (and, to some extent, of Brecht's epic theatre) has been to halt the monopoly on Western stages of a prevalent unilateral, naturalistic theatrical culture. In so doing, the Theatre of Cruelty paved the way for a different brand of theatre bent on diversifying dramatic representation through multiple rhetorical and formal devices. It is on the basis of this diversification of theatrical modalities that the culture of a postmodernist performance strategy is feasible. Yet, unlike modernist productions, postmodernist performance cannot thrive on a purely experimental platform, because even though this performance domain is inevitably shaped by experimental methods (e.g. emphasis on gesture and symbolism), it also draws on its conventional, naturalistic heritage by relying on speech and dialogue, a humanist foundation that has stood the test of time.

Interestingly, the humanist ingredient, which underscores the actor's body and language as the centre of attraction on stage, constitutes the thematic core of the Francisco Nieva Theatre Company's Manifesto. In its rather short bilingual document, the company makes some striking affirmations:

> The company's most valuable contribution is that of a concept whereby the literary text and the plastic image come together into a theatrical whole. The effect of this is a more balanced and clear – in short, more varied theatre – than has been created by others who have gone beyond modernity without giving up their prejudices. This European new wave, which attempts to maintain the theatre's humanist legacy as well as its experimental tendencies, constitutes the axis of our work. All of this has allowed the Theatre Company to make advances in its assertion of modern European values. (Official pamphlet, Francisco Nieva Theatre Company, 1988)

On the basis of these words, it is clear that what Nieva seeks to achieve as a director is consistent with what he does in his literary production as a whole, namely, to neutralize the prejudicial dominance of modernist abstract experimentalism and to infuse his theatre with humanistic principles centred on the actor and his/her speech. The resulting balance (between the dramatic text and plastic imagery), to which the manifesto vaguely refers as the 'European new wave', is, in my view, an unequivocal mark of a postmodernist performance strategy. In the hybrid vigour of Nieva's theatre, this interactive relationship – the wholesome marriage between the literary text and the performance text – is fully accomplished and enables his work to thrive where the avowed experimentalism of most avant-garde and neo-avant-garde theatre has waned.

Nieva's position regarding the text–performance dynamic is very clear: 'Without belittling the importance of other factors, language is the great mediator of theatre' (1996c, 82). This insistence on language as primary resource for his stage productions fully supports the rhetorical claims made in the manifesto. One should, however, not be misled by Nieva's words into thinking that he pays less attention to the non-literary dimension of the theatre, for this is not the case. In this respect, it would be stretching the matter to compare him with, say, Beaumarchais, Racine or even Shakespeare. It is, thus, compelling to heed Maria M. Delgado's call (2003) on theatre critics to go beyond the written text if one is to assess properly Spanish theatre history. In Nieva's case, what is important is the balance he establishes between the various elements that go into making the stage production – music, lighting, décor, costume, etc., without excluding the role of language. The foundation of that global vision, for which he won the National Theatre Award in 1980, lies in his professional work as a director and designer, an experience that preceded his career as a playwright. Throughout his adventures in Paris, Venice and (East) Berlin, it was for his painting and set design that Nieva was known. Among some of his most famous set designs are those he made for Ionesco's *Exit the King* (his first set design ever in Spain that also gained him wide recognition), *The New Tenant* and *Macbeth* (of which he was also the translator). Others are Shaw's *Pygmalion*, Weiss's *Marat Sade*, Sartre's *The Condemned of Altona*, Frich's *Biography: A Game*, Miller's *After the Fall*, Büchner's *The Death of Danton* and Claudel's *The Satin Slipper*. In (East) Berlin, Nieva collaborated with Walter Felsenstein as designer of several operas and ballets, including Prokofiev's *Cinderella* at the Komische Oper. Between 1964 and 1968, he worked with José Luis Alonso and later with Adolfo Marsillach on several projects and soon became acknowledged as one of Spain's top designers. Indeed, it was not until 1969 that he actually moved away from his primary career as a painter and designer and became a full-time playwright, although he had been writing plays all along.[5]

With respect to Nieva's experience as a director, it is worth noting, besides his own works, Manuel de Falla's *La vida breve*, an opera he directed in 1999 to inaugurate Madrid's Royal Theatre after it had been shut down for many years. In 2001, he returned to the same theatre to direct Luis de Pablo's *La señorita Cristina*. And in 2004, at the age of 80, he capably directed Joaquín and Serafín Álvarez Quintero's plays, *La mala sombra* and *El mal de amores*. These recent works of Nieva crowned a long history of stage direction – Calderón's *The Phantom Lady* in New York, Jarry's *King Ubu* (of which he was also the translator), Duque de Rivas's *Don Álvaro*, Mozart's *Don Giovanni*, etc.

In effect, Nieva brings to the stage a loaded experience in scenic techniques and management to complement the literary component of his theatrical enterprise. That said, his strength remains firmly grounded in the construction of characters from a linguistic point of view. Like Jacques Copeau, he frames his productions in such a way as to project the textual reality, which the spectator is invited to contemplate. Imagining the text's scenic representation, he works on how best to employ non-verbal devices to communicate to the audience that which is impossible to capture in the dramatic text.[6] Nieva's grandiose, allegorical narrative is comparable to Baroque or Romantic theatre, requiring what he calls ' "a super-imposed" interpretation, like a visual stylization of the concept itself' (1990a, 43). That is, the signifying processes that underlie the dialogue tend to transcend denotative, logical transcription of concepts. It must be stressed, however, that unlike many post-modern writers and theatre practitioners, this playwright harbours no aversion to the use of language with conventional meaning; a level of flexibility manifested in the dialogue witnessed in such works as *No es verdad, Caperucita y el otro* or *El baile de los ardientes*. No wonder, as director Nieva is extremely faithful to the literary text. Rarely does he modify the dramatic text in any significant measure when directing his plays.[7]

Surprising though it may sound, Nieva's emphasis on the literary text is not unique even within the framework of contemporary experimental theatre. On the contrary, the emphasis re-inforces what some theorists have pointed out as a trend in postmodern theatre. Fischer-Lichte best represents this viewpoint. She underlines language and the body precisely as epitomizing what she refers to as 'the project of postmodernist theatre'. Using Robert Wilson's performance modes as her analytical point of departure, Fischer-Lichte notes that the rediscovery of poetic language, in combination with a rediscovery of the human body, is a fundamental value equal to the reinvention of a new humanism, which, in her view, constitutes the project of postmodernist theatre. 'By foregrounding body and language', she observes, 'theatre recalls the possibilities and conditions that are innate to human beings, and exposes them to the reflecting gaze of the spectator' (1996, 298). Even before Fischer-Lichte, Veronica Hollinger, one of the few who use the term 'postmodernist theatre' positively, affirms what some would have considered until recently as blasphemy: 'in its own very different way(s), postmodernist theater is also involved in a mimetic enterprise. It too endeavors to mirror the real.' But then she adds:

> Within the postmodern cultural fields, however, there has occurred a drastic alteration in the ways in which aspects of the real have come

to be defined. Language is an arbitrary system of signs which are culturally produced and which undergo constant transformation; the mediation of language and other culturally defined codes creates a permanent division between the real and our interpretation of it . . . (1992, 184–5)

Outside of academic debate, the reality of theatrical practice proves Hollinger's point. As Gay McAuley demonstrates in her accomplished study *Space in Performance: Making Meaning in the Theatre*, despite all the assault by contemporary theorists on the function of the written text in the performance process, the directors who have dominated theatrical production in Europe in recent years have not rejected the old tradition. As if making a case for postmodernist theatre without mentioning the *p* word, McAuley insists that these theatre artists have drawn on the traditional repertoire, radically reinterpreting plays from the past and borrowing from the traditions of neighbouring cultures (210–15).

The observations made by Fischer-Lichte and Hollinger (and McAuley to some extent) lead me to affirm the following. In classifying postmodernist theatre, it is perhaps necessary to draw a distinction between performance-based works and text-based categories such as Nieva's. Performance-based theatre, as promoted by Artaud or Beckett, borders on what is perhaps best defined as high-modernist, since this kind of theatre delicately marks the frontier between avant-gardism and postmodernism. In this sense, holding other factors constant, it seems to me that text-valued experimental playwrights such as Francisco Nieva (Valle-Inclán and, to some extent, Jerónimo López Mozo are also good examples) represent postmodernist theatre at its most balanced because of their humanistic and comprehensive vision. Moreover, in targeting the reader as effectively as the spectator, this brand of poetic theatre provides the reader with an intellectual satisfaction that a combination of factors – poor stage direction, mediocre acting, inadequate material resources, even mechanical failure – can deny the keen spectator before a live performance.

Nieva does not undertake a formal training of his actors; neither does he follow any specific acting method such as the Actors Studio or Stanislavsky's system. Instead, he gives his actors ample room to improvise and to shine on stage.[8] Still, because his theatre demands a certain type of actor, he does uphold a certain degree of expectations. In an article, '*El baile de los ardientes*' (1990), he lays out some of these expectations, saying that the actor of his work must, first and foremost, grasp his intentions in a simple way and master his/her role. He expects his actors to act in a spontaneous, almost naturalistic, fashion even though his allegorical diction generally contradicts the logic of the actors' linguistic system. At rehearsals, he then goes about measuring and improving their expressive skills and gestural movements until they are fully in tune with the spirit of theatricality and stylization that the text projects. Because of the intertextual sophistication of Nieva's theatre, Juan José Granda insists that it is important that directors and actors of his works be adequately trained and knowledgeable about artistic movements and their philosophy if they are to render proper interpretation of these works.[9] This need probably explains why Nieva's theatre company was almost exclusively composed of young graduates and students of Madrid's Royal School of Drama, that is, disciples of his own dramatic ideas.

Having described in general terms the dramatic principles that guide the performance practices of Nieva and his theatre company, let me now focus on a couple of his stage productions to elucidate my observations. In analysing these performances, I seek to draw attention to his role as a director and designer, especially to the diversity of theatrical traditions from which he borrows, and to the ways in which the literary text interacts with the 'performance text' (to borrow Marco de Marinis's term). The analysis involves the production of *Corazón de arpía* (Heart of a Harpy) (1989) and *Las aventuras de Tirante el Blanco* (The Adventures of Tirant Le Blanc) (1978).[10]

CORAZÓN DE ARPÍA ON STAGE

Corazón de arpía premièred on 2 February 1989 at Madrid's Sala Olimpia thanks to a subsidy received by Guillermo Heras, the director of the National Centre for New Theatrical Tendencies at the time. The technical team was made up as follows: Nieva as director and set designer, Tomás Marco as musician, Granda as lighting technician, Floyd Pierce as choreographer and Juan Antonio Cidrón as costume designer (Nieva worked with Cidrón in this capacity as well). Composing the cast are Paco Torres (Músico-Relator), Luis Hostalot (Luciano), Anna Ricci (Dirce), Francisco Maestre (Creonte), Pilar Ruiz (Bacante) and Manuel F. Nieves (the faun).

From the inaugural drumbeat, which quickly merges with Mozart-like classical tunes that introduce the stage action, to the final voodoo-like operatic dance, Nieva, in less than two hours, takes the spectator through centuries of theatrical culture, combining diverse modes, concepts and practices into one complex mythical experience. Action, costume, acoustics, special effects, décor, the actors' bodies – these are all dotted with signs that accentuate the performance's heterogeneous artistry. What the performance text presents, however, are not abstractions of absurdity in Beckett fashion; neither does the event agitate any structural anarchic tendency. Rather, the diffused and puzzling situations rest on, and are counterbalanced by, a plot that is lineally enacted in such a way that the story nevertheless unravels with a logical rhythm. The introductory music, played by flute and drum, sets the play in a once-upon-a-time frame, which harks back to the Renaissance and at the same time stirs echoes of classical Greek and Roman theatre. This escape into the past, initiated via acoustic sounds, extends itself smoothly into the rigour of speech: the narrator (Músico-Relator) steps in with pronouncements to set up and to prepare the audience for the story, just like the historical Italian *commedia dell'arte*. The scenery, with a dark-blue skydrop, gives the impression of a peaceful dawn enhanced by a peaceful operatic melody. However, the commanding presence of a huge golden sun projected onto the skydrop gives the ambivalent look of sunset.

The décor is as economical as it is suggestive; the sets and props are constructed strictly to intensify and to relay the message behind the drama. In this, Nieva clearly draws inspiration from the dramatic model of Brecht, who revolutionized set design by detaching it from its illusionist and decorative function and accorded it an exclusively utilitarian value.[11] It must, however, be pointed out that Nieva's inspiration in Brecht is discriminating and eclectic. Whereas Brecht launched an assault on all stage make-up, Nieva tends to match his minimalist strategy with a certain measure of plasticity (scenic painting, for example) moulded along Romantic traditions. Indeed, his newspaper column, 'Ni teatro pobre ni teatro rico, sino todo lo contrario' (1997b), is a strong defence of the practice of traditional scenic painting. Not persuaded by those who charge that scenic painting is a step backward, Nieva asks: 'But what does it mean in true art to take a backward step? Does Picasso not paint in neoclassical style [or] in Romanic style . . .?' (1997b, 236).[12] Having said that, *Corazón*'s economical design was probably compelled more by financial limitations than by principle, since typically Nieva's set design is much more complex and elaborate than what one witnesses on this particular occasion.[13] Even so, for this Spanish designer, what is important is not the material object per se. It is the concept behind it, that is, the way in which the material object serves as a symbolic ingredient to illuminate and to enrich the work as a whole. Even when grandiose, setting in Nieva's theatre is never designed as a decorative piece.

In the *Corazón* show, this minimalist technique is expressed in the way in which human puppets are used as props. Whenever the props need to be rearranged, the puppets simply move around and reposition themselves or transform themselves into new shapes altogether. The only sets or props that one sees on stage through-out the play are a straw hut, a straw tower, a windmill (which later turns into a bread-making oven), two vertical dry straws and a tree trunk, which serves as Dirce's stool. The sets/props, con-structed with elongated silhouettes, are distinct from one another but do share a unified design: their shapes create the impression of a pre-modern universe reminiscent of a remote African cottage. This purported distance from the audience's familiar, modern space is further emphasized by the interjection throughout the performance of different noises and typical bird sounds of a natural environment. Like Brecht, Nieva creates a narrator who constantly plays various instruments – drums, castanets, cymbals, a bell, a conga and a xylophone. As in Brechtian theatre, these sounds are not exactly musical to the ears but rather intensify the spectacle's rustic and mysterious sensation, often disturbing the audience's composure in such a way as to divert its attention from the dramatic action.

The exaggerated size of the fiery sun, which sporadically trans-forms itself into the moon, recalls Lorca's allegorical use of the moon as a mysterious participant in human affairs. As is typical of Nieva's theatre, however, that mysterious atmosphere is saturated

with erotic symbolism. The giant chimney that juts out of the hut
at about forty-five degrees can be seen as a phallic symbol. Still
more revealing are the shape and material content of the tower.
Looking like a penis with hairy testicles flanked by two tall straws,
the tower projects the image of a male–female sexual intercourse.
Even the shape of the oven entrance and the back-and-forth
movement of the puppet (which stretches its head to collect money
and to hand out bread) serve to produce the same erotic effect.
Furthermore, the humanization of the sets/props creates a visual
double in which the human and the inanimate cohabit. This
anthropomorphism in turn accentuates the metadramatic and
non-illusionist dimensions of the theatrical text. The designer makes
no pretence of illusion; he deliberately reveals the feet of the
human sets (the stagehands), and at one moment during the play,
these sets dance passionately all over the stage to a ballet beat.
When the season changes from winter to spring, the two main sets
in a cinematographic style transform themselves into Bacante
and the faun, who continue to play their main dramatic roles.

The audience's attention is especially directed onto the actors'
speech and what Fischer-Lichte calls the actor's body-text, that is,
the synthesis of his/her gestural, proxemic and paralinguistic
signs (1992, 192). Like Fyodor Komissarzhevsky, Nieva sees the
actor as the depository of multiple dramatic expressions, from
music and song to dance, mime and interpretation. In the *Corazón*
show, the faun and the Harpy embody this function, representing
the performance's ultimate instrument of theatricality. The faun's
appearance recalls the rural deities of Roman mythology whose
tail, horns and legs resemble those of a goat. Besides its double
blend of humanity and animality, Nieva's faun especially distinguishes itself by its erotic endowment: gifted with an extra-long
tail and a very hairy chest, he/it presents a visual image that
invokes the classical Eros-ridden centaur. The faun's anthropo-
morphous character further foregrounds the mythological context
within which the play is set: the context of the *Golden Ass*, which
is basically the story of a man turned into an ass.

The embodiment of the double, manifested as a fusion of the
human and the animal, is even more visually accomplished in the
construction of Dirce as a character. Drawing on Greek mythology,
Nieva recreates his own version of the Harpy, designing her as a
beautiful woman with wings and three sets of breasts that chirps

like a bird. Made of flexible steel bars wrapped in cloth and manipulated by an invisible stagehand, Dirce's wings bestow on it/her multiple identities: while it/she looks like a huge bird, it/she could very well be seen as an oversized insect, a Medusa, a bat, a lobster, a scorpion, even an octopus. Yet it/she is neither the beast that the visual image seems to portray, since it/she boasts of being the master of several skills: it/she says that it/she is a poet, it/she plays the harp, writes hymns and can foretell the future. Although chained, it/she exhibits a royal pomp that is enhanced by Luciano's tearful subservience to its/her unbridled desire. What Nieva does, therefore, is to unite in Dirce and the faun two extremes on the basis of classical mythology, which he reconstructs with his own symbolic attributes in order to project a subversive image of modern Spanish society; a creative distinction rarely witnessed on the Spanish stage.

The classical underpinning of the devices employed in the staging of *Corazón de arpía* is interlaced with puppetry, a modern technique inspired by Edward Gordon Craig's *Über-marionette*. As one knows, Craig's acting style de-emphasizes the actor's personal emotion and experiences and privileges his/her role as a puppet reduced to action, rhythm and words. Nieva makes use of Craig's concept to enhance the fantastic facet of his own stage, but *h e* maintains the value of the written text. In the *Corazón* show, the characters, extreme and static, carry representational attributes instead of self-identity signals. For example, so blinded is Bacante by her own coquetry that, unable to talk to Luciano in a normal voice, she speaks all the time like an excited whining child. No less effective is the function of the costume design in reinforcing the characters' image as puppets. Thus, Bacante's loose, pale look visually casts her more like a bewitched puppet than as a genuine romantic lover. Luciano's clean-cut physique amidst a thoroughly rural background makes him stand out as a Pinocchio, a naïve buffoon, before the beastly self-assurance of Dirce and Creonte.

The same spirit of puppetry is expressed in the operatic song and dance led by Anna Ricci (Dirce). As the show ends, Ricci delivers a first-rate solo with only two lines – 'Quiero ser una diosa para sobrevivir' (To survive, I wish to be a goddess) – to which Luis Hostalot (Luciano) melodiously responds, '¡Oh! suerte veleidosa, lo bello es no morir' (Oh! Fickle fate, how wonderful it is not to die). As soon as the rest of the actors join in, however, the serious, melodramatic tone shifts into an out-of-step choreography and a hallucinatory jubilation akin to a feast of fools or a Balinese *topeng panca*. What is more, the puppet-like facial gestures and the exaggerated movements, directed by the narrator (now in the role of director of the chorus), concur with the excessive alliter-ation and childish repetitive sounds that make up the song:

> Ser felices como dices, buscar paces y solaces, con tus vicios y solsticios, y tus males animales. Animales con sus males, con sus vicios y solsticios . . .

> [Be happy as you say, seek peace and solace, with your vices and indulgences, and your primitive tribulations. Animals with their tribulations, with their vices and indulgences . . .]

(Note that rhyme and alliteration, important elements of the song, are lost in translation.) In this musical integration, one hears

7. *Corazón de arpía* (Heart of a Harpy), directed, with a set designed by Francisco Nieva. Sala Olimpia, Madrid, 1989. Photo by Chicho, courtesy of Centro de Documentación Teatral, Madrid.

the echo of such postist poems as Gabino-Alejandro Carriedo's 'Soneto de la mujer gorda' (A Sonnet of the Fat Woman) or segment II of Ángel Crespo's 'Aire preso a Carlos Edmundo de Ory' (Captive Air to Carlos Edmundo de Ory'), where what matters, above all, is not logical meaning but rhythm and sounds. Overall, Nieva draws on conventions characteristic of Roman comedies and of the *género chico*, while combining his borrowings with contemporary Spanish *zarzuela*, just like Molière, who takes motifs from the Italian *commedia* and recycles them into a French farcical model of the *comédie française*. Even though Tomás Marco is the one charged with the music in this case, Nieva's skill as a musician has had a significant bearing on the production's musical composition. One can see, therefore, that in order to direct a Nieva play successfully, the director not only requires a certain degree of attraction to or knowledge of classical forms but he/she must also know how to employ and project those forms and ideas from a modern perspective.

So complex is the diversity of the artistic resources employed by Nieva in the staging of *Corazón de arpía* that critics have had to struggle to frame the production within a definite aesthetic category. In his review, Eduardo Galán describes the performance as 'a mixture of genres' (1989, 36). For his part, Lorenzo López Sancho, unable to settle on any single definition, observes:

> *Corazón de arpia* could very well be a mythological play. Undecided, however, the critic is unsure if it is exactly that. This play is not a lyrical one-act farce developed along the lines of the so-called 'género chico' . . . Neither does it fall completely within the category that, careful of not pigeonholing himself, [Nieva] has designated as 'Furious Theatre'. It is neither an up-beat pastiche like *No es verdad . . .* nor is it comparable to the provocative and burlesque *Te quiero, zorra*, although it does share a direct affinity with this last-mentioned piece. (1989, 91)

Drama, dance, opera, *zarzuela*, ballet, pantomime, song, puppet show, cinematographic techniques, projection of silhouettes, admixture of sounds and lighting, fireworks – together these modes and techniques interact to accord the play a hybrid quality in which the postmodernist distinction of its director comes to light. In an article, 'New Models, New Visions: Some Notes toward a

Poetics of Performance' (1977), Jerome Rothenberg argues that postmodernist performance establishes a continuum, rather than a barrier, between various conventionally defined arts and non-arts, between poetry and prose, between music and noise, between dance and normal locomotion such as jumping, walking or running. There is 'no hierarchy of media in the visual arts,' he goes on, 'no hierarchy of instrumentation in music, and . . . qualitative distinctions between high and low genres and modes (opera and vaudeville, high rhetoric and slang) are no longer operational' (13). Even though Rothenberg's comments may be most applicable to the radical experimental techniques of, say, the Spanish in-dependent theatre movement, they do aid the Nieva spectator in comprehending the fluid and pluralist disposition of his perform-ance praxis.

The porous and unstable character of *Corazón*'s performance mode is in tandem with this play's subversive rhetorical under-current. In an important study of the representational (symbolic) nature of theatrical objects and performance, Umberto Eco affirms that '[a] semiotics of the mise-en-scène is constitutively a semiotics of the production of ideologies' (1977, 117). Eco's words make strong resonances in *Corazón*. As the human sets and props take their final bows alongside the characters at the close of the action, the play's underlying message remains obscure. Each character remains within his/her own limited space, making the show seem more about a principle or an ethic than about the characters themselves. My best guess is that the play's ethic centres on Dirce's transformation (from a caged exhibit to a dignified lady about to be sanctified). Nevertheless, this ethic is subversive and not didactic. The idea is that, in Spanish theatrical tradition, the Harpy's changed circumstances could not have been possible within the context of Catholic severity unless Dirce repented and received absolution. That indispensable medium of repentance is an imprint of Spanish Baroque and neoclassical theatre: the urgency to sustain the dichotomy between good and evil and to force that which is deemed as good to prevail at the close of the drama. By dignifying the Harpy in this case and by promising it/her a non-repentant consecration as a goddess, Nieva fuses the terms of morality and breaks down the old barrier of having to do according to old traditions. In this sense, the playwright-director works from within theatre's pagan foundations to create a satire of a modern society's malaise, one represented by Luciano's hypocritical inhibitions. In this connection with the past, Nieva follows the convention of the vulgar, ludic flavour of Roman theatre (thoroughly expressed through costume design), rather than the ritualistic festivity of Greek theatre. Consequently, one can say that *Corazón de arpía*'s ethical paradigm is consistent with that of modern Spanish society, which increasingly grows less concerned about religion-based morality. This peculiarly rhetorical and aesthetic welding of old and new paradigms is a postmodernist mechanism employed by Nieva to forge onstage a revised version of an entrenched system of Spanish theatrical practice.

LAS AVENTURAS DE TIRANTE EL BLANCO ON STAGE

Begun in 1978 and completed in 1986, *Las aventuras de Tirante el Blanco* is an adaptation of Joanot Martorell's fifteenth-century romance novel. The performance event, which inaugurated the activities of the Francisco Nieva Theatre Company, premièred in July 1987 at Mérida's Roman Theatre at the invitation of that city's annual international festival. Assisted by Granda, Nieva directed the play and was also its designer. Against *Corazón de arpía*'s modest cast of six, the production of *Las aventuras* features a cast of sixteen who play roles representing as many as thirty-three characters.

The play's atmosphere is steeped in conventions of the *auto sacramental* and of the *capa y espada* (cloak-and-dagger). Like *Corazón de arpía*, musical notes introduce the action, with the initial palace tunes gradually merged into melodious organ sounds that ceremoniously greet the magical appearance of God (played by Pedro del Río, a famous actor of Calderón's plays). Clothed in majestic resplendence, with glistening gloves and a mask, this masculine God arises in an explosive fire of lights that suddenly reveals his presence. Tall mirrors, installed on the back wall, reflect this character's image in a triple perspective as if to register a visual impression of the Holy Trinity he embodies. This initial angelic tone and spiritual suggestiveness quickly give way to a secular atmosphere, however. In a typical metadramatic style that recalls the narrator's opening speech in *Corazón de arpía*, the almighty figure faces the audience and exclaims,

No os asustéis, que soy Dios . . . Como sabéis, hubo un tiempo más grosero y vulgar que éste, pero muy lleno de sorpresa, porque entonces gustaba yo de bromear y hacer fiesta exagerada con las cosas de la tierra.

[Don't be frightened, for I am God . . . As you know, there once was a more uncouth and a more vulgar era, albeit it was full of surprises, for, at that time, I used to take tremendous delight in playing jokes and making merry with the things of the earth.]

In this heroically delivered discourse, even before the drama is set in motion, the character dismisses any possible speculations about him and about the play as instruments of Christian morality: he metadramatically reminds the audience that he is actually a force of pagan divinity who promotes earthly vulgarities.

This ethical ambivalence, which evinces the character's subversive hypostasis as God and King of England, also expresses itself in the combination of visual symbols – especially costume style – that reinforce the controversial actions of Liduvina and Sabena, two court ladies who enter the stage upon the divine figure's disappearance. Their innocence as virgins is transparent in their nun-like costumes, whose appealing yellowish colour, matching that of the tent in which they are rolled onto the stage, concertedly evokes typical colours of the altar and of the priest's cassock. Even the tent is shaped like an enlarged host (in which the Eucharist is kept). The air of purity radiated by Liduvina's and Sabena's virgin identity, which the costume is intended to highlight, is corrupted by their profane action, that is, their examination of Tirante's private parts. What the designer has done here is to evoke typical Baroque theatrical imagery and then subvert it by conferring upon it apparently contentious qualities, an unmistakable trademark of Nieva's dramaturgy.

This ironic or paradoxical merging of ethical and aesthetic modes, expressed in the performance's body-text (costume, gesture, action, speech), sweeps across the production in other visually concrete ways. For example, La Reposada is dressed in a black gown, symbolic of her mourning, but the long dress, with its low bust line, looks more like a wedding gown. Her dramatic appearance as a mermaid erases any assurances about her self-identity. Apparently cast in fibreglass with a metal mesh frame, this huge, highly eroticized figure of a mermaid comes decorated with an elaborate headpiece, its style drawn from cabaret or possibly from popular carnival conventions. The perceived physical incongruity between her enormous size and the small ship before which she emerges parallels the metaphysical disjunction embedded in the sudden appearance of her deceased husband El Gran Podrido as a living corpse that interacts with living beings. El Gran Podrido's speech, his gestures and his movements, so adroitly acted by Manuel Palenzuela, inevitably bring into play typical cinemato-graphic devices inspired by Luis Buñuel or by the surrealist paintings of Salvador Dalí. The dead-living man's appearance in the lit self-driven coffin, from which his horrifying enunciations are electronically emitted, evidences a skilful director's modern treatment of an old Romantic artistic motif, very much like productions of the Cleveland (Ohio) Public Theatre such as *The Fable of the Cloister of Cemeteries* (1997), *Renfield* (1997), *A Brief Chronology of the Human Race* (1997) and *Transformations of Lucius* (1996 and 1998). Similarly, a Romantic aura invades the stage when it turns dark blue, creating a feeling of potential danger parallel to that associated with *El baile de los ardientes* when Cambicio puts out to sea. Even the costume and the physical spaces and their vertical lines invoke the appearance of nineteenth-century Romantic opera. These diverse cultural traditions are further boosted by a Renaissance theatrical instrument. The music that introduces Princess Ricomana is not the old Greek, flute, harp and drum piece heard in *Corazón de arpía*; it is music that proceeds from the Renaissance. Note also that the undue attention paid by Liduvina and Sabena to the monkey and the parrot as pets touches on a typical habit associated with the Renaissance. Even the plot contains elements taken from a popular English myth – King Arthur and the sword. Here too, Nieva aptly distinguishes the symbolic originality of Tirante's sword from Arthur's: the exaggeration of the length and shape of Tirante's sword (called Maldonado), with which he never parts even when asleep, impels the spectator to see it as a penile extension.

A comparison between Nieva's performance strategy and that of Baz Luhrmann in *Moulin Rouge* (2001) could help us better comprehend the core of Nieva's role as director within a post-modernist paradigm. Set in Paris in the 1900s, Luhrmann's film is a labyrinthine merger of speech and song, opera and drama,

popular music and exotic dance, with a mixture of famous late
twentieth-century musical voices such as Madonna, Gloria Estefan,
U2, Kiss, Phil Collins, Gloria Gaynor, Paul McCartney and
Whitney Houston. What is especially remarkable is the surprising
blend or adulteration of these voices with other musical types.
For example, Elton John's piece is done on the basis of opera
music, Sting's music is sung to tango rhythms, while Indian music
and dance and *The Sound of Music* blend with techno-pop,
which, in turn, suddenly gives way to drama rehearsals that end
up in a major theatrical show. Still, the performance, which
invigorates the underlying theme of love, becomes one dangerous,
suspense-packed exercise in metadrama, perfectly fusing life and
art onstage (when the Duke's vengeful intervention is seen by the
play's audience as part of the performance). Even though Luhrmann's
film is obviously more vivid, with more powerful effects than any
Nieva show, both do share strong resemblances: the action of the
male bride, the coordinated ballet-style dance with undertones of
puppetry, the gelatine breasts served on a platter, etc. No less is
the film's aesthetic plurality in tune with its ethical make-up: the

8. *Las aventuras de Tirante el Blanco* (The Adventures of Tirant le
Blanc), directed, with a set designed by Francisco Nieva. Roman Theatre,
Mérida, 1987. Photo by Chicho, courtesy of Centro de Documentación
Teatral, Madrid.

fusion of truth and lie, joy and anger, certainty and confusion, past and present, reality and dream, love and hatred . . . 'You've never seen anything like it' is what *Time Magazine* says in its review of this film. The point is this: the great paradox of the ultimate postmodernist piece of work such as *Moulin Rouge* is that its cut-and-paste reinscription, which makes you feel like saying it is all déjà vu, as Roger Copeland has said about post-modernist literature, is ironically what accords the work its merit of originality, because the work's interlaced constitution comes to assume an overall identity that distinguishes it from previous forms. Put differently, what makes one see the intertextual value of the postmodernist work as 'just plain derivative or downright plagiaristic' (Copeland 1991, 76), is the same thing that impels another to say, 'You've never seen anything like it.' In post-modernism, hybrid impurity is the basis for singularity. A superior grasp of this paradox greatly enhances one's appreciation of post-modernist literature in general and of the underlying mechanics of Nieva's theatre specifically.

In the sea of competing modes and trends, what serves as the unifying framework behind the production of *Las aventuras* is the sense of play and irrationality in which the show is steeped. Tirante's sleep journey and his resurrection from the dead, El Gran Podrido's dead living (or living death) and his escape in the stone coffin, the automatic release of the sword from the rock, even the ominous trumpet cacophony that always announces the arrival of La Reposada – these and several other situations in the play inject strong poetic or surrealist notes. As in *Corazón*, the ludic tone of the action is most vividly expressed in the actors' body-text as puppets. In this connection, it should be noted that, for all its grotesqueness, *Las aventuras* was initially intended as a children's play until Nieva's friend José María Morera persuaded him against that goal (Nieva 1996c, 79–80). In the performance, the acting is highly stylized. The scale of the presentation, the tendency to make everything larger than life (a characteristic trait of German and French Romantic operas), translates itself here into a hyperbolic portrayal of royalty and an inflated caricature of reality in general. The excessive courtly manners and gestures; the burlesque caricature of Algeciras, who mostly speaks in the infinitive mode; the puppet-like appearance and infantile speech of the porters at the gates of Constantinople; the town-crier's

clownish look; the quixotic contrast between the tiny Tirante
before a bodily Doncellón; the colossal gold-plated puppet-like
head of the lion (even the letter it holds between its teeth looks more
like a scroll); the virgins' childlike speech pattern and their exaggerated
adoration of the pets; the oversized fish mask (reminiscent of
Greek tragedy) worn by the stagehand who pulls along the ship –
collectively these emblematic stage devices and calculated arrange-
ments cast an aura of comical or grotesque puppetry over the
play's movement, even as the plot structure remains fairly Aristotelian.

These signs of puppetry, the product of a skilled designer's
effort, create for the actor a crisis of conflict, because although the
actor is unable to identify well with the unorthodoxy embodied by
the character, the mechanics of Nieva's drama compel him/her
to manipulate the character constantly without actually putting
his/her inner emotions on display. Identification with Nieva's
characters can be a challenging task because the weird disposition
and conduct of characters embodied as animals, androgynous
beings, Harpies and phallic creatures can distance and estrange
the very actors who represent them. At the same time, if the action
is to appear credible, the highly metaphoric language and the
stylized mannerism of the characters need to be imbibed and
integrated into the actor's linguistic and behavioural repertoire.
The dialectic of this difficulty – the need for identification (between
actor and character) and the impossibility of its complete realization
– makes Nieva confess on the occasion of *Corazón*'s staging:

> In the first place, the actor is of utmost importance because he/she is
> the one who contributes the most. But then comes the need to make
> the necessary effort to become fully accustomed to the costume, for
> example. The actor must get used to his/her costume, his/her shell,
> to becoming the character that never really existed until now. And all
> this is difficult, it is very important to carry out, and it takes a lot of
> effort. (Nieva and Ricci 1989, 37)

This seemingly naturalistic call on the actor – an antithetical
call to Artaud's proposition that the actor should not transmit
anyone else's message – has paradoxically produced in Nieva's
shows not a realistic effect but rather a theatricalized one. Nieva's
call for identification could not have produced a naturalistic effect

because the characters, being puppet-like, already establish the basis for a non-realistic representation. If anything, the closer the Nieva actor identifies with the character, the less illusory and the more theatrical the visual effect becomes. After all, with all that has been said about the conceptual differences between Brecht and Stanislavsky, much more unites both theorists than separates them. Stanislavsky never really demanded total identification, nor did Brecht ever reject it outright (Saura 2001, 120); it has always been a question of degree. Needless to say that were total identification possible, Anna Ricci would not have sung or spoken the way she does in *Corazón de arpía*, since a Harpy is unable to display that level of rationality. And were she to distance her own emotions completely from Dirce (the Harpy), her speech and actions would have seemed ridiculous, since obviously her life experience does not resemble that of a Harpy. What one learns from the underlying philosophy of the acting style promoted by Nieva is that, in postmodernist performance, as opposed to avant-garde histrionics, one does not have to call on actors' preservation of distance in order to create a stylized effect.[14]

In the staging of *Las aventuras*, the importance of speech most clearly manifests itself in the way in which the audience reacts to it. Of the twenty-five instances of audience laughter that I recorded during the taped performance, only five had to do directly with the action; the rest were all in response to the humour and wit that the characters' words projected. Suffice a couple of examples. When Don Kirieleisón de Montalván appears at the city gates of Constantinople as a tall man with an extraordinarily long beard, he draws no audience reaction. The theatre roars with laughter, however, when the portress verbally calls attention to his size: '¡Uy, qué regalo de hombre! Tan alto y con esas barbas tapabocas . . . ¿Por dónde os sale la voz?' (Goodness, what a gift of a man! So tall and with so much beard covering his mouth . . . How does one hear your voice?). To which Don Kirieleisón responds with a pun, 'Me sale de las narices. No me despiertes el genio, montón de poquita cosa, y ábreme esa puerta o la tumbo de dos patadas' (It comes through my nostrils. Don't get me going, you mediocre thing, and open that door for me before I knock it down). Additionally, several instances of oxymoron enunciated by María Asquerino (La Reposada) draw heavy laughter from the audience. Here are a few examples:

Son falsos esos diamantes, Doncellón. Falsos como la conciencia de Judas, que Dios tenga en su Gloria. Sólo puedo negociarlos yo, que soy fraudulenta.

[Those diamonds are false, Doncellón, as false as the conscience of Judas. May God keep him in his glory. I am the only one capable of trading them, since I am fraudulent.]

Soy viuda; soy tan viuda que me estoy quedando ciega de no ver a mi marido. ¡Oh, quisiera morir! Ayudadme.

[I am a widow, so much of a widow that I am becoming blind from not being able to see my husband. Oh, how I wish to die! Help me!]

Ah, qué bien sienta hacer el mal. Es una virtud. Yo he sido siempre virtuosa en el mal y así, Dios me tiene que ayudar. No dejará que triunfen mis enemigos, menos virtuosos que yo.

[Ah, how great it feels to do evil. It is indeed a virtue. I have always been virtuous by doing bad, and so I pray God help me. God will not allow my enemies to triumph, for they are less virtuous than I am.][15]

Artaudian theatre may view with suspicion literary emphasis in performance, but it seems to me that Nieva's celebration of language within avant-garde aesthetic paradigms is a more balanced onstage strategy than what Veronica Hollinger calls 'the wordless alienation of an exhausted high modernism' (1992, 187). The avant-garde director, placing little premium on the dramatic text, reorganizes, if not destroys, the script. The informed postmodernist director, with an elaborate text he/she trusts, does not have to ignore the script; instead, he/she calls for strict adherence to it, because he/she knows, as Douwe Fokkema has suggested, that textual contexts, made up of signs with conventional meanings, are still valid in the postmodernist work. It is hard to imagine Nieva writing a play such as *The Future Is in Eggs* or *It Takes All Sorts to Make a World*, works in which all that Ionesco does is to indulge in a uniform repetition of meaningless sentences. Neither is it possible for Nieva to follow the purist dictum of a play such as *Breath*, in which no characters or dialogue appear except one long sigh. As he so perceptively puts it, 'to rid the theatre of conventionalism is to rid it of its charm and magic. One never does things repeatedly in the same manner, [since] the meaning of the very convention changes' (Nieva 1997b, 236). The most basic form of such theatrical 'conventionalisms' is speech, against which, I might add, it is fruitless to fight. This postmodernist mode of thinking largely informs Francisco Nieva's stage praxis.

The variety of the technical devices and strategies employed in the production of *Las aventuras* corresponds with and supports the rhetorical platform on which the drama rests. The rhetorical platform coincides with the value system represented by La Reposada as a subversive character. And no one understands that role better than the widow herself: 'Escándalo, moralidad, desatino y mala pata. Ése es mi lema' (Scandal, morality, folly and bad luck. That is my motto), she thunders as she argues with a bewildered Tirante at the Constantinople court. If La Reposada's words reveal any conceptual contradiction (between scandal and morality), the contradiction disappears in the end before Tirante's newly adopted moral philosophy:

> Todos vivimos bajo un hechizo mayor y las hechiceras son las más hechizadas de todos. ¿No lo entiendes? Escúchame, Carmesina, quiero revelarte un secreto. El bien y el mal, juntos, forman un hechizo que nos confunde y que no se termina jamás.

> [We all live under a great spell, and sorceresses are the most bewitched of all. Don't you understand? Listen to me, Carmesina. Let me tell you a secret: together Good and Evil form a spell that confuses us endlessly.]

With these words, Tirante echoes the same principles underlying La Reposada's pagan doctrine; he thus parts company symbolically with such characters as Cambicio (*El baile de los ardientes*), Silverio (*Malditas sean Coronada y sus hijos*) and Luciano (*Corazón de arpía*), for whom morality signifies a hierarchical order of right and wrong. His new identity embraces such characters as El Conde Jorbatán (*El baile*), Coronada (*Coronada y el toro*), Nosferatu (*Nosferatu*) and Creonte (*Corazón*), who all exemplify a vision of ethical relativism and freedom. Thus, when at the point of his death Tirante (the traditional hero) pardons La Reposada (the traditional villain), his dramatic gesture rhetorically supports the performance's postmodernist underpinning. As 'God' revealingly affirms in his final intervention as *deus ex machina*, what reigns supreme is Tirante's scandalous conversion, embodied by him as a fusion of the old and the new order, and the failed God-ordained pursuit of honour and glory:

> [Y]a es tiempo de que te revele que el verdadero ideal eres tú. Sí, querido, eres tú. Un ideal viejo y nuevo, porque en la eternidad los extremos se juntan y son la misma cosa. (TC 1135)

> [It is now time for me to make you see that the true ideal is you. Indeed, my dear, it is you. An old and a new ideal, for in eternity extremes are joined to become one.]

As Nieva has so pertinently asserted, '[p]rogress is not about destroying but about accumulating' (1990b, 86). In his adventures of the stage, he has invented no extraordinary scenic styles. At the same time, it is hard to isolate any single school of thought as the predominant thread of inspiration behind his stage direction and design. What he has done instead is to break down barriers, displaying onstage a conjunction of old conventions derived from classical Roman and Greek theatres and traditional Spanish dramaturgy inspired by such playwrights as Calderón, Arniches, Ramón de la Cruz, Lope de Vega, etc. These conventions are then interlaced with modern scenic techniques popularized by such theatre artists as Craig, Appia, Brecht, Artaud, Copeau and Valle-Inclán. This eclectic recycling of classical modes in light of modern scenic models to promote a distinctive poetic theatre is an unmistakable identity of Nieva's postmodernist stage praxis.

SPECTATORSHIP

In an article entitled 'El público ideal', Nieva establishes unambiguously the intellectual standard he expects from his spectators:

> In order to reach out to spectators who are artistically inclined, their level of education ought to be high. A dramatist needs to elect: either to write for a wide audience or for a cultured one, and he/she must know the degree to which both groups blend into each other. A cultured audience, that is, an artistically inclined audience, is one that brings with it novelty and diversity. It is also an audience that selects the best available mix of a given moment. (1996f, 160)

He goes on to explain:

> Writing for an artistically inclined audience is not the same thing as writing for a few snobs removed from shared experiences. It is not writing for a contemptible minority, a few pedants who think they are above good and evil. It means dreaming of an ideal audience and considering it as co-creator of the drama's propositions, an audience open to diversity and disposed to upholding tightly those propositions. It is liberating to write for those who understand, to conquer them, for the goal is to refine the audience, to homogenize it, to consider it all as one, artists and artistically inclined audiences alike. (ibid.)

What is key is to determine whether or not Nieva's expectations do correspond with the actual composition of his audiences, that is, with the category of people who in reality go to see his plays on a regular basis. In Madrid, his audiences tend to be composed mainly of young people – especially students – and academics, in addition to a few older, non-academic individuals who understand and enjoy his theatre. This is an audience that, because of its familiarity with contemporary dramatic trends or because of its open-mindedness and tolerance, tends to appreciate the complexities of Nieva's theatre and accepts its unorthodox ideas.[16]

But how does one explain this clustered, minority spectatorship, when Nieva's theatre is a relentless effort at inclusion? The fact is that the selective make-up of his theatre's receptive composition is imposed by circumstances and not by choice. Some factors, especially those related to the ethical connotations of his theatre, make it difficult for more conservative social categories to embrace his work. In an article, 'Tres historias íntimas' (1998), Juan José Granda expresses this problem as a systemic one, showing that average audiences and actors are generally ill-prepared for Nieva's unconventional linguistic style. He blames this lack of preparedness and appreciation on the absence of drama schools and appropriate curricula to educate the Spanish public and theatre artists in alternative ethical and aesthetic values. Granda adds that, without a language school, Nieva's theatre, like that of Valle-Inclán, will always be questioned by those who see themselves as 'masters of modernity'. In this sense, the widely academic and youthful constituency that Nieva commands can be seen as a logical response to the open-mindedness that his subversive theatre requires. This situation, however, exposes what I believe to be a lamentably legitimate quandary with which the postmodernist writer in general is faced, namely, the discord between the literary work's integrationist goal and the handicap the work suffers from its limited reception.

In a concluding statement that she makes after a lengthy discussion of Robert Wilson's postmodern performance, Katherine Arens notes, '[p]ostmodern performance will not work without a postmodern audience that understands plurality, referential insecurity, and individual significance instead of the security of the group' (1991, 40); a perceptive observation that resonates with Fischer-Lichte's own view on the subject. Fischer-Lichte (1996) likens the postmodern theatre spectator to the Baroque prince, saying that he was the only one whose view of the stage's scenic world remained undistorted by perspective and that he was the ideal actant in the social, economic and political world, since he was God's representative. Postmodernist theatre, contends this theatre semiotician, bestows the sovereignty of the Baroque prince on its individual spectators, whom she defines as 'any member of a secular, plural, democratic society' who is 'willing and able to claim responsibility for the theatrical semioseis and their results'. Thus, Fischer-Lichte concludes, postmodernist theatre may be taken as a kind of aesthetic *Vor-Schein*, because 'it realizes and demands a community in which the totally divergent life-projects of the individual members, all of equal rights and value, can peacefully coexist with each other side by side' (300). Indeed, it makes sense to expect that, as a cultural trend, postmodernism will be more decisively rooted in cultures that are open to pluralist ideals. Since cultural agents tend to be individuals who may differ from one another in significant ways, it is important that these individuals be open-minded if they are to respond to an art form that endorses the principle of diversity. Logically, then, disturbing as it may sound, postmodernist theatre can be discriminatory, unless the general public – often conservative – is willing to respond positively to the integrationist agenda of this kind of theatre. This cultural factor, in my view, explains the limited receptive configuration of Nieva's defiant theatre in a culture that has only within the past decade begun to adopt a more open attitude toward social taboos such as homosexuality.

Another dimension of the spectatorship associated with Nieva's theatre that needs to be addressed is the part it plays (or is expected to play) in his stage productions. Nieva's theatre makes no pretext to involve the audience directly. Although a keen admirer of Jacques Copeau – a pioneer in developing forms of communication between audiences and the stage – his performances are in no way comparable to, say, The Squat Theatre of New York, whose 1979 presentation of *Andy Warhol's Last Love* involved live spectators composed of passers-by. Neither has Nieva ever constructed any play mainly for non-conventional spaces, which tend to promote higher actor–audience interaction. The reality is that, even if he had wanted to produce that kind of theatre, it would not have been feasible because spaces with such characteristics are often not available in Madrid where his productions are based.[17] Much easier has been the reconfiguration of stages to adapt to the festive disposition of his drama, an outstanding example being the 1997 production of *Pelo de tormenta* at the María Guerrero Theatre. On this occasion, the director rearranged the stage in such a way that the Italian three-quarter theatre was transformed into a thrust stage that placed the front row in the heat of the action. Similarly, in the production of *Las aventuras*, during the royal toast given to welcome Tirante and El Doncellón to Sicily, the action moves down into the pit where the actors sit at a long banquet table next to the audience. The notion, especially upheld by avant-garde theatre artists, that the proscenium stage belongs to the archaic repertoire of naturalistic theatre is not tenable in Nieva's dramatic arena. Critics are sometimes surprised that Nieva's work is staged in traditional theatres such as the María Guerrero. Yet it is hard to imagine the staging of a play such as *El rayo colgado* on the street, on a boat, or in an abandoned storehouse without serious technical problems, since the function of the underground cave, for example, is central to the show's success. Unlike avant-garde theatre, Nieva's postmodernist theatre harbours no craving to be different; rather, it relies on conventional resources, including conventional spaces, to fashion theatrical forms that nevertheless stand out. Again, this postist-inspired mode of modernizing traditional resources distinctly sets him apart from the performance methods of the Spanish independent theatre movement, which is by far more radically avant-garde in its representations.

Of course, direct audience involvement does not represent the only form of audience participation. Participation in Nieva's theatre is perceivable in the manner in which rarity, wit and humour are combined to engage the audience with the action.[18] Since it is difficult for Nieva's audiences to identify readily with the stage action, what he creates is not so much for self-identification as it is for alternative ways of reading and interpreting the performance text. A world apart, framed within a magical atmosphere, Nieva's theatre invites the spectator who is unable to penetrate that universe to watch from his/her own standpoint and to develop the drama in his/her imagination. He invites the audience to participate, therefore, in order to recreate that immense intellectual space. He reiterates this emphasis on the audience's creative role in a 1991 article: 'Theatre is not something determinate but rather a potential of suggestiveness that must be realized on daily basis, and the audience always has the last word. Theatre and audiences are in constant evolution' (1991b, 79). As a director, then, Nieva may very well set himself apart from those, like Brecht, who insist on distancing the actor from the character, but as a true postmodernist, he is aligned with the avant-garde in embracing the audience's role as a 'fourth creator' empowered to complete the signifying process initiated by the writer, the director and the actor.

Postmodernist theatre is indeed possible, and Francisco Nieva's theatre, I believe, is a bona fide testimony. Even though as a concept postmodernism stands on unstable grounds, historical perspective has made it easier to determine its central principles and to affirm more comfortably its legitimate links with the theatre. In order to establish a playwright such as Nieva as a postmodernist, one should not focus on isolated aspects of his theatre, which by themselves parallel other artistic currents. Instead, one must take into account the aggregate whole formed by the composite interaction of the multivalent dimensions that define his artistic universe. These dimensions are the following: a postist ideological foundation, a theatrical resistance to unilateral modes of classification, the critique of authority and glorification of the marginalized, the dramatization of paradox and contradiction, an interplay of representation and theatricality and an exaltation of open theatre. Other facets are: the supreme role of the literary text in performance, reliance on humanistic devices within experimental paradigms, the reconstruction of classical forms on the basis of modern theatrical strategies and the dissolution of the dichotomy between actor identification and the preservation of distance. When these features are collectively contemplated, one finds in Nieva justifiable grounds on which to assert the validity of the notion of a postmodernist theatre. His identity as a postmodernist with postist roots also brings into focus the historical significance of the *Postismo* movement and, consequently, of Spain's role in the formulation of literary postmodernism as a whole. It was Francisco Nieva who in the 1950s and 1960s ushered onto the Spanish stage the postmodernist wave for which Valle-Inclán's innovations paved the way earlier in the twentieth century. He is the pivot around which the culture of postmodernist Spanish theatre spins, a culture of rupture and renewal that runs parallel to the socio-political and literary coordinates unique to Spain. Perhaps a broader recognition of his historical importance as a theatre artist will serve to reinforce the need to advance the discussion on postmodernist theatre beyond Anglo-American models, which have predominantly shaped the theoretical and historical boundaries of postmodernism.

NOTES

¹ Because of a common tendency to misuse the terminology associated with postmodernism, it is necessary to make a few clarifications. My use of the terms *postmodernity* and *postmodern* corresponds with Jean-François Lyotard's in *La condition postmoderne* and, ironically, with Fredric Jameson's in *Postmodernism, or, The Cultural Logic of Late Capitalism*: 'an underlying transition from an industrial to a post-industrial social matrix' or 'the state of the world after modernity', as Hans Bertens describes it (1997, 7–8). I use *postmodernism* – still following Bertens – in reference to either a lifestyle phenomenon (similar to the terms described in the preceding sentence) or to its manifestation as the new artistic practices that emerged in the 1950s. Where I differ from Bertens, and most people, is that my use of the term *postmodernist* – not postmodern – strictly refers to postmodernism's artistic or typological manifestation. In this regard, a 'postmodern writer' refers to any writer in the postmodern contemporary context, whereas a 'postmodernist writer' necessarily employs devices or strategies associated with this cultural current. Throughout this study, I use the capital *P* whenever I refer to postmodernism or *postismo* as a movement, and I use the small *p* in reference to the two currents as aesthetic categories.

² The system of documentation I follow is the author-date system. For the benefit of those readers not familiar with this method, this means that citations within the text, enclosed in parentheses, consist of the author's surname (omitted when clear from the context), the year of publication of the work and, where appropriate, the relevant page number(s), in that order. Multiple works by the same author in the same year are differentiated through the use of letters following the year of publication.

³ This is not the place to attempt to address the tired question of whether or not Spain has even experienced the reality of modernity at all. Let me simply reaffirm Juan Antonio Ramírez's humorous way of addressing the issue:

> Does the modern exist? Yes, and there you have the modern art museums to prove it. Obviously, governments do not spend money on institutions that contain or promote things that do not exist. Recent polls show that the great majority of people have seen with their own eyes pieces of modern art, which exists with a greater degree of evidence than UFOs. (1986, 16)

Regarding the topical lack of coincidence between Western Modernism and Hispanic *Modernismo* (a bourgeois artistic movement of the late nineteenth century influenced by French Parnassianism and Symbolism), the following studies could be consulted: Iris Zavala (1988); Richard Caldwell (1993); John Butt (1993); Dolores Romero López (1997); and Christopher Soufas (1997). Whatever the differences may be between the two concepts of modernism, what is of interest in the context of postmodernism is that, during the early part of the twentieth century, the process of Castilian adaptation to the conditions of modernity synchronized aesthetically with that of Europe in concrete forms such as the avant-garde, a process viewed by Bou and Soria Olmedo as creating a genuine basis for the study of authors and works whose strategies are now characterized as postmodernist (Bou and Soria 1997, 397).

[4] Some of the principal figures of the Generation of 1982 listed by Amestoy are José Sanchis Sinisterra, Vicente Molina Foix, Miguel Medina Vicario, José Luis Alonso de Santos, Rodolf Sirera, Fermín Cabal, Lourdes Ortiz, Francisco Melgares, Sebastián Junyent, Álvaro del Amo, Juan Antonio Hormigón and Fernando Savater.

[5] Antonio Sánchez draws a distinction between the historical avant-garde and what he calls the contemporary avant-garde. Whereas the historical avant-garde refers to the 1920s, with its clearest manifestation in such movements as *Ultraísmo*, Surrealism or Dada, the contemporary avant-garde covers the period from the 1980s onward. Sánchez, however, notes that this latter group is mainly composed of alternative theatre groups such as Els Joglars, Els Comediants, La Cubana, Dagoll-Dagom and La Fura dels Baus (2000, 103–5).

[6] It must be pointed out that the experimental works of alternative theatre groups such as Els Joglars, Els Comediants or La Fura dels Baus have sometimes been categorized as postmodernist. As will be seen, Nieva's brand of postmodernism, which places emphasis on the dramatic text, varies a great deal from the performance style of the independent theatre movement.

[7] Johannes Birringer's theoretical stance on postmodernist theatre was expressed a few years earlier in *Theatre, Theory, Postmodernism* (1991), but I find the argument in his 1997 article much clearer and more forcible.

[8] Indeed, the statistics, reported toward the end of 2003 by the National Institute for the Performance Arts and Music, show a positive development for the performance arts in Spain. According to the report, published by Carlos Galindo (2004) in the Madrid daily *ABC*, from September 2002 to August 2003 stage performances (of which the theatre occupied 58.39 per cent in Madrid and 54.19 per cent in Barcelona), recorded an increase in spectatorship by 11 per cent in Madrid and 14 per cent in Barcelona, an encouraging outlook that the cinema did not share. Moreover, in Madrid, except for a small drop during the 2000–1 season, the increase in spectatorship has been consistent since 1999: 2,674,130 (1999–2000), 2,660,644 (2000–1), 2,700,210 (2001–2) and 3,011,805 (2002–3). This trend is parallel to the case of Barcelona, where the only drop in spectatorship occurred in 2001–2. Similarly, the number of performances has increased in both cities since 1999, except for a drop in Madrid in 2002–3: 9,187 (1999–2000), 9,564 (2000–1), 10,276 (2001–2) and 10,127 (2002–3). In Barcelona, the figures have been one-directional: 8,234 (1999–2000), 8,287 (2000–1), 8,470 (2001–2) and 8,513 (2002–3). In light of such figures, Julio Huélamo, the director of Madrid's Centre for Theatrical Documentation, maintains that

the theatrical scene in Spain is enjoying 'good health' and that this growth augurs well for the future of the Spanish performance arts in general.

⁹ Recalling Paul Virilio's view that the technologies of the electronic age enable a new visual perception detached from human beings, Fischer-Lichte (1996) contends that postmodernist theatre engenders a contrary effect, which she calls 'the aesthetics of disruption'. 'By insisting on the simultaneous physical presence of actors and spectators, by challenging the creative potential in the eye of the beholder', asserts this theatre semiotician, '[postmodernist theatre] confirms its premise that aesthetic perception is the same as sensuous perception, based on and tied to the body of the perceiver, made possible and determined solely by it'. She goes on to say that the theatrical aesthetics of disruption cannot be derived from so-called zapping, that is, switching between TV channels because the eye of the spectator in this case does not wander but is permanently fixed on the same spot. 'In a certain light', insists Fischer-Lichte, 'one might even characterize the zapping as an attempt of the media user to simulate the theatrical experience of the wandering eye before the TV set without being able or actually forced to mobilize it.' She then concludes that the disruption created by the gaze of the spectator in postmodernist theatre, on the contrary, is a direct result of its free movement within the time–space continuum (299).

CHAPTER I: *POSTISMO*, POSTMODERNISM, THEATRE

¹ There is controversy over the importance of *Postismo*'s remote origins. Whereas Jaume Pont (1987) insists on the movement's Madrid birth, Gianna Prodan (1989) calls attention to the significance of a previous, Italian phase, between 1928 and 1932, when Eduardo Chicharro Jr and the Spanish painter Gregorio Prieto became friends at Rome's Fine Arts Academy of the Gianicolo. In Rome, the two experimented with surrealist photography (Chicharro's father was then the director of the Spanish Academy in the Italian capital). Pont accuses Prieto's self-promotion as the movement's genesis by charging that it is an attempt on Prieto's part to reduce the historical *Postismo*, particularly its literary underpinning, to a simple matter of 'resurgence' or to a simple episodic diary related to the context of experimentation in photography (42–3).

Rafael de Cózar underscores the significance of *Postismo*'s historical co-incidence with what he refers to as the second European avant-garde; a post-World War II new wave symbolized by such movements as *Letrista* (founded in France in 1945), *Espacialismo* and *Concretismo*. The primary focus of these movements, Cózar points out, was to launch an attack on the formal unity of language (1989, 15).

² Besides Eduardo Chicharro's *Música celestial y otros poemas* (1974, 271–312), from which my own citations are taken, the manifesto texts can also be found in the following sources: Jaume Pont (1987, 246–93); Carlos Edmundo de Ory (1970, 279–306) (the Fourth Manifesto is excluded); and Raúl Herrero (1998, 255ff.).

³ I am indebted to Jaume Pont, whose seminal work, *El postismo: un movimiento*

estético-literario de vanguardia (1987), has facilitated my research on the *Postismo* movement.

4 For another perspective on Spain's role in the development of postmodernism, see Ramón Esquerra's entire entry on the term (as defined by Onís) in his 1938 literary vocabulary book *Vocabulario literario*, p. 246.

5 For a list of early postist literature and its editorial information, see Pont (1987, 16–21).

6 For a semiotic analysis of the interconnections between the avant-garde and postmodernism as they relate to theatre, see Erika Fischer-Lichte's essay 'Avant-garde and Postmodernism: Theatre between Cultural Crisis and Cultural Change' (1991).

7 It is worth documenting the allusions that Nieva himself has made to the connection between *Postismo* and Postmodernism. See his article 'El "Postismo" una vez más' (1984) and his 1987 interview with Vicente Mosquete. His newspaper column, '¿Cómo saber si somos postmodernos?' (1998), was in response to a paper (entitled 'Francisco Nieva, dramaturgo posmodernista') that I had presented a few days earlier at Madrid's Royal School of Drama.

8 Given that Fernando Arrabal's links with *Postismo* have been documented, I would like to make a few comments on his association with this Spanish movement. Not only has Arrabal himself publicly expressed his ideological debt to *Postismo* (see Arrabal 1977), a few studies have framed his theatre within postist conceptual parameters. A good example is José Manuel Polo de Bernabé's 'El teatro de Fernando Arrabal: vanguardia e ideología' (1981). In this study, Polo de Bernabé methodically applies postist theory to Arrabal's work, but besides a parenthetical reference to this playwright's collaboration with two postists – José F. Arroyo and Gabino Alejandro Carriedo – on a film project, the reader is left to wonder about the true nature of Arrabal's link with the movement. This question is addressed effectively by Ángel Berenguer. Perhaps the one critic who most rigorously studies Arrabal's connection with *Postismo*, Berenguer admits no dependence whatsoever on Arrabal's part on postist principles. He goes on to say that Arrabal never played an integral role in the movement's activities, and when he made contact with the postist poets, this happened during the later phase of the movement's development (1977, 44). Indeed, Arrabal's name does not appear in the list of thirty-four prepared by Gianna Prodan (1989, 2) to identify those who in one way or another associated themselves with *Postismo* during its existence. Moreover, the extent of postist influence on Arrabal is actually limited to his very early theatre, written between 1952 and 1959 – *Pic-Nic, El Triciclo* and *El cementerio de automóviles* – and, in his study of the topic, it is to this phase that Berenguer exclusively limits himself. Even if traces of postist aesthetics – imaginative creativity, madness, humour, linguistic rupture, etc. – can be detected in Arrabal's later theatre, as expressed in his Panic concept, the tendency is more evidenced toward the dictates of surrealism than toward those of *postismo*. Consequently, easy though the temptation has been to create an affinity between Nieva and Arrabal, not only does the kind of study I propose disallow an equal footing between the two playwrights as far

as *Postismo* is concerned, but the study employs postist aesthetics as a means of laying the basis of a postmodernist dramaturgy, to which Arrabal's unabashed experimentalism, in my view, does not exactly conform.

[9] For complete details on Nieva's biography, see his memoirs *Las cosas como fueron* (2002). Antonio González (1980), Francisco Peña (2001) and José Monleón (1976) serve as useful biographical sources as well. A comprehensive list of Nieva's works can be found in Peña's book and on Nieva's webpage, *www.franciscomeva.com.*

[10] Some of the playwrights in whom García Ruiz traces this poetic or idealist thread are Miguel de Unamuno, Valle-Inclán, Azorín, Ramón Gómez de la Serna, Jacinto Grau, García Lorca, Enrique Jardiel Poncela, Alejandro Casona, Edgar Neville, Miguel Mihura as well as more recent or contemporary playwrights such as Rafael Alberti, Valentín Andrés Álvarez, Claudio de la Torre, José López Rubio and Antonio Buero Vallejo (59–123).

[11] Nieva's direct link with key figures of the European avant-garde needs to be emphasized. In Paris, where he led a remarkably bohemian life in the early 1950s, he met with Ionesco, Adamov and Beckett in the cafés of Saint-Germain even before these writers became world-famous. Such was his rapport with these writers that Ionesco would later pay him visits at his drama studio in Madrid. He witnessed Brecht and his Berliner Ensemble's performance at the Théâtre des Nations, an experience that impressed him and influenced his theatre a great deal. Nieva also interacted frequently with Georges Bataille, since his wife Geneviève Escande was the one who helped fund Bataille's journal *Critique* by using the resources of the French Research Centre for Scientific Investigation. The climax of Nieva's Paris experience, however, was when he came to know Artaud's writings through the help of Colette Allendy, a close family friend of the French theorist (Artaud had died a few years before Nieva arrived in France). Nieva also developed relationships with several figures of the painting world — Joan Arp, Constantin Brancusi, Pierre Alechinsky and Philippe Dotremont — and he met Charles Aubrun, Robert Marrast and Georges Wilson. In (East) Berlin he became friends with the musician Paul Dessau. Mention must also be made of his special relationship with Visconti, Barthes, Weiss, Strehler, Octavio Paz and Walter Felsenstein, the German opera director. By the time Nieva returned to Spain in 1963, therefore, he was virtually intoxicated with unorthodoxy, thanks to his exposure to avant-garde and radical ideas. In short, Paris accorded his postist formation an adequate medium of expression that his motherland avidly kept in check: 'The fact is that, returning to Spain eight or ten years ago with my head full of Wilde, Bataille, Jarry, Artaud and Genet meant returning to ask for a post in the Carabanchel prison, not in its political science department but in that of perverse sciences' (Nieva 1973a, 21). Let me add that Nieva's extensive reading and his close association with so many European intellectuals have made him a living encyclopaedia, a well-versed personality of the highest order. One need only interview him or read his memoirs to confirm my assertions.

[12] The categories, established by Nieva in 1980, are 'Teatro Furioso' (Furious Theatre) (TF), which is highly surrealist and hermetic in orientation; 'Teatro de Farsa y Calamidad' (Theatre of Farce and Calamity) (TFC) in which the

characteristics that delineate TF are still present but considerably mitigated; and 'Teatro de Crónica y Estampas' (Theatre of Chronicle and Imprint), which consists of an adaptation of Mariano José de Larra's play *No más mostrador*. Added to these categories in 1991 are 'Teatro Inicial' (Early Works), two plays called 'Reópera' (Operatic Open Theatre), 'Tres Versiones Libres' (Three Adaptations) and 'Teatro en clave de brevedad' (Short Plays). Jesús María Barrajón's article 'Sobre la clasificación del teatro de Francisco Nieva' (1994) is devoted to the confusion and problems created by these new classifications. Barrajón does not see TF and TFC as two simultaneous expressive forms but as a sign of a writer struggling to gain an effective medium of communicating his ideas (6). Katarzyna Górna-Urbanska earlier criticized the same classifications (1987, 23), although her own grouping along thematic lines is questionable.

[13] Nieva's newspaper articles, published between 1985 and 1995 mainly in the Madrid newspaper *ABC*, were reprinted by Espasa Calpe in 1996 under the general title, *El reino de nadie*. My citations of most of Nieva's newspaper articles are taken from this 1996 collection. Another collection of his articles is *En tela de juicio*, which was published in 1988 by ARNAO Ediciones. Twelve articles from this earlier collection are reprinted in *El reino de nadie*.

It is perhaps worth pointing out that Nieva's (postmodern) passion for artistic pluralism is consistent with his practice of ideological tolerance outside the literary universe as well. Although a Leftist, Nieva never aligned himself with the politics of the socialist government of the 1980s. Instead of the pro-government daily *El País*, he opted for the relatively conservative daily *ABC* to editorialize most of his ideas during that period. In part, Nieva's decision stems from a commitment not to undermine the independence of his art, especially in the face of a democracy that turned out to control the theatre so heavily. In the context of a Spain that has compelled generations of its citizenry to follow a tragic political divide, often sacrificing art for politics, Nieva's non-conformist disentanglement from that schism is commendable indeed. In an interview with him (in November 1998), he gave me what may be considered a 'postmodern' response when I asked him about his sentiments regarding his nationality: 'No me considero español. Me considero ciudadano del mundo' (I don't consider myself a Spaniard. I consider myself a citizen of the world). Only much later, when I read Ory's poem 'Todos somos extranjeros' (We are all foreigners) did I realize the postist percussions behind those words.

[14] Even though María Francisca Vilches de Frutos (1999) classifies Nieva in what she calls the Symbolist Generation, his name is absent from George E. Wellwarth's list of Spanish 'underground' dramatists, a list that serves as basis for Vilches de Frutos's own classifications. Wellwarth (1972) correctly excludes Nieva not only because this playwright chronologically precedes the Symbolist Generation but also because he differs from it ideologically. In her essay, Vilches de Frutos groups the principal exponents of the Symbolist Generation in the following order: a) those who were born in the 1920s: José Bellido, José Martín Elizondo, José Martínez Ballesteros, Francisco Nieva, Luis Riaza, Miguel Romero Esteo and José Ruibal; b) those born in the 1930s and 1940s: Jesús Campos, Ángel García Pintado, Agustín Gómez Arcos, Jerónimo López

Mozo, Manuel Martínez Mediero, Luis Matilla, Alberto Miralles and Diego Salvador.

[15] All citations from Nieva's 'Breve poética teatral' (1980) will henceforth be indicated by the abbreviation BP.

[16] For example, in an interview with Santiago Trancón, Nieva minimizes Valle-Inclán's influence on him (1982, 25), but in his memoirs and on several other occasions, he mentions Valle-Inclán as a model that inspires his dramaturgy.

[17] There are numerous critical references to the affinity between the dramatic works of Nieva and Valle-Inclán. See, for example, Claudia Schaefer, 'Francisco Nieva in the Shadow of Goya, Valle-Inclán, and the Aesthetic of the *Esperpento*' (1989). Schaefer calls the painter the grandfather of the *esperpento*, Valle-Inclán as its father and Nieva as heir to their artistic legacy. See also Jesús Rubio Jiménez, 'Prolegómenos para un estudio de las relaciones entre Francisco Nieva y Valle-Inclán' (1994). Peña's *El teatro de Francisco Nieva* (2001, I, 134–8) is also specific about aspects of Valle-Inclán's theatre that are present in Nieva. Nieva's own 'Virtudes plásticas del teatro de Valle-Inclán' (1967) reflects his ideological debt to Valle-Inclán. For a discussion of Valle-Inclán's general role in the development of contemporary Spanish theatre, see Frank P. Casa, 'The Assimilation of Ramón del Valle-Inclán's Dramas into Contemporary Spanish Theater' (1988) or Robert Lima's numerous studies on this playwright.

CHAPTER II: CRUELTY AND PARADOX

[1] This short, artless piece was published in *El Español*, Madrid, 7 April 1945.

[2] Colette Allendy was the wife of René Allendy, Artaud's private physician and close friend. She was one of those who contributed financially toward the foundation of the Alfred Jarry Theatre in which Artaud's ideas were espoused at the time.

[3] All quotations of Nieva's plays are taken from his *Teatro completo* (1991c), volumes 1 and 2. The quotations are indicated in the text with the use of the abbreviation TC. The composition dates of the plays are found in parentheses following their titles. Those dates separated by a slash show the year in which the composition was started and completed.

[4] For a useful discussion of the apocalypse as a salient feature of postmodernist theatre, see Veronica Hollinger, 'Playing at the End of the World: Postmodern Theater' (1992). See Eduardo Chicharro's article 'Posología y uso' (1971–2), where he describes *postismo*'s inspiration in the apocalypse. The apocalyptic theme is pervasive in Nieva's drama, including *¡Viva el estupor!* (Long Live the Wonder!) (2005), one of his two latest plays. Moisés Pérez Coterillo makes a brief reference to this theme in *Pelo de tormenta* (Tresses of Turmoil (1961)), *Nosferatu* and *Coronada y el toro* (Coronada and the Bull (1974)) (1975, 30–8). Górna-Urbanska (1987, 24–34) and Emil George Signes (1982, 157–65) also make a survey of the topic in several of Nieva's plays.

[5] Another play in which Nieva's paradoxical vision of pain is well developed is *El maravilloso catarro de Lord Bashaville* (The Marvellous Catarrh of Lord

Bashaville) (1967). In this piece, a British dandy called Lord Bashaville suffers a chronic catarrh for which he has become famous, but the antidote he employs to cure his illness rather perpetuates it: he lives in a suffocating heat produced by lamps that burn at unusually high temperatures under his mattress, and he refuses to let in fresh air. At the same time, he commands his servant to saturate his body periodically with cold water and to hurl eggs at his chest to control the pain.

[6] In a study of Genet and his work, Georges Bataille shows how the French playwright bestows royalty on crime by mingling the taste for scandal with the taste for piety. In his conceptual approach to scandal, Genet artistically creates for himself a boundless sovereignty, what Bataille describes as 'the power to rise, indifferent to death, above the laws which ensure the maintenance of life' (1973, 155).

[7] Bataille's words also connect with Michel Foucault's politics of transgression. For Foucault, transgression is not a negative act of subversion but a progressive strategy intended to forge alternative possibilities by way of anarchy. In 'A Preface to Transgression', his essay on Nietzsche and Bataille, he asserts: 'Transgression . . . is not related to the limit as black to white, the prohibited to the lawful, the outside to the inside, or as the open area of a building to its enclosed spaces. Rather, their relationship takes the form of a spiral which no simple infraction can exhaust . . .' Foucault goes on to say that transgression 'contains nothing negative, but affirms limited being–affirms the limitlessness into which it leaps as it opens this zone to existence for the first time' (1980, 35).

[8] For a systematic conceptual approach to the question of evil as a competitive partner of good, see John Kekes's study, *Facing Evil* (1990).

[9] For further details on Cubist theatre, see J. Garrett Glover, *The Cubist Theatre* (1983). It must be pointed out, however, that Cubist theatre is mainly concerned with stage décor and costume design.

[10] *El rayo colgado* was launched as a short story entitled 'El valle de Porrerito' (The Valley of Porrerito). Directed by Juan José (Juanjo) Granda, this play was first staged in July 1980 in Vitoria by the Denok Cooperative. It was later staged at the Sala Olimpia on 20 September of the same year. The performance received mixed reviews. Several critics (Barea (1980), García Osuna (1980), Haro Tecglen (1980), Fernández Santos (1980)) praised the sophistication and appeal of the stage décor but underscored poor acting as a noticeable weakness.

[11] A clear example of the complexity of Nieva's language, this text presents serious difficulties for translation, and my own is by no means perfect. Sor Isena's words, sometimes made up by Nieva, sometimes lifted from historical context, are left open to multiple interpretations. It seems to me that Nieva has characteristically inserted these words within a distant historical past, within (Jewish and Arabic) speech systems of fourteenth-century Toledo. 'Catafú' sounds like an animal (probably a cat's) sound made up of 'cata' and 'fu', and whereas 'malbaratillo' exists as a word (a second-hand shop or stall), it appears here as a neologism, composed of 'mal' (bad) and 'barato' (cheap), but, ultimately, without any clear meaning. St Bartolo is invented, as is 'siniestraria'. 'Que en la . . . encapillada' could very well be a reference to the Inquisitors, promoters of sinister justice within the Church, against whom

Isena seeks protection. The way in which the word 'rajatabla' is used here nullifies its denotative value, making it a hopeless curse that is difficult to capture adequately in English. One can see, then, why few translations of Nieva's plays exist.

[12] For further details on the *auto sacramental*, see Alexander A. Parker (1943), Bruce W. Wardropper (1967), Donald Thaddeus Díetz (1973) and Louise Fothergill-Payne (1977).

[13] One cannot fully appreciate postmodernist literature without taking into account its vital connection with Romanticism. For an account of that connection, see Gerald Graff's 'The Myth of the Postmodernist Breakthrough' (1973).

[14] For further details on verbal contradiction in Nieva's drama, see Francisco Peña's introduction to his edition of *El teatro gótico: La señora Tártara, El baile de los ardientes* (1996).

CHAPTER III: METATHEATRICALITY

[1] Of course, before Richard Hornby, several studies had appeared on the scene: Robert J. Nelson's *Play within a Play* (1958), James L. Calderwood's *Shakespearean Metadrama* (1971), Robert Egan's *Drama within Drama* (1975) and Sidney Homan's *When the Theatre Turns to Itself* (1981). Still, none shows the same degree of clarity and efficacy in their classifications as Hornby's work does.

[2] *Centón de teatro* contains a metaplay called *El drama rápido* (Fast Drama), which Francisco Peña published in his 2002 re-edition of the collection.

[3] I must mention three previous studies of metatheatricality in Nieva's work. Phyllis Zatlin's 'Metatheatricalism and Nieva's *Sombra y quimera de Larra*' (1989) concentrates on Nieva's adaptation of the nineteenth-century essayist Mariano José de Larra's *No más mostrador*. Zatlin's article 'La meta-teatralidad de Francisco Nieva' (1994) is an expose of several plays in which the metadramatic technique is used. A more recent study is A. David Hitchcock's 'A Theater Posed against Itself' (2001), which explores the link between *Tórtolas* and the Theatre of Cruelty. José A. Hernández (1986) had earlier studied *Tórtolas* on the basis of Artaud's dramatic theory.

[4] Ramón de la Cruz Cano y Olmedilla (1731–94), perhaps the most prominent playwright in Madrid toward the end of the eighteenth century, is best known for his *sainetes* (some examples are *La civilización* (1763), *El deseo de seguidillas* (1769), *El poeta aburrido* (1773) and *Los locos con juicio* (1778)). Ramón de la Cruz also wrote metaplays using popular forms of the *sainete* (a one-act farce), classified as *sainetes de costumbres teatrales* that metadramatically explore the world of actors and acting companies. Examples of such plays are *El teatro por dentro* (1768), *El huésped consolado* (1776) and *El repente de los cómicos* (1781).

[5] For further details on space design in *Tórtolas*, see Carlos A. Rabassó and Fco. Javier Rabassó, 'La derterminación del espacio poético en *Tórtolas, crepúsculo y . . . telón*' (1993).

[6] Premiered along with *Te quiero, zorra* (I Love You, Bitch) (1987) in February 1988 at El Escorial's Coliseo Carlos III, this short piece was later performed at

Madrid's Teatro del Círculo de Bellas Artes. In July 1994, it was again staged along with *Te quiero, zorra* and *Caperucita y el otro* (Red Riding Hood and the Other) (1968) under a general title, 'Le retable de damnées', at the Avignon Theatre Festival in Paris. The triptych was again performed in May 1995, under the direction of Agathe Alexis, at Jorge Lavalli's Théâtre National de la Colline.

[7] Nieva was most likely inspired by Pirandello's piece in writing his own. Note, for example, that he published an article in *ABC* in praise of the Italian playwright (see Nieva 1996d).

[8] Despite the incisive impression that Brecht's distantiation theory has made on modern theatre, one cannot fail to acknowledge the scepticism held against his theory by some critics. For example, Ronald Speirs argues that, in practice, the spectator is not really free in Brechtian theatre as claimed and that, instead of argument and reason, he/she is affected by suggestion and feelings just like in any other theatre types. Because the epic narrator tends to define or influence the audience's mind, Speirs contends, no pure independence of mind can be attributed to him/her. The wit and rhetorical elegance of the narrator makes him/her an attractive object of identification. Brecht's devices merely shift the focus of identification away from the protagonist onto the various expressions of authorial point of view (1994, 26–41).

[9] Emil George Signes portrays the 'ceremonia negra' as a Black Mass designed to mock the Roman Catholic Mass: 'An altar of filth is raised for the ceremony, which parodies the Eucharist by transforming something even less than human (Liliana the goat) into something divine (Venus) sent to bestow grace upon whomever is in attendance (Luis)' (1982, 188). The Black Mass, I might add, represents Genet's supreme metaphor for portraying a world in which God appears in every sign of degradation, which this French playwright sees as a sacred ceremony.

[10] It is, nevertheless, worth keeping in mind the long debate over the nature of Aristotelian Tragedy, especially the compelling contributions of D. D. Raphael in *The Paradox of Tragedy* (1960). In this book, Raphael dismisses *catharsis* as 'old game', questions the conceptual basis of fear and pity and argues against the logic behind *hamartia*. Instead, he sees in Tragedy a conflict between inevitable power, which he calls 'necessity', and 'the reaction to necessity of self-conscious effort' (25).

CHAPTER IV: SEXUAL POLITICS, GENDER POLITICS
AND THE POPULAR

[1] For background notes on Ramón de la Cruz, see note 4 of chapter III.

[2] Nieva's idea of the popular is transparent in María Cruz García de Enterría's dictionary definition of the term. In *Diccionario de literatura popular española*, this critic points out that the Marxist definition of the term is reductionist because the popular cannot simply be relegated to the subaltern. As such, she devotes a good part of her definition to explaining the long historical interconnection between the popular and the *culto* (the cultured).

³ The *género chico* originated in Madrid around the 1868 Revolution in the tradition of the *Teatro por horas* (theatre by the hour). It refers to the one-act play with a one-hour limit on the duration of its performance, but from about 1915 onward the term came to designate only short one-act plays accompanied by music. In her entry under 'género chico' in *Diccionario de literatura popular española*, María Pilar Espín Templado lists the dramatic sub-genres to which the *género chico* gave birth: the *sainete* or *pasillo*, the short *zarzuela* and the *parodia*. Other modern versions are the *juguete*, the *revista* and the *opereta*. Some of the genre's key representatives who figure in Espín Templado's list are Ricardo de la Vega, Javier de Burgos, Tomás Luceño, M. Ramos Carrión, Vital Aza, Sánchez Pastor, F. Pérez y González, all of them members of the 1868 Generation. Of the 1898 Generation are C. Fernández-Shaw, J. López Silva, C. Lucio, F. Manzano and Carlos Arniches. More than any other, the writer who left an incisive imprint on Nieva is Arniches, whose plays he often watched in Madrid theatres as a child.

⁴ The *verbena* – Madrid's version of the *romería* and of the Andalusian *feria* – is an open-air popular festival designed, like the carnival, to transgress the authority of social regulation, something akin to the Greek Bacchanal or the Roman Saturnalia. What Nieva proposes in his festive drama is to restore to the *verbena* the attributes he considers lost amidst modernity: supernatural science, myth and symbolism, communal spirit and permissiveness (see Nieva 1973c, 25).

⁵ My reference to sex and sexuality should be understood not only in terms of physiological arousal and genital activity but especially in terms of Foucault's definition of sex, namely,

> that agency which appears to dominate us and that secret that which seems to underlie all that we are, that point which enthralls us through the power it manifests and the meaning it conceals, and which we ask to reveal what we are and to free us from what defines us . . . that [through which] each individual has to pass in order to have access to his [or her] own intelligibility . . . to the whole of his [or her] body . . . to his [or her] identity. (1978, 155–6)

⁶ Freud presents civilization as a dualistic struggle between the instinct of life (Eros) and the instinct of destruction (Death or Thanatos). Parallel to this paradigm, this psychoanalyst develops his theory of 'the pleasure principle' (the unconscious, animal impulses in human beings) and 'the reality principle' (the awareness of social limitations), both of which must be sustained in good balance in order to ensure civilization's survival. Guilt, argues Freud, arises from one's struggle between these polarities (1962, 64–80).

⁷ See Patricia W. O'Connor, 'A Theater in Transition: From Paternalism to Pornography' (1988), where she studies the proliferation in Spanish theatre of sex and nudity during the transition from the Franco dictatorship to democracy. In this essay, O'Connor examines plays dealing with sex and nudity that were produced during the period in question, raising very important questions about the future of Spanish erotic theatre.

⁸ Written in Paris in 1961, it took more than twenty-five years before *Pelo de tormenta* was staged. This play was reportedly rejected four times by Franco's censors, so its ideological severity eventually waned, and by the time

it was granted permission, no one was interested any longer in performing it (Nieva 1997c, 20). The 1997 performance, directed by Juan Carlos Pérez de la Fuente at Madrid's María Guerrero Theatre, was hailed as the theatrical event of the year in Spain.

[9] For a philosophical and literary discussion of cigarettes, see Richard Klein, *Cigarettes Are Sublime* (1993).

[10] Unlike Freud, Marcuse calls for a resexualization of humanity as the basis for a sound civilization. Freud argues that, for civilization to sustain itself, one's 'pleasure principle' (the unconscious instincts) needs to be restrained because, in his view, the uncontrolled Eros is as dangerous as Thanatos, the death instinct. Marcuse questions the Freudian necessity of heterosexual and genital norms that safeguard social welfare, contending that sexual perversions are often expressions of a rebellion against the procreative condition that Freud imposes on sexuality (see Weeks 1985, 160–70 and Marcuse 1955, 11–126).

[11] In his study of Calderón's *autos*, Alexander A. Parker makes reference to the *loa* to *La Segunda Esposa* where the following dialogue takes place between two characters:

PASTOR   . . . decidme, aquellas torres
o triunfales carros que
el aire ocupan disformes,
¿para qué fin aquí están?

LABRADOR   A fin de hacer las mejores
fiestas que pudo la idea
inventar.

PASTOR   ¿Qué son?

LABRADOR   Sermones
puestos en verso, en idea
representable cuestiones
de la Sacra Teología,
que no alcanzan mis razones
a explicar ni comprender
y el regocijo dispone
en aplauso de este día. (Parker 1943, 62–3)

[SHEPHERD   . . . tell me, those towers
or triumphant chariots that
fill the air in a deformed shape,
what are they here for?

PEASANT   To make the best
feasts that the mind can ever
invent.

SHEPHERD   And what are these feasts?

PEASANT   Sermons
in verse, and in
dramatic form questions
of Sacred Theology,

which my thoughts cannot
explain or understand
and which the jubilant celebration reveals
through the applause of this day.]

[12] For a reprint of some of these *aleluyas*, see Rafael Gayano Lluch, *Aucología valenciana: estudio folklórico* (1942, 107–11).

[13] To show the avant-garde foundations of this time concept, it may be worth citing at length Genet's own observations. In *Reflections on the Theatre*, this French writer affirms:

> Among other things, the goal of the theatre is to take us outside the limits of what is generally referred to as 'historical' time but which is really theological. The moment the theatrical event begins, the time which will elapse no longer belongs to any calibrated calendar. It transcends the Christian era as it does the revolutionary era. Even if that time which is called 'historical' – I mean the time that flows from some mythical and controversial event, also known as Advent – does not disappear completely from the spectators' consciousness, another time, which each spectator lives to the full, then unfolds, and as it has neither beginning nor end, it destroys the historical conventions necessitated by social life, and at the same time destroys social conventions as well, not for the sake of just any disorder but neither for the sake of a liberation – the theatrical event being suspended, outside of historical time, on its own dramatic time – it is for the sake of a vertiginous liberation . . .
>
> Trapped in a time named for, calculated from, an event that is of interest only to the West, the world is in serious danger, if it accepts this time, of emphasizing it according to celebrations in which the whole world will be trapped. (1972, 64–5)

[14] Like *Pelo de tormenta*, *Coronada y el toro* premiered at Madrid's María Guerrero Theatre, but much earlier, in April 1982. A resounding success, the performance was directed by Nieva himself at the invitation of José Luis Alonso, this playhouse's director at the time.

[15] In her analysis of Coronada's domestication of the bull, Phyllis Zatlin affirms that, whereas the concealment of the female – Zebedeo's suppression of Coronada – is viewed in the play as a sane and expected act, the concealment of the macho (the bull) and of his taming is denounced by the patriarchal powers (1996, 311).

[16] The funeral procession scene evokes a popular customary practice during *ferias* and *romerías* in small towns throughout Spain. The processions of Santa Marta de Ribaterme serve as a strong example.

[17] For her part, Iride Lamartina-Lens says of Hombre-Monja:

> Inherent in his/her philosophy of life is the conscious acceptance of the intrinsic interplay of the masculine and feminine in all humans. This androgynous god allows the human psyche the possibility of savoring the entire range of human experience. Once freed of the rigid sex role assignment according to gender alone, the individual can choose from a myriad of possibilities that before were [inaccessible] to members of either sex. (1989, 18)

[18] Hombre-Monja's role in the play foregrounds the important theme of homo-sexuality in Nieva's drama, a theme I explore in 'Francisco Nieva y la homo-sexualidad' (2005). In this essay, I maintain that what Nieva exalts in his theatre is not homosexuality per se but bisexuality especially. I lay out this playwright's double approach to the question of homosexuality in the context of Spain's homosexual identity politics. In his theatre, Nieva advocates sexual emancipation, including homosexuality, and he suggests the need for gays to come out of the closet. At the same time, he transcends essentialist categorizations of homosexuality, implying that it is meaningless to define the fluid nature of identity on the basis of such categories as homosexual, heterosexual, bisexual, etc. In the history of Spanish theatre, few playwrights present (homo)sexuality more provocatively and more consistently on stage than Francisco Nieva has done.

From the 1990s, a growing critical interest in Spanish gay culture has emerged, although a complete document on the history of Spanish gays remains absent. I am referring to such authors as Óscar Guasch Andreu (1991), Juan Vicente Aliaga and José Miguel G. Cortés (1997), Javier Gafo (ed.) (1997), Ricardo Llamas (1998), Gustav Malone (1998), José Antonio Nieto (ed.) (1998) and Alberto Mira (1994, 2000). In the United States and England, outstanding are the studies of Paul Julian Smith (1992, 1996), Emilie L. Bergmann and P. J. Smith (1995), Robert Richmond Ellis (1997), David William Foster and Roberto Reis (eds.) (1996), Sylvia Molloy and Robert McKee Irwin (eds.) (1998).

[19] So vulgar and so grotesque is the portrayal of Nieva's female characters that one wonders if this playwright's pro-female stance is sincere. Nieva seems to address this issue in an article, 'La mujer maldita' (1988b), by saying that his aggressive approach springs in part from a profound desire to restore what he considers to be the old, pre-puritanical image of the bad woman. In the past, contends Nieva, women who displayed cultural irregularities or permis-siveness were seen as a sign of progress within their ethnic group. Only in their being marginalized were such women able to give full vent to their intense and distinct erotic feelings. At the root of this cultural factor lies an even deeper, real-life inspiration, namely, Nieva's numerous encounters with crooked and abusive women, including his own mother's emotional abuse of him as a child. For example, in his memoirs, he states, '[m]y mother was, internally, what is called "a tremendous woman". That female tremendous-ness constitutes one of the foundations of my theatre, and it is reflected in the types that I label "muddy women", who only externally resemble the literary type seen in *La Celestina*' (2002, 29). Aware, or perhaps guilty, of his aggressive portrayal of women, Nieva goes on to defend himself, saying that he has never considered himself anti-feminist because he, simply, is not. For him, women are just as bad as men, even if their badness shows itself in different ways (195). In part, Nieva's liberal presentation of women could be his way of overturning the paranoia and insecurity his mother embodied as a woman whom he saw as being subjected to severe social scrutiny and a quest for affection and love.

[20] Since its appearance in 1499, *The Celestina* was first entitled *Comedia de Calisto y Melibea* and later *Tragicomedia de Calisto y Melibea* before its definitive title in 1519.

CHAPTER V: PERFORMANCE

1 Nieva's first stage production ever was *Es bueno no tener cabeza* (It Is Good
To Be Headless) (1966), which he wrote in Dublin. It is also a piece that
happens to be his first published work. Directed by Santiago Paredes with a
cast of students from Madrid's Royal School of Drama, the performance took
place in June 1971 at this school, where Nieva was teaching at the time.
Attended mostly by his students and a few invited guests, this secretly
organized show had no repercussions in the daily press of the time and was
suppressed by the police after only two days on stage (for further details, see
Nieva 2002, 418–25).

2 Of course, the characteristic complexity of Nieva's theatre presents no
acceptable excuse for its isolation from the support of directors and public
institutions. In the 1980s, literary critics never grew tired of expressing their
sentiment against what they saw as an injustice against a formidable talent.
This overwhelming sentiment could be summed up in an extended
commentary in which Fernando Lázaro Carreter laments the marginalization
of Nieva's major works from the Spanish stage (1989, 14).

3 The Francisco Nieva Theatre Company's formation was announced with the
staging in July 1987 of *Las aventuras de Tirante el Blanco* (The Adventures of
Tirant Le Blanc) (1978) at Mérida's Roman Theatre. Following this
production was the performance in February 1988 of *Te quiero, zorra* and
No es verdad. Directed by Granda, this last-mentioned performance took
place at Madrid's Círculo de Bellas Artes. Next were *Corazón de arpía*
(Heart of A Harpy) (1989), staged in February 1989 at the Sala Olimpia, and
El baile de los ardientes (The Dance of the Passionate) (1975), which was
staged at the Albéniz Theatre in March 1990. The company's last performance took place in August 1992 with *Los españoles bajo tierra* at Bilbao's
Arriaga Theatre.

4 Of course, the debate over the role of the text vis-à-vis performance began
long before the 1960s. Marvin Carlson discusses this topic in depth in chapter
17 of *Theories of the Theatre* (1993), where, for example, he mentions Joel
Elias Spingarn (1875–1939) as one of the earlier defenders of the text.

5 Besides Nieva's memoirs, see also Óscar Cornago Bernal (2000) for useful
details on Nieva's set design projects in collaboration with Adolfo Marsillach:
After the Fall, Biography: A Game (pp. 501–6) and Molière's *The Hypocrite*
(pp. 624–7). For those interested in seeing photographs of Nieva's set design,
the National Theatre Museum in Almagro houses a very large collection of
photos of his stage productions. A good collection of printed versions can be
found in Andrés Peláez and Fernanda Andura (eds) (1990).

6 My assertions are sometimes based on my interviews with Granda. Some of
my affirmations regarding Nieva's production methods and his audiences are
derived from taped interviews I conducted between November 1998 and July
2002 with Nieva and with a few individuals who are well versed in his
dramaturgy (my references to these interviews are all subsequently noted).
Granda, a professor of acting and stage direction (he was also the director of
Madrid's Royal School of Drama from 1999 to 2003), was Nieva's ex-student
and close friend. A co-founder of Nieva's theatre company, Granda has

collaborated with the playwright on several performance projects and directed a couple of his plays. José María Pedreira (Nieva's partner) and Julia Trujillo are two of Nieva's most regular actors who have played major roles in several of his plays.

[7] Julia Trujillo confirms Nieva's faithfulness to the text. In my interview with this actress, she insists that Nieva admires surprises and allows the actors' personality to flourish on stage, but when it comes to the script, Trujillo points out, 'not a single sentence can be altered'. Indeed, when I took the liberty of reading some of Nieva's plays while watching the shows on video, I noted only negligible differences between the original text and the onstage dialogue.

[8] José Pedreira (in my July 2002 recorded interview) and Anna Ricci (Nieva and Ricci 1989, 37) concur with Trujillo in her assertion that Nieva allows his actors a great deal of freedom to improvise onstage.

[9] These assertions are based on my July 2002 recorded interview with Granda.

[10] My analysis of *Corazón de arpía* and *Las aventuras de Tirante el Blanco* is based on video recordings of these performances that Francisco Nieva made available to me.

[11] For a persuasive argument in support of Brecht as a postmodernist playwright, see chapters 5 and 6 of Elizabeth Wright, *Postmodern Brecht: A Re-Presentation* (1989).

[12] A useful source for comprehending the philosophy behind Nieva's set design is his *Tratado de escenografía* (2000b). Although this book is primarily concerned with the general evolution of set design (from Greek theatre to the contemporary period), the information it provides is a good guide into the psychology of Nieva as a designer.

[13] See Nieva's memoirs *Las cosas como fueron* (2002, 598–601), where he discusses financial difficulties related to the staging of *Corazón de arpía*.

[14] A close observation of the acting model upheld by Nieva appears to be in consonance with David George's triadic theory. In an essay (1989), George postulates a new role for performance in a postmodern culture. He argues that this new role, which is fundamentally subversive, may now be about to replace the old (modernist) cultural paradigm by a new (postmodernist) one, 'which instead of trying to heal a split world, reverses the procedure: explodes all units, locates the kernel of doubt in all securities, the paradox in all truths, the difference in all identity' (74). George fashions for this new performance order a new 'triadic theory of acting' to replace what he sees as 'the contradictory binary of classical acting theories which will either have the actor disappear into the role or preserve some distance' (79).

[15] For a detailed analysis of Nieva's use of language, see Jesús María Barrajón, *La poética de Francisco Nieva* (1987). See also Carlos Bousoño, 'El Teatro Furioso de Francisco Nieva' (1991).

[16] I have not come across any written documentation on the general make-up of Nieva's audiences. Thus, I have had to rely on interviews with Nieva, Granda, José Pedreira and Julia Trujillo, who all concur with the assertions I have made in regard to the general receptive composition of Nieva's theatre.

[17] For an empirical analysis of the problem of theatre spaces and of the general situation of Spanish actors during the Franco period, see Emeterio Díez, 'La situación laboral del actor bajo el Franquismo' (2001).

[18] Gay McAuley has mapped out various forms of audience participation throughout theatre history, emphasizing what she calls the energy exchange among and between spectators and performers. She mentions as part of this exchange 'the play of looks' (from spectator to actor, from actor to spectator and from spectator to spectator). In McAuley's view, this energy exchange, particularly transmitted through the gaze, is a participatory medium that energizes actors a great deal (1999, 235–77).

REFERENCES

A. Translations of Nieva's Plays

Nieva, Francisco (1976). *La carroza di piombo incandescente* [*La carroza de plomo candente*]. Ed. Franco Quadri. Trans. María Luisa Aguirre D'Amico. Venice: La Biennale di Venezia.

—— (1982). 'The Blazing Carriage: Black Ritual in One Act' [*La carroza de plomo candente*]. Trans. Emil George Signes. In 'The Theatre of Francisco Nieva: A Summary, Analysis, and Bibliography, together with an Edition and Translation of *La carroza de plomo candente*'. Unpublished Ph.D. thesis, Rutgers University, The State University of New Jersey, pp. 259–322.

—— (1985). *Coronada and the Bull* [*Coronada y el toro*]. Trans Emil G. Signes. In Marion Peter Holt (ed.), *Drama Contemporary: Spain. Plays by Antonio Buero Vallejo, José Martín Recuerda, Jaime Salom, Francisco Nieva*. New York: Performing Arts Journal Publications, pp. 191–229.

—— (1994). *Le retable des damnées: trois pièces en un acte* [*Caperucita y el otro, Te quiero, zorra, No es verdad*]. Arles: Actes Sud.

—— (1997). *Wolfsbräute* [*Te quiero, zorra, Caperucita y el otro, No es verdad, El combate de Ópalos y Tasia*]. Trans. Angélica Bécker. Merlín Theatre, Munich.

—— *It's Not True* [*No es verdad*]. Trans. Phyllis Zatlin. Unpublished. *www.rci.-rutgers.edu/~estrplay/nieva.htm*

—— *Red Riding Hood, Part II* [*Caperucita y el otro*]. Trans. Phyllis Zatlin. Unpublished. *www.rci.rutgers.edu/~estrplay/nieva.htm*

—— *Watch Out for Wolves* [*Caperucita y el otro, Te quiero, zorra, No es verdad*]. Trans. Phyllis Zatlin. Unpublished. *www.rci.rutgers.edu/~estrplay/nieva.htm*

B. Works Cited

Abbott, Anthony S. (1989). *The Vital Lie: Reality and Illusion in Modern Drama*. Tuscaloosa and London: University of Alabama Press.

Abel, Lionel (1963). *Metatheatre: A New View of Dramatic Form*. New York: Hill and Wang.

Aggor, Komla (1998). 'Evil and Cure: Francisco Nieva's *Nosferatu* and the Theater of Cruelty'. *Revista Hispánica Moderna* 51:391–405.

—— (1999). 'Ceremony in Francisco Nieva's *La carroza de plomo candente*'. *Estreno* 25, 1:36–41.

—— (1999). 'Francisco Nieva's *Pelo de tormenta* and the Politics of Eroticism'. *Hispanófila* 127:37–52.

—— (2000). 'Francisco Nieva, Postmodern Playwright'. *Hispanic Review* 68, 4:429–52.

—— (2005).'Francisco Nieva y la homosexualidad'. In Jesús María Barrajón (ed.), *Francisco Nieva*. Madrid: Editorial Complutense, pp. 165–80.

Aliaga, Juan Vicente and Cortés, José Miguel G. (1997). *Identidad y diferencia. Sobre la cultura gay en España.* Barcelona and Madrid: Editorial Gay y Lesbiana.

Amestoy Egiguren, Ignacio (1996). 'Un realismo posmoderno'. *ADE Teatro* 50:91–3.

—— (1997). 'La literatura dramática española en la encrucijada de la posmodernidad'. *Ínsula* 601–2:3–5.

Amezúa, Efigenio (1974). *La erótica española en sus comienzos.* Barcelona: Editorial Fontanella.

Amorós, Andrés (1986). Preface to Andrés Amorós (ed.), *La carroza de plomo candente. Coronada y el toro.* Madrid: Espasa Calpe, pp. 9–45.

Ansón, Luis María (2002). 'Nieva'. Review of F. Nieva, *Las cosas como fueron. Memorias. La Razón* (Madrid), 3 April, 3.

Arens, Katherine (1991). 'Robert Wilson: Is Postmodern Performance Possible?' *Theatre Journal* 43, 1:14–40.

Arrabal, Fernando (1977). 'Salud, amigos'. *El País*, 10 April, 15.

Artaud, Antonin (1958). *The Theater and Its Double.* Trans. Mary Caroline Richards. New York: Grove Press.

Aszyk, Urszula (1995). 'Francisco Nieva: en busca de la teatralidad total'. In Alfonso de Toro and Wilfried Floeck (eds), *Teatro español contemporáneo: autores y tendencias.* Kassel: Edition Reichenberger, pp. 243–73.

Bakhtin, Mikhail (1984). *Rabelais and His World.* Trans. Hélène Iswolsky. Bloomington: Indiana University Press.

Ballesteros, Jesús (1989). *Postmodernidad. decadencia o resistencia.* Madrid: Editorial Tecnos.

Barea, Pedro (1980). 'Denok: *El rayo colgado,* de F. Nieva. En busca de la totalidad'. Review of F. Nieva, *El rayo colgado.* Denok Theatre Cooperative, Madrid. *Pipirijaina* 17:48–9.

Barrajón, Jesús María (1987). *La poética de Francisco Nieva.* Ciudad Real: Diputación Provincial de Ciudad Real.

—— (1991). 'Teatro de farsa y calamidad'. Introduction to F. Nieva, *Teatro completo.* Vol. 2. Toledo: Servicio de Publicaciones de la Junta de Comunidades de Castilla–La Mancha, pp. 585–602.

—— (1994). 'Sobre la clasificación del teatro de Francisco Nieva'. *Ínsula* 566:5–6.

Barth, John (1977). 'The Literature of Exhaustion'. In Malcolm Bradbury (ed.), *The Novel Today: Contemporary Writers on Modern Fiction.* Glasgow: Fontana/Collins, pp. 70–83.

Bataille, Georges (1962). *Erotism: Death and Sensuality.* Trans. Mary Dalwood. San Francisco: City Lights Books.

—— (1973). *Literature and Evil.* Trans. Alastair Hamilton. London: Calder and Boyars.

Bauman, Zygmunt (1993). *Postmodern Ethics*. Oxford and Cambridge, MA: Blackwell.

Berenguer, Ángel (1977). Introduction to Fernando Arrabal, *Pic-Nic, El triciclo, El laberinto*. Madrid: Ediciones Cátedra, pp. 11–122.

Bergmann, Emilie L. and Smith, Paul Julian, eds (1995). *¿Entiendes?: Queer Readings, Hispanic Writings*. Durham, NC, and London: Duke University Press.

Bertens, Hans (1986). 'The Postmodern *Weltanschauung* and its Relation with Modernism: An Introductory Survey'. In Douwe Fokkema and Hans Bertens (eds), *Approaching Postmodernism*. Amsterdam and Philadelphia: John Benjamins Publishing Company, pp. 9–51.

—— (1997). 'The Debate on Postmodernism'. In Hans Bertens and Douwe Fokkema (eds), *International Postmodernism: Theory and Literary Practice*. Amsterdam and Philadelphia: John Benjamins Publishing, pp. 3–14.

Birringer, Johannes (1991). *Theatre, Theory, Postmodernism*. Bloomington and Indianapolis: Indiana University Press.

—— (1997). 'Postmodernism and Theatrical Performance'. In Hans Bertens and Douwe Fokkema (eds), *International Postmodernism: Theory and Literary Practice*. Amsterdam and Philadelphia: John Benjamins Publishing, pp. 129–40.

Blau, Herbert (1977). 'Letting Be Be Finale of Seem: The Future of an Illusion'. In Michel Benamou and Charles Caramello (eds), *Performance in Postmodern Culture*. Milwaukee: Center for Twentieth-Century Studies, University of Wisconsin; Madison: Coda Press, pp. 59–77.

Bolton, Richard (1986). 'The Modern Spectator and the Postmodern Participant'. *Photo Communique* 8, 2:34–45.

Bou, Enric and Soria Olmedo, Andrés (1997). 'Postmodernity and Literature in Spain'. Trans. Elizabeth Rhodes. In Hans Bertens and Douwe Fokkema (eds), *International Postmodernism: Theory and Literary Practice*. Amsterdam and Philadelphia: John Benjamins Publishing, pp. 397–403.

Bousoño, Carlos (1990). 'Un nuevo dramaturgo en la Academia: Francisco Nieva, el más alto estilo'. In Andrés Peláez and Fernanda Andura (eds), *Exposición antológica Francisco Nieva*. Teatro Albéniz, March–May, pp. 70–4.

—— (1991). 'El Teatro Furioso de Francisco Nieva'. Introduction to F. Nieva, *Teatro completo*. Vol. 1. Toledo: Servicio de Publicaciones de la Junta de Comunidades de Castilla–La Mancha, pp. 261–88.

Bravo, Julio (1986). 'El dramaturgo Francisco Nieva es, desde ayer, miembro de la Real Academia Española'. *ABC*, 18 April, 57.

Breuer, Josef and Freud, Sigmund (1957). *Studies on Hysteria*. Trans. James Strachey. New York: Basic Books.

Bristow, Joseph, ed. (1992). *The Importance of Being Earnest and Related Writings*. London and New York: Routledge.

Brown, Erella (1992). 'Cruelty and Affirmation in the Postmodern Theater: Antonin Artaud and Hanoch Levin'. *Modern Drama* 35, 4:585–606.

Burton, R. W. B. (1980). *The Chorus in Sophocles' Tragedies*. Oxford and New York: Oxford University Press.

Butt, John (1993). '*Modernismo* and Modernism'. In Richard Cardwell and Bernard McGuirk (eds), *¿Qué es el Modernismo? Nueva encuesta, nuevas lecturas*. Boulder: Society of Spanish and Spanish-American Studies, pp. 39–58.

Calderwood, James L. (1971). *Shakespearean Metadrama: The Argument of the Play in 'Titus Andronicus', 'Love's Labour Lost', 'Romeo and Juliet', 'A Midsummer Night's Dream', and 'Richard II'*. Minneapolis: University of Minnesota Press.

Caldwell, Richard (1993). 'Degeneration, Discourse and Differentiation: *Modernismo frente a noventa y ocho* Reconsidered'. In Luis González-del-Valle (ed.), *Critical Essays on Literatures of Spain and Spanish America*. Anejo de Anales de la Literatura Española Contemporánea. Boulder: University of Colorado Press, pp. 29–46.

Carlson, Marvin (1993). *Theories of the Theatre: A Historical and Critical Survey, from the Greeks to the Present*. Ithaca and London: Cornell University Press.

Caro Baroja, Julio (1979). *El carnaval (Análisis histórico-cultural)*. Madrid: Taurus Ediciones.

Carriedo, Gabino-Alejandro (1991). 'Postismo, postistas y filopostistas' (1949). In Amador Palacios, *Jueves postista (El papel de Ciudad Real en el Postismo. Los artículos de* Lanza). Ciudad Real: Diputación de Ciudad Real – Área de Cultura, pp. 97–9.

Casa, Frank P. (1988). 'The Assimilation of Ramón del Valle-Inclán's Dramas into Contemporary Spanish Theater'. In Martha T. Halsey and Phyllis Zatlin (eds), *The Contemporary Spanish Theater: A Collection of Critical Essays*. Lanham, New York and London: University Press of America, pp. 163–77.

Castillo Buils, David (1989). 'La plurilingüe lengua: el lenguaje poético postista'. *Ínsula* 510:12–13.

Chicharro Jr, Eduardo (1971–2). 'Posología y uso'. *Trece de Nieve* 2:45–8.

—— (1974). *Música celestial y otros poemas*. Ed. Gonzalo Armero. Madrid: Seminarios y Ediciones.

Cixous, Hélène (1984). 'Aller à la mer'. Trans. Barbara Kerslake. *Modern Drama* 27, 4:546–8. Originally published in *Le Monde*, 28 April 1977.

Copeland, Roger F. (1991). 'A Post Mortem for the Post-Modern' *Theater ??*, 3:67–77.

Cornago Bernal, Óscar (2000). *Discurso teórico y puesta en escena en los años sesenta: la encrucijada de los 'realismos'*. Anejos de Revista de Literatura 50. Madrid: Consejo Superior de Investigaciones Científicas. Instituto de la Lengua Española.

Cossío, José María de (1931). *Los toros en la poesía castellana (Estudio y antología)*. Madrid: Compañía Ibero-Americana de Publicaciones.

Cózar, Rafael de (1989). 'El postismo en el contexto de la vanguardia'. *Ínsula* 510:13–16.

Cramsie, Hilde F. (1984). *Teatro y censura en la España franquista: Sastre, Muñiz y Ruibal*. New York, Berne and Frankfurt: Peter Lang.

De Marinis, Marco (1993). *The Semiotics of Performance*. Trans. Áine O'Healy. Bloomington and Indianapolis: Indiana University Press.

Debicki, Andrew P. (1988). 'Poesía española de la postmodernidad'. *Anales de literatura española* 6:16–80.

Delgado, Maria M. (2003). *'Other' Spanish Theatres: Erasure and Inscription on the Twentieth-Century Spanish Stage*. Manchester and New York: Manchester University Press.

Deming, Robert H. (1974). *Ceremony and Art: Robert Herrick's Poetry*. The Hague and Paris: Mouton.

Derrida, Jacques (1978). *Writing and Difference*. Trans. Alan Bass. Chicago: University of Chicago Press.

Diamond, Elin (1996). 'Brechtian Theory / Feminist Theory: Toward a Gestic Feminist Criticism'. In Carol Martin (ed.), *A Sourcebook of Feminist Theatre and Performance: On Stage and beyond the Stage*. London and New York: Routledge, pp. 120–35.

Diccionario de literatura popular española (1997). Salamanca: Ediciones Colegio de España.

Dietz, Bernd (1989). 'El postismo y su lugar en la poesía española contemporánea'. *Ínsula* 510:9.

Díetz, Donald Thaddeus (1973). *The 'Auto Sacramental' and the Parable in Spanish Golden Age Literature*. Chapel Hill, NC: Department of Romance Languages, University of North Carolina.

Díez, Emeterio (2001). 'La situación laboral del actor bajo el Franquismo'. *ADE Teatro* 84:108–18.

DiGaetani, John L. (1991). *A Search for a Postmodern Theater: Interviews with Contemporary Playwrights*. New York, Westport and London: Greenwood Press.

Dolan, Jill (1991). *The Feminist Spectator as Critic*. Ann Arbor: University of Michigan Press.

Eco, Umberto (1977). 'Semiotics of Theatrical Performance'. *The Drama Review* 21, 1:107–17.

—— (1983). 'A Correspondence with Umberto Eco'. Interview by Stefano Rosso. Trans. Carolyn Springer. *Boundary 2* 12, 1:1–13.

—— (1989). *The Open Work*. Trans. Anna Cancogni. Cambridge, MA: Harvard University Press.

Egan, Robert (1975). *Drama within Drama: Shakespeare's Sense of His Art in 'King Lear', 'The Winter's Tale', and 'The Tempest'*. New York: Columbia University Press.

Ellis, Robert Richmond (1997). *The Hispanic Homograph: Gay Self-Representation in Contemporary Spanish Autobiography*. Urbana and Chicago: University of Illinois Press.

Esquerra, Ramón (1938). *Vocabulario literario*. Barcelona: Editorial Apolo.

Esslin, Martin (1971). *Brecht: The Man and His Work*. Garden City, NY: Doubleday and Company.

Fernández Santos, Ángel (1980). '*El rayo colgado*'. Review of F. Nieva, *El rayo colgado*. Denok Theatre Cooperative, Madrid. *Cambio 16*, 3 October, n.p.

Ferreras, Juan Ignacio (1988). *El teatro en el Siglo XX (Desde 1939)*. Madrid: Taurus.

Fischer-Lichte, Erika (1991). 'Avant-garde and Postmodernism: Theatre between Cultural Crisis and Cultural Change'. In Ingeborg Hoesterey (ed.), *Zeitgeist in Babel: The Postmodernist Controversy*. Bloomington and Indianapolis: Indiana University Press, pp. 216–28. Reprinted in E. Fischer-Lichte, *The Show and the Gaze of Theatre: A European Perspective*. Iowa City: University of Iowa Press, 1997, pp. 261–74.

—— (1992). *The Semiotics of Theater*. Trans. Jeremy Gaines and Doris L. Jones. Bloomington and Indianapolis: Indiana University Press.

—— (1996). 'The Return of the Text: Implied Ethics of Postmodern Theatre'. In Gerhard Hoffman and Alfred Hornung (eds), *Ethics and Aesthetics: The Moral Turn of Postmodernism*. Heidelberg: Universitätsverlag C. Winter, pp. 293–301.

Floeck, Wilfried (1997). 'Escritura dramática y posmodernidad. El teatro actual, entre neorrealismo y vanguardia'. *Ínsula* 601–2:12–14.

—— (1999). 'Teatro y posmodernidad en España'. In Martha T. Halsey and Phyllis Zatlin (eds), *Entre actos: diálogos sobre teatro español entre siglos*. University Park, PA: Estreno, pp. 157–64.

—— (2004). 'El teatro actual en España y Portugal en el contexto de la postmodernidad'. *Iberoamericana* 4, 14:47–67.

Fokkema, Douwe (1997). 'The Semiotics of Literary Postmodernism'. In Hans Bertens and Douwe Fokkema (eds), *International Postmodernism: Theory and Literary Practice*. Amsterdam and Philadelphia: John Benjamins Publishing, pp. 15–42.

Foster, David William and Reis, Roberto, eds (1996). *Bodies and Biases: Sexualities in Hispanic Cultures and Literature*. Minneapolis and London: University of Minnesota Press.

Foster, Hal, ed. (1983). 'Postmodernism: A Preface'. In Hal Foster (ed.), *The Anti-Aesthetic: Essays on Postmodern Culture*. Port Townsend, WA: Bay Press, pp. ix–xvi.

Fothergill-Payne, Louise (1977). *La alegoría en los autos y farsas anteriores a Calderón*. London: Támesis.

Foucault, Michel (1978). *The History of Sexuality*. Trans. Robert Hurley. Vol. 1. New York: Pantheon Books.

—— (1980). 'A Preface to Transgression'. In Donald F. Bouchard (ed. and trans.), *Language, Counter-Memory, Practice: Selected Essays and Interviews*. Ithaca: Cornell University Press, pp. 29–52.

Freud, Sigmund (1962). *Civilization and Its Discontents*. Ed. James Strachey, New York: W. W. Norton & Company.

Gafo, Javier, ed. (1997). *La homosexualidad: un debate abierto*. 2nd edn. Bilbao: Editorial Desclée de Brouwer.

Galán, Eduardo (1989). 'Francisco Nieva, un disidente teatral vigente en la escenografía española, entre la pantomima y el texto'. Review of F. Nieva, *Corazón de arpía*, Francisco Nieva Theatre Company, Madrid. *Ya*, 3 February, 36.

Galindo, Carlos (2004). 'Los teatros madrileños superaron la pasada temporada los tres millones de espectadores'. *ABC*, 21 January, 70–1.

García Delgado, Fernando (1975). 'Francisco Nieva, un dramaturgo español en el silencio'. *Ínsula* 343:4.

García Garzón, Juan Ignacio (1997). 'Teatro total: *Pelo de tormenta*, furiosa e irónica reópera de Francisco Nieva'. Review of F. Nieva, *Pelo de tormenta*. National Drama Centre, Madrid. *ABC*, 21 March, 91.

García Osuna, Carlos (1980). '*El rayo colgado*, de Francisco Nieva'. Review of F. Nieva, *El rayo colgado*. Denok Theatre Cooperative, Madrid. *El Imparcial*, 25 September, n.p.

García Ruiz, Víctor (1999). *Continuidad y ruptura en el teatro español de la posguerra*. Pamplona: EUNSA.

García Templado, José (1992). *El teatro español actual*. Madrid: Anaya.

Gayano Lluch, Rafael (1942). *Aucología valenciana: estudio folklórico*. Valencia: Hijo de F. Vives Moras.

Geis, Deborah R. (1993). *Postmodern Theatric(k)s: Monologue in Contemporary American Drama*. Ann Arbor: University of Michigan Press.

Genet, Jean (1960). *The Blacks: A Clown Show*. Trans. Bernard Frechtman. New York: Grove Press.

—— (1972). *Reflections on the Theatre and Other Writings*. Trans. Richard Seaver. London: Faber and Faber.

George, David (1989). 'On Ambiguity: Towards a Post-Modern Performance Theory'. *Theatre Research International* 14, 1:71–85.

Gilmore, David D. (1998). *Carnival and Culture: Sex, Symbol, and Status in Spain*. New Haven and London: Yale University Press.

Girard, René (1986). *Violence and the Sacred*. Trans. Patrick Gregory. Baltimore and London: Johns Hopkins University Press.

Glover, J. Garrett (1983). *The Cubist Theatre*. Ann Arbor: UMI Research Press.

Gómez de la Serna, Ramón (1957). *Nuevas páginas de mi vida*. Valencia: Editorial Marfil.

Góngora, Luis de (1939). *Poemas y sonetos*. Buenos Aires: Editorial Losada.

González, Antonio (1980). Introduction to Antonio González (ed.), *Malditas sean Coronada y sus hijas. Delirio del amor hostil*. Madrid: Ediciones Cátedra, pp. 9–44.

Goodall, Jane (1993). 'Postmodernism and the Discipline of Drama/Theater Studies'. *American Studies International* 31, 2:24–30.

—— (1994). 'Cruelty and Cure'. In Gene A. Plunka (ed.), *Antonin Artaud and the Modern Theater*. Rutherford, Madison and Teaneck: Fairleigh Dickinson University Press; London and Toronto: Associated University Presses, pp. 51–65.

Górna-Urbanska, Katarzyna (1987). 'Viaje al teatro de Francisco Nieva'. *Cuadernos El Público* 21:21–61. Originally written as Part 2 of BA thesis, University of Warsaw, 1984.

Gortari, Carlos (1975). 'Malditamente consagrado: Francisco Nieva'. *Reseña de literatura, arte y espectáculos* 12, 88:14–16.

Graff, Gerald (1973). 'The Myth of the Postmodernist Breakthrough'. *TriQuarterly* 26:383–417.

Granda Marín, Juan José (1998). 'Tres historias íntimas'. *Minerva*, January, 3.

A Greek–English Lexicon (1925). Oxford: Clarendon Press.

Groden, Michael and Kreiswirth, Martin, eds (1994). *The Johns Hopkins Guide to Literary Theory and Criticism*. Baltimore and London: Johns Hopkins University Press.

Guasch Andreu, Óscar (1991). *La sociedad rosa*. Barcelona: Editorial Anagrama.

Haro Tecglen, Eduardo. (1980). 'Humor y mística'. Review of F. Nieva, *El rayo colgado*. Denok Theater Cooperative, Madrid. *El País*, 21 September, 31.

—— (1988). 'Ejercicios de estilo'. Review of F. Nieva, *Te quiero, zorra* and *No es verdad*. Francisco Nieva Theatre Company, Madrid. *El País*, 29 February, 34.

—— (1997). 'Mucho Nieva'. Review of F. Nieva, *Pelo de tormenta*. National Drama Centre, Madrid. *El País*, 22 March, 32.

Hassan, Ihab (1980). 'The Question of Postmodernism'. In Harry R. Garvin (ed.), *Romanticism, Modernism, Postmodernism.* Lewisburg: Bucknell University Press; London and Toronto: Associated University Presses, pp. 117–26.

—— (1986). 'Pluralism in Postmodern Perspective'. *Critical Inquiry* 12, 3:503–20.

Hernández, José A. (1986). 'El teatro de la crueldad en *Tórtolas, crepúsculo y . . . telón* de Francisco Nieva'. *Estreno* 12, 2:72–4.

Herrero, Raúl, ed. (1998). *Antología de la poesía postista.* Zaragoza: Igitur.

Heuvel, Michael Vanden (1991). *Performing Drama / Dramatizing Performance: Alternative Theater and the Dramatic Text.* Ann Arbor: University of Michigan Press.

Hitchcock, A. David (2001). 'A Theater Posed against Itself: Nieva's Metadramatic *Tórtolas, crepúsculo y . . . telón*'. *Gestos* 32:75–88.

Hoffman, Ernst Theodor Amadeus (1840). *Contes fantastiques.* París: Perrotin.

Hollinger, Veronica (1992). 'Playing at the End of the World: Postmodern Theater'. In Patrick D. Murphy (ed.), *Staging the Impossible: The Fantastic Mode in Modern Drama.* Westport and London: Greenwood Press, pp. 182–96.

Holloway, Vance R. (1999). *El posmodernismo y otras tendencias de la novela española (1967–1995).* Madrid: Editorial Fundamentos.

Homan, Sidney (1981). *When the Theatre Turns to Itself: The Aesthetic Metaphor in Shakespeare.* Lewisburg: Bucknell University Press; London and Toronto: Associated University Presses.

—— (1989). *The Audience as Actor and Character: The Modern Theater of Beckett, Brecht, Genet, Ionesco, Pinter, Stoppard, and Williams.* Lewisburg: Bucknell University Press; London and Toronto: Associated University Presses.

Hornby, Richard (1986). *Drama, Metadrama, and Perception.* Lewisburg: Bucknell University Press; London and Toronto: Associated University Presses.

Huerga Murcia, Antonio J. and Toño Martínez, José, eds (1900). *La polémica de la posmodernidad.* Madrid: Ediciones Libertarias.

Hunt, Lynn (1991). 'The Many Bodies of Marie Antoinette: Political Pornography and the Problem of the Feminine in the French Revolution'. In Lynn Hunt (ed.), *Eroticism and the Body Politic.* Baltimore and London: Johns Hopkins University Press, pp. 108–30.

Hutcheon, Linda (1988). *A Poetics of Postmodernism: History, Theory, Fiction.* London and New York: Routledge.

—— (1989). *The Politics of Postmodernism.* London and New York: Routledge.

Innes, Christopher (1993). *Avant-Garde Theatre, 1892–1992.* London and New York: Routledge.

Jencks, Charles (1996). *What is Post-Modernism?* 4th edn. London: Academy Editions.

—— ed. (1992). *The Post-Modern Reader.* London: Academy Editions. New York: St. Martin's Press.

Kaye, Nick (1994). *Postmodernism and Performance.* New York: St. Martin's Press.

Kekes, John (1990). *Facing Evil.* Princeton: Princeton University Press.

Kitazawa, Masakuni (1992). 'Myth, Performance, and Politics'. *The Drama Review* 36, 3:160–73.

Klein, Richard (1993). *Cigarettes Are Sublime*. Durham, NC: Duke University Press.

Kristeva, Julia (1977). 'Modern Theater Does Not Take (A) Place'. Trans. Alice Jardine and Thomas Gora. *Sub-Stance* 18–19:131–4.

Kroker, Arthur and Cook, David (1986). *The Postmodern Scene: Excremental Culture and Hyper-Aesthetics*. New York: St. Martin's Press.

Krysinski, Wladimir (1990). 'Estructuras evolutivas "modernas" y "postmodernas" del texto teatral en el siglo XX'. Trans. Milena Grass. In Fernando de Toro (ed.), *Semiótica y teatro latinoamericano*. Buenos Aires: Editorial Galerna/ IITCTL, pp. 147–80.

Lamartina-Lens, Iride (1989). 'Masculine, Feminine and Androgynous Sex Roles in Nieva's Theater: The Case of *Coronada y el toro*'. *Estreno* 5, 2:17–19.

Lamont, Rosett C. (1995). 'The Bitches and Werewolves of Nieva's *Retable*'. *Western European Stages* 8, 1:35–40.

Landeira, Ricardo (1987). 'Veinte años más de paciencia: crítica y teatro españoles de 1960 a 1980'. In Juan Emilio Aragonés (ed.), *Veinte años de teatro español (1960–1980)*. Boulder: Society of Spanish and Spanish-American Studies, pp. 5–9.

Larson, Harold Mark (1993). 'Francisco Nieva's "Teatro Furioso": Analysis of Selected Plays'. Unpublished Ph.D. thesis, Ohio State University.

Latorre, Joaquín (1969). *Los españoles y el VI mandamiento*. Barcelona: Ediciones 29.

Lázaro Carreter, Fernando (1989). '*Corazón de arpía*, de Francisco Nieva'. Review of *Corazón de Arpía*. Francisco Nieva Theatre Company, Madrid. *Blanco y negro*, 26 February, 14.

Lemaitre, Georges (1947). *From Cubism to Surrealism in French Literature*. Cambridge, MA: Harvard University Press.

Lewis, Allan (1972). *Ionesco*. New York: Twayne Publishers.

Lima, Robert (2001). '*Nosferatu*: A Play on the Vampire by Francisco Nieva'. *Modern Drama* 44, 2:232–46.

Llamas, Ricardo (1998). *Teoria torcida: prejuicios y discursos en torno a 'la homosexualidad'*. Madrid: Siglo Veintiuno Editores.

London, John (1997). *Reception and Renewal in Modern Spanish Theatre: 1939–1963*. London: Modern Humanities Research Association.

López Sancho, Lorenzo (1989). 'Erotismo y transgresión: *Corazón de arpía*, de Francisco Nieva'. Review of *Corazón de arpía*. Francisco Nieva Theatre Company, Madrid. *ABC*, 4 February, 91.

—— (1993). 'Los vampiros modernizados de *Aquelarre y noche roja de Nosferatu*'. Review of F. Nieva, *Nosferatu*. National Centre for New Tendencies in Stage Performance, Madrid. *ABC*, 29 May, 95.

Lyotard, Jean-François (1984). *The Postmodern Condition: A Report on Knowledge*. Trans. Geoff Bennington and Brian Massumi. Minneapolis: University of Minnesota Press.

Malinowski, Bronislaw (1949). *Sex and Repression in Savage Society*. London: Routledge and Kegan Paul.

Malkin, Jeanette R. (1999). *Memory-Theater and Postmodern Drama*. Ann Arbor: University of Michigan Press.

Malone, Gustav (1998). *Homosexualidad: gays y lesbianas, una alternativa sin tabúes*. Barcelona: FAPA Ediciones.

Marcuse, Herbert (1955). *Eros and Civilization: A Philosophical Inquiry into Freud.* Boston: The Beacon Press.

Martin, Wallace (1980). 'Postmodernism: Ultima Thule or Seim Anew?' In Harry R. Garvin (ed.), *Romanticism, Modernism, Postmodernism.* Lewisburg: Bucknell University Press; London and Toronto: Associated University Presses, pp. 142–54.

Mayhew, Jonathan (1994). *The Poetics of Self-Consciousness: Twentieth-Century Spanish Poetry.* Lewisburg: Bucknell University Press; London and Toronto: Associated University Presses.

McAuley, Gay (1999). *Space in Performance: Making Meaning in the Theatre.* Ann Arbor: University of Michigan Press.

McGlynn, Fred (1990). 'Postmodernism and Theater'. In Hugh J. Silverman (ed.), *Postmodernism – Philosophy and the Arts.* New York and London: Routledge, pp. 137–54.

McHale, Brian (1982). 'Writing about Postmodern Writing'. Review article on *A Rhetoric of the Unreal: Studies in Narrative and Structure, Especially of the Fantastic,* by Christine Brooke-Rose; *After the Wake: An Essay on the Contemporary Avant-Garde,* by Christopher Butler; *Horizons of Assent: Modernism, Postmodernism, and the Ironic Imagination,* by Alan Wilde. *Poetics Today* 3, 3:211–27.

Millett, Kate (1970). *Sexual Politics.* New York: Doubleday.

Mira, Alberto. (1994). *¿Alguien se atreve a decir su nombre?: enunciación homosexual y la estructura del armario en el texto dramático.* Valencia: Universitat de València.

—— (2000). 'Laws of Silence: Homosexual Identity and Visibility in Contemporary Spanish Culture'. In Barry Jordan and Rikki Morgan-Tamosunas (eds), *Contemporary Spanish Cultural Studies.* London: Arnold; New York: Oxford University Press, pp. 241–50.

Molloy, Sylvia and McKee Irwin, Robert, eds (1998). *Hispanisms and Homosexualities.* Durham, NC, and London: Duke University Press.

Monleón, José (1976). *Cuatro autores: José María Rodríguez Méndez, José Martín Recuerda, Francisco Nieva, Jesús Campos.* Granada: Universidad, Secretariado de Extensión Universitaria, Gabinete de Teatro.

Navajas, Gonzalo (1987). *Teoría y práctica de la novela española postmoderna.* Barcelona: Edicions del Mall.

—— (1993). 'Una estética para después del posmodernismo: la nostalgia asertiva y la reciente novela española'. *Revista de occidente* 143:105–30.

—— (1994). 'Posmodernidad – Posmodernismo. Crítica de un paradigma'. *Ínsula* 570–1:22–6.

—— (1996). *Más allá de la posmodernidad. Estética de la nueva novela y cine españoles.* Barcelona: EHB.

Navas Ocaña, María Isabel (2000). *El Postismo.* Cuenca: El Toro de Barro.

Nelson, Robert J. (1958). *Play within a Play: The Dramatist's Conception of His Art. Shakespeare to Anouilh.* New Haven: Yale University Press.

Nieto, José Antonio, ed. (1998). *Transexualidad, transgenerismo y cultura: antropología, identidad y género.* Madrid: TALASA Ediciones.

Nietzsche, Friedrich Wilhelm (1964). 'The Birth of Tragedy'. In Albert Hofstadter and Richard Kuhns (eds), *Philosophies of Art and Beauty.* New York: Random House, pp. 496–554.

Nieva, Francisco (1967). 'Virtudes plásticas del teatro de Valle-Inclán'. *Primer Acto* 82:12–21. Originally published as 'Vertus plastiques du théâtre de Valle-Inclán' in *Le théâtre moderne*. Paris: Éditions du CNRS, 1958.

—— (1973a). 'Auto-biobibliografia'. *Primer Acto* 153:18–21.

—— (1973b). 'El bloque temático del Teatro Furioso'. In Miguel Bilbatúa (ed.), *Riaza, Hormigón, Nieva: Teatro*. Madrid: Cuadernos para el Diálogo (EDICUSA), pp. 162–4.

—— (1973c). 'Confesiones en voz alta'. Interview by Moisés Pérez Coterillo and Santiago de Las Heras. *Primer Acto* 153:22–5.

—— (1973d). 'En torno a una nueva escritura "teatrante"'. In Miguel Bilbatúa (ed.), *Riaza, Hormigón, Nieva: Teatro*. Madrid: Cuadernos para el Diálogo (EDICUSA), pp. 155–61.

—— (1976a). Interview by Miguel A. Medina Vicario. In M. A. Medina Vicario (ed.), *El teatro español en el banquillo*. Valencia: Fernando Torres Editor, pp. 57–64.

—— (1976b). 'Pequeña teoría sobre un teatro histórico-didáctico'. In F. Nieva, *Sombra y quimera de Larra (Presentación alucinada de 'No más mostrador')*. Madrid: Editorial Fundamentos, pp. 5–28.

—— (1978). 'Francisco Nieva y el lenguaje teatral'. Interview by Blanca Berasategui. *ABC*, 22 January, 28.

—— (1980). 'Breve poética teatral'. In Antonio González (ed.), *Malditas sean Coronada y sus hijas. Delirio del amor hostil*. Madrid: Ediciones Cátedra, pp. 98–117.

—— (1981). 'Autobiografia'. *Triunfo* 35, 7:55–63.

—— (1982). 'Francisco Nieva: "a la búsqueda del gran teatro" '. Interview by Santiago Trancón. *Primer Acto* 194:23–6.

—— (1984). 'El "postismo" una vez más'. *ABC*, 22 July, 3.

—— (1987). 'Con Francisco Nieva: el amor y la gloria'. Interview by José Luis Vicente Mosquete. *Cuadernos El Público*, February, 5–19.

(1988a). *En tela de juicio: la literatura y la vida, la moda y el teatro*. Madrid: ARNAO Ediciones.

—— (1988b). 'La mujer maldita'. In F. Nieva, *En tela de juicio. La literatura y la vida, la moda y el teatro*. Madrid: ARNAO Ediciones, pp. 257–61.

—— (1990a). '*El baile de los ardientes*'. *Primer Acto* 232:41–3.

—— (1990b). 'Francisco Nieva'. Interview by María Victoria Cansinos. In Andrés Peláez and Fernanda Andura (eds), *Exposición antológica Francisco Nieva*. Teatro Albéñiz, March–May, pp. 84–7. First published in *El Socialista*, 31 March 1989.

—— (1991a). 'Esencia y paradigma del Género Chico'. Induction Speech into the Spanish Royal Academy of Language. In F. Nieva, *Teatro completo*. Vol. 2. Toledo: Servicio de Publicaciones de la Junta de Comunidades de Castilla–La Mancha, pp. 1335–50.

—— (1991b). 'El mundo azaroso de la adaptación'. *Primer Acto* 237:77–9.

—— (1991c). *Teatro completo*. 2 vols. Toledo: Servicio de Publicaciones de la Junta de Comunidades de Castilla–La Mancha.

—— (1994). *Nosferatu*. Madrid: Sociedad General de Autores de España.

—— (1996a). 'Arte vivo y arte sepulcral'. In F. Nieva, *El reino de nadie*. Madrid: Espasa Calpe, pp. 212–16. Originally published in *ABC*, 20 September 1992.

—— (1996b). 'El auroral teatro de Lorca'. In F. Nieva, *El reino de nadie*. Madrid:

Espasa Calpe, pp. 124–31. Originally published in *El País*, 19 August 1986.

—— (1996c). 'De cómo llegué a hacer una comedia que se llamó *Las aventuras de Tirante el Blanco*'. In F. Nieva, *El reino de nadie*. Madrid: Espasa Calpe, pp. 79–83. Originally published in *ABC*, 20 November 1990.

—— (1996d). 'Ese diablo de Pirandello'. In F. Nieva, *El reino de nadie*. Madrid: Espasa Calpe, pp. 109–13. Originally published in *ABC*, 20 September 1986.

—— (1996e). 'La inclemente modernidad de Ramón'. In F. Nieva, *El reino de nadie*. Madrid: Espasa Calpe, pp. 275–9. Originally published in *ABC*, 26 January 1992.

—— (1996f). 'El público ideal'. In F. Nieva, *El reino de nadie*. Madrid: Espasa Calpe, pp. 160–4. Originally published in *ABC*, 1 November 1992.

—— (1996g). *El reino de nadie*. Madrid: Espasa Calpe.

—— (1996h). 'El teatro libertino'. In F. Nieva, *El reino de nadie*. Madrid: Espasa Calpe, pp. 30–4. Originally published in *ABC*, 21 February 1988.

—— (1996i). 'Un teatro sin escritores'. In F. Nieva, *El reino de nadie*. Madrid: Espasa Calpe, pp. 58–61. Originally published in *ABC*, 23 January 1994.

—— (1997a). 'Mi viejo teatro inesperado'. Programme Notes, *Pelo de tormenta*. Centro Dramático Nacional, Madrid.

—— (1997b). 'Ni teatro pobre ni teatro rico, sino todo lo contrario'. *ABC*, 1 June, 236.

—— (1997c). '*Pelo de tormenta*'. *ADE Teatro* 58–9:19–26.

—— (1997d). 'Reflexiones sobre *Pelo de tormenta*'. In *Pelo de tormenta*. *Cuaderno pedagógico* 3. Madrid: Centro Dramático Nacional, pp. 17–20.

—— (1998). '¿Cómo saber si somos postmodernos?' *La Razón* (Madrid), 13 December, 5.

—— (2000a). 'Arcaísmo y vanguardia en *Nosferatu*'. In F. Nieva, *Nosferatu (Aquelarre y noche roja de)*. *Reópera*. Zaragoza: Libros del Innombrable, pp. xi–xxxi.

—— (2000b). *Tratado de escenografía*. Madrid: Editorial Fundamentos.

—— (2002). *Las cosas como fueron. Memorias*. Madrid: Espasa Calpe.

—— (2005). *¡Viva el estupor! Los mismos (Dos comedias televisivas)*. Juan Francisco Peña (ed.), Madrid: Espasa Calpe.

Nieva, Francisco and Ricci, Anna (1989). 'Una obra dedicada al espíritu griego de los andaluces: una mezcla explosiva'. Interview by Paula Lara. *Diario de Córdoba*, 7 April, 37.

Núñez de Velasco, Francisco (1614). *Diálogos de contención entre la milicia y la ciencia*. Valladolid: Imprenta de Iuan Godinez de Millis.

O'Connor, Patricia W. (1988). 'A Theater in Transition: From Paternalism to Pornography'. In Martha T. Halsey and Phyllis Zatlin (eds), *The Contemporary Spanish Theater: A Collection of Critical Essays*. Lanham, New York and London: University Press of America, pp. 201–13.

Ory, Carlos Edmundo de. (1970). *Poesía, 1945–1969*. Ed. Félix Grande. Barcelona: EDHASA.

Palacios, Amador (1989). 'Gabino-Alejandro Carriedo y Ángel Crespo en el postismo'. *Ínsula* 511:15–16.

Parker, Alexander A. (1943). *The Allegorical Drama of Calderón: An Introduction to the Autos Sacramentales*. Oxford and London: The Dolphin Book.

Pavis, Patrice (1992) *Theatre at the Crossroads of Culture.* Trans. Loren Kruger. London and New York: Routledge. (Chapter on postmodernist theatre originally published in *Modern Drama* 29, 1 (1986):1–22.)

Peláez, Andrés and Andura, Fernanda, eds (1990). *Exposición antológica Francisco Nieva.* Teatro Albéñiz, March–May.

Peña, Juan Francisco (2001). *El teatro de Francisco Nieva.* 2 vols. Madrid: Universidad de Alcalá de Henares.

—— ed. (1996). *Teatro gótico: La Señora Tártara. El baile de los ardientes,* by F. Nieva. Madrid: Espasa Calpe.

—— ed. (2002). *Centón de Teatro 2,* by F. Nieva. Alcalá de Henares: Servicio de Publicaciones, Universidad de Alcalá.

Pérez Coterillo, Moisés (1975). Introduction to F. Nieva, *Teatro Furioso.* Madrid: Editorial Akal-Ayuso, pp. 7–38.

—— (1982). 'Liquidación irónica de la España negra'. Preview of F. Nieva, *Coronada y el toro.* National Drama Centre, Madrid. *ABC,* 24 April, 94–5.

Picó, Josep, ed. (1988). *Modernidad y postmodernidad.* Madrid: Alianza Editorial.

Piga, Domingo (1979). 'Problemas del teatro popular'. In Sonia Gutiérrez (ed.), *Teatro popular y cambio social en América latina: panorama de una experiencia.* Ciudad Universitaria Rodrigo Facio, San José: Editorial Universitaria Centroamericana, pp. 66–75.

Pinillos, José Luis (1998). *El corazón del laberinto: crónica del fin de una época.* Madrid: Espasa Calpe.

Pirandello, Luigi (1998). *Six Characters in Search of an Author.* Trans. Edward Storer. Mineola, NY: Dover Publications.

Pizzato, Mark (1998). *Edges of Loss: From Modern Drama to Postmodern Theory.* Ann Arbor: University of Michigan Press.

Plunka, Gene A. (1994). 'The Suffering Shaman of the Modern Theater'. In Gene A. Plunka (ed.), *Antonin Artaud and the Modern Theater.* Rutherford, Madison and Teaneck: Fairleigh Dickinson University Press; London and Toronto: Associated University Presses, pp. 3–36.

Polo de Bernabé, José Manuel (1981). 'El teatro de Fernando Arrabal: vanguardia e ideología'. *Anales de la Literatura Española Contemporánea* 6:173–82.

Pont, Jaume (1987). *El postismo: un movimiento estético-literario de vanguardia.* Barcelona: Edicions del Mall.

—— (1998). *La poesía de Carlos Edmundo de Ory.* Lleida: Ediciones de la Universitat de Lleida.

Portoghesi, Paolo (1983). *Postmodern: The Architecture of the Postindustrial Society.* New York: Rizzoli International Publications.

Prodan, Gianna (1989). 'La imagen gráfica del postismo'. *Ínsula* 511:1–2, 27.

Quevedo y Villegas, Francisco de (1932). *Obras completas.* Ed. Luis Atrana Marín. Madrid: M. Aguilar.

Rabassó, Carlos A. and Rabassó, Fco. Javier (1993). 'La determinación del espacio poético en *Tórtolas, crepúsculo y . . . telón*'. In C. A. Rabassó and F. J. Rabassó, *Pedrolo, Nieva, Arrabal: Teatrología del vanguardismo dramático. Aproximaciones hermenéutico-fenomenológicas al teatro español contemporáneo.* Barcelona: Editorial Vosgos, pp. 47–123.

Ramírez, Juan Antonio (1986). 'Catecismo breve de la (post)modernidad'. In Antonio J. Huerga Murcia and José Tono Martínez (eds), *La polémica de la posmodernidad*. Madrid: Ediciones Libertarias, pp. 15–25.

Raphael, D. D. (1960). *The Paradox of Tragedy*. London: George Allen & Unwin.

Reinhardt, Nancy (1983). 'New Directions for Feminist Criticism in Theatre and the Related Arts'. In Elizabeth Langland and Walter Gove (eds), *Feminist Perspective in the Academy: The Difference It Makes*. Chicago and London: University of Chicago Press, pp. 25–51.

Ricoeur, Paul (1967). *The Symbolism of Evil*. Trans. Emerson Buchanan. New York, Evanston and London: Harper and Row Publishers.

—— (1981). *The Conflict of Interpretations: Essays in Hermeneutics*. Ed. Don Ihde. Evanston: Northwestern University Press.

Rodríguez Méndez, José María, ed. (1972). *Comentarios impertinentes sobre el teatro español*. Barcelona: Ediciones Península. Quoted in Alberto Romero Ferrer, *El género chico: introducción al estudio del teatro corto fin de siglo (de su incidencia gaditana)*. Cádiz: Servicio de Publicaciones de la Universidad de Cádiz, 1993, pp. 45.

Romero López, Dolores (1997). 'Hispanic *Modernismo* in the Context of European Symbolism: Towards a Comparative De/construction'. *Orbis Litterarum* 52:194–210.

Rosset, Clément (1993). *Joyful Cruelty: Toward a Philosophy of the Real*. Ed. and trans. David F. Bell. New York and Oxford: Oxford University Press.

Rothenberg, Jerome (1977). 'New Models, New Visions: Some Notes toward a Poetics of Performance'. In Michel Benamou and Charles Caramello (eds), *Performance in Postmodern Culture*. Milwaukee: Center for Twentieth-Century Studies, University of Wisconsin; Madison: Coda Press, pp. 11–17.

Rubio, Fanny (1976). *Revistas poéticas españolas, 1939–1975*. Madrid: Ediciones Turner.

Rubio Jiménez, Jesús (1991). 'Prolegómenos para un estudio de las relaciones entre Francisco Nieva y Valle-Inclán'. *Ínsula* 566:14–15.

Ruiz Ramón, Francisco (1995). *Historia del teatro español: Siglo XX*. 10th edn. Madrid: Ediciones Cátedra.

Sánchez, Antonio (2000). 'Postmodernism and the Contemporary Spanish Avant-garde'. In Barry Jordan and Rikki Morgan-Tamosunas (eds), *Contemporary Spanish Cultural Studies*. London: Arnold; New York: Oxford University Press, pp. 101–10.

Sartre, Jean-Paul (1963). *Saint Genet: Actor and Martyr*. Trans. Bernard Frechtman. New York: George Braziller.

Saura, Jorge (2001). '¿Existen actores brechtianos?' *Primer Acto* 287:120–4.

Savramis, Demosthenes (1974). *The Satanizing of Woman: Religion versus Sexuality*. Trans. Martin Ebon. New York: Doubleday.

Schaefer, Claudia (1989). 'Francisco Nieva in the Shadow of Goya, Valle-Inclán, and the Aesthetic of the *Esperpento*'. *Estreno* 15, 2:12–16.

Schlueter, June (1979). *Metafictional Characters in Modern Drama*. New York: Columbia University Press.

—— (1985). 'Theatre'. In Stanley Trachtenberg (ed.), *The Postmodern Moment*. Westport and London: Greenwood Press, pp. 210–28.

Shank, Theodore (1992). 'The Shock of the Actual: Disrupting the Theatrical Illusion'. In Patrick D. Murphy (ed.), *Staging the Impossible: The Fantastic Mode in Modern Drama.* Westport and London: Greenwood Press, pp. 169–81.

Signes, Emil George (1982). 'The Theatre of Francisco Nieva: A Summary, Analysis, and Bibliography, Together with an Edition and Translation of *La carroza de plomo candente*'. Unpublished Ph.D. thesis, Rutgers University, The State University of New Jersey.

—— (1988). 'Francisco Nieva: Spanish Representative of the Theater of the Marvelous'. In Martha T. Halsey and Phyllis Zatlin, *The Contemporary Spanish Theater: A Collection of Critical Essays.* Lanham, New York and London: University Press of America, pp. 147–61.

Simard, Rodney (1984). *Postmodern Drama: Contemporary Playwrights in America and Britain.* Lanham, New York and London: University Press of America.

Smedes, Lewis B. (1984). *Sex for Christians.* Grand Rapids: William B. Eerdmans Publishing.

Smith, Paul Julian (1992). *Laws of Desire: Questions of Homosexuality in Spanish Writing and Film, 1960–1990.* Oxford: Oxford University Press; New York: Clarendon Press.

—— (1996). *Vision Machines: Cinema, Literature and Sexuality in Spain and Cuba, 1983–93.* London and New York: Verso.

Soufas, Christopher (1997). 'The Generation of 1927 and the Question of Modernity'. *Anales de la Literatura Española Contemporánea* 22, 2:283–97.

Soyinka, Wole (1976). *Myth, Literature, and the African World.* London, New York and Melbourne: Cambridge University Press.

Speirs, Ronald (1994). 'The Theatre of Bertolt Brecht: Theory and Practice'. In Brian Docherty (ed.), *Twentieth-Century European Drama.* New York: St. Martin's Press, pp. 26–41.

Summers, Montague (1960). *The Vampire: His Kith and Kin.* New York: University Books

Szabolcsi, Miklós (1971). 'Avant-garde, Neo-avant-garde, Modernism: Questions and Suggestions'. *New Literary History* 3, 1:49–70.

Thomson, Philip (1972). *The Grotesque.* London: Methuen and Co Ltd.

Tono Martínez, José (1986). Foreword to Antonio J. Huerga Murcia and José Tono Martínez (eds), *La pólemica de la posmodernidad.* Madrid: Ediciones Libertarias, pp. 9–11.

Toro, Alfonso de (1990). 'Hacia un modelo para el teatro postmoderno'. In Fernando de Toro (ed.), *Semiótica y teatro latinoamericano.* Buenos Aires: Editorial Galerna / IITCTL, pp. 13–42.

Ubersfeld, Anne. (1989). *Semiótica teatral.* Trans. Francisco Torres Monreal. Madrid: Ediciones Cátedra; Murcia: Universidad de Murcia.

Umbral, Francisco (1987). *Guía de la Posmodernidad: crónicas, personajes e itinerarios madrileños.* Madrid: Ediciones Temas de Hoy.

—— (1989). 'Paco Nieva'. Review of F. Nieva, *Corazón de arpía.* Francisco Nieva Theatre Company, Madrid. *Diario 16*, 10 February, 4.

Valdés, Mario J. (1994). 'The Invention of Reality: Hispanic Postmodernism'. *Revista Canadiense de Estudios Hispánicos* 18, 3:455–68.

Van der Naald, Anje C. (1981). *Nuevas tendencias en el teatro español: Matilla, Nieva, Ruibal*. Miami: Ediciones Universal.

Vilches de Frutos, María Francisca (1999). 'La Generación Simbolista en el teatro español contemporáneo'. In Martha T. Halsey and Phyllis Zatlin. *Entre actos: Diálogos sobre teatro español entre siglos*. University Park, PA: Estreno, pp. 127–36.

Wardropper, Bruce W. (1967). *Introducción al teatro religioso del siglo de oro. Evolución del auto sacramental antes de Calderón*. 2nd edn. Salamanca: Anaya.

Watt, Stephen (1998). *Postmodern / Drama: Reading the Contemporary Stage*. Ann Arbor: University of Michigan Press.

Waugh, Patricia (1989). *Feminine Fictions: Revisiting the Postmodern*. London and New York: Routledge.

Weeks, Jeffrey (1985). *Sexuality and Its Discontents: Meanings, Myths, and Modern Sexualities*. London: Routledge and Kegan Paul.

—— (1986). *Sexuality*. Chichester: Ellis Horwood; London and New York: Tavistock Publications.

—— (1989). *Sex, Politics and Society: The Regulation of Sexuality since 1800*. 2nd edn. London and New York: Longman.

Wellwarth, George E. (1972). *Spanish Underground Drama*. State College: Pennsylvania State University Press.

Wright, Elizabeth (1989). *Postmodern Brecht: A Re-Presentation*. London and New York: Routledge.

Zatlin, Phyllis (1989). 'Metatheatricalism and Nieva's *Sombra y quimera de Larra*'. *Gestos* 4, 7:65–73.

—— (1994). 'La metateatralidad de Francisco Nieva'. *Ínsula* 566:12–14.

—— (1996). 'Atacando al patriarcado: los ejemplos de Gala y Nieva'. *Boletín de la Fundación Federico García Lorca* 19, 20:301–16.

Zavala, Iris (1988). 'On the (Mis-)Uses of the Post-Modern: Hispanic Modernism Revisited'. In Theo D'haen and Hans Bertens (eds), *Postmodern Fiction in Europe and the Americas*. Amsterdam: Rodopi, pp. 83–113.

INDEX